BEN

My life changed at a football match, but not the way you're thinking. There wasn't a glorious goal after magnificent teamwork that inspired me to greater things. As my dad and I watched The Posh slide to another disappointing loss, he told me my mum was ill. That ruined football. We only went to one more game after that and I spent ninety minutes on edge, wondering if he had something else awful to say.

I'd loved it until then. Not just the game but the whole day out. We went twice a year as we had little money, or anything else decent for that matter. My dad worked long hours to buy tickets, but did so, he alleged, with a smile. It was our thing, together. Of course, we took my friend Jonty, so it was always fun.

Dad's words were. 'Your mother's got an illness. You're old enough to understand.' I wasn't. There are illnesses and sicknesses. Who'd have known? She had one and, even though I didn't know it then, he already had the other.

Considering my line of work, I expect Mum will outlive us all. My dad was sick with a different beast. His was a snarling, relentless entity that would leave this sixteen-stone man a bedridden skeleton in twelve short months, like two sorrowful eyes on shrunken parchment. He was a great man, a kind man, and then a dead man. He didn't deserve that, and neither did we.

Life isn't fair.

I know that now.

PART I

ADULT CUSTODY

1

27TH AUGUST 2014

The banging on the wing reaches a new level of fury and drags me from my daydream. I understand what this means. Decision time.

I pull the sheet of paper I've used to cover the observation panel out of the way and look down the wing. The Senior Officer plods up the steps to the top landing like an enormous, cumbersome troll. It's him, and that's bad news. It's likely we'll get hurt during the upcoming 'incident', but if this man is in charge it'll be inescapable. He'll make sure of it.

I let the paper – which, ironically, is the notice that Jake has been placed on report – drop back into place, and glance round at the other two occupants. One is conscious, one is not. Our cell is what's affectionately known as a big double. It's three times the normal size. The ground floor ones are often saved for inmates in wheelchairs. Yes, the disabled break the law too. The upper landing cells like this are usually occupied by those who run the wings. Prisoners, obviously, not staff. If you haven't been to jail you might assume that given the choice, which most aren't, you would want your own space. That's not the case as often the most powerful inmates share with their friends. If you're locked up for twenty-two hours a day, any company can be safer than your own.

Our 'hostage' is lying on his back on the floor next to the bunks, sweating like a boxer on his stool at the end of the eleventh round. God knows what he's taken, but he's currently no use to anyone. It's a shame because he's a threatening individual and perfectly suited to our current predicament. Many people remind you of animals and birds, but Donny was the first person I met who resembled a bull. His huge head is perched on comically narrow shoulders, but his back and arms are enormous. His legs, although powerful, are too short for his body and he seems to walk hunched forward as though he's about to charge. His piggy suspicious eyes usually tell of poor eyesight, but they're rolled back in his head, indicating no one is home.

Jake looks like a hungry crow. He's sizing me up as though he's eyeing risky roadkill on a motorway, head bobbing from side to side, feeding off the nervous look I'm giving him.

'What's going on?' he asks.

'It's the SO, coming for a chat. The one you said strangled you!' I shout to be heard over the din.

'The big one? Senior Officer Cave? I told him I'd walk. You were there, you heard me. He smashed my head against the window bars. Grabbed me by the neck, you know, with both hands. It took four men to pull him off me. That man is tapped, and it was him that did Will, I know it.'

That is another reason for our situation. Someone went in on Jake's earlier pad mate and beat him senseless. Jake thinks it was Cave. Breakfast was late, as the man had been blue-lighted away. Even though this isn't an unusual event in a prison, Jake wants revenge. This SO is the eye of Jake's storm. The man has been present as long as I've been coming here. I've no idea what happened in his life to make him so full of hate and malice, but it must've been truly appalling.

Rage, frustration and spite pour off him like the smoke from a volcano just before she erupts. To Jake, though, it's as if every single backhand, clenched fist, missed birthday, broken promise, late night drunken visit, unwanted probing finger and dismissive stare over the past twenty years have evolved into a human being. This creature has then been sent here to haunt Jake. Until I saw it was Cave who had come to talk to us, I wasn't sure we'd follow our plan through. I know now it is inevitable.

The main reason we've barricaded the cell door and taken a 'hostage' is different for all three of us. This is Donny's cell and I doubt he has a decent motive. For that you need high-order thinking skills, which require a minimum level of intelligence and nurture denied to him. Donny's previous cellmate was on the wrong end of a screwdriver in the workshop a few days earlier and will be in hospital. Assuming he's still alive. So, we're in Donny's cell, because mine and Jake's is tiny since we've only just arrived. Jake said there will be more room to fight. That comment seemed funny all those hours ago.

I stare at Donny as I ponder his thought processes. As I do, his eyes roll back into place and he pants like an exhausted racehorse after an arduous steeplechase. His cellmate was the brains of the operation. If you had met him, you would realise what a worrying statement that was. No wonder they got caught. He agreed to be our hostage because Jake suggested it, and hinted it would be a laugh. It may have seemed that way. Now we are going through with it, the feeling has changed.

What we've done is barricaded Donny's cell door at final bang up: about 7 p.m. We then told the officer who was locking the doors we had a hostage who we'd hurt if we didn't get what we wanted. Our barricade is, more or less, some soaking-wet mattresses and a few plastic chairs with some towels on top to make it look more substantial. Pathetic really. The SO could push them over by himself and drag us out by our ears. However, we have obscured the observation panel, so they don't know what's going on for sure and will need to follow their procedures. Health and safety, I expect. First, they send in a negotiator to help us see the error of our ways. They've sent the wrong guy for that. Cave may be evil but he isn't easily fooled. He'll know there isn't a hostage, and he also knows how it will end. We will lose.

2

Donny splutters a strangled, congested cough, and I raise an eyebrow at Jake.

'Do you think he's going to be OK?'

Jake comes and stands next to me, and we stare down at Donny, frowning, in the way you might at finding a huge jellyfish marooned by the tide.

'I'm not sure, he looks wasted.'

'What's he taken?'

'Spice. He loves it.'

'It looks like he's taken a lot.'

'He knows what he's doing.'

Spice and other legal highs are the new scourge of the prison system. They're chemicals produced in dodgy labs that mimic the effects of mind-altering drugs. You've a good idea of what will happen if you stick to the old tried and tested drugs, but these newer processed products have crazy side effects, causing fits, seizures and tremors. Someone told me they could make the heart explode. Prison rumour, I should think, but what is true, is many have died taking it. It's categorised as an unauthorised substance because its formula is not classified as an illegal drug, so it's hard to prosecute for bringing it in. It also doesn't show up on mandatory drug tests. Therefore, it is everywhere.

The law is changing soon, to make it illegal to have anything like this, but that's not a deterrent. The problem is that it's cheap and easily available. A friend of ours, Dan, bought some off the Internet once. Cost him twelve pounds and a gall bladder.

Jake has smoked it in our cell previously. It was as if someone had set fire to a tractor tyre. It was suffocating, and we shouted and screamed to get out of there. The officers thought we were faking it and denied our requests for fresh air. Eventually they released us and Jake got carried to Healthcare. Even he won't touch it now and he has zero regard for his own welfare, so that is saying something. As my mum used to say, 'He may be daft, but he's not stupid.'

Donny is stupid.

Jake shrugs.

'Let's face it, he's an oxygen waster. It's not like he'll be missed. The world will be a better place for his absence too. Besides, I can think of worse ways to go.'

Harsh. That's Jake all over. He prides himself on caring about nothing and no one. I shake my head, but I'm not surprised. I wonder if he'd be as disparaging over my twitching body. Jake leans against the window, wearing his best prison face. Everyone here has one. A face that says, nothing bothers me, I don't care and you can't reach me. It's bluster. They hurt. They know they're wasting time in a vicious warehouse. Locked in cages like animals while their life ticks by. Aware that when they rejoin the world it'll be to a life that's broken, and they will lack the money, skills, or knowledge to repair it. Even Jake is different on the other side of the prison gates. He's not the incredible prick he is in here. There he is fun, still nuts, but almost likeable.

I saw these faces when I first arrived. Thought what a hard place

I had been sent to. I put on my own mask of anger and indifference, and that's how I know these facades are untrue, because I care. I have things and people to lose. I will ache when they are gone.

That brings me to what Jake and I get out of it. He's one of the rare few who have nothing. There's no one to send him money or clothes, no one waiting for his call, and no one to meet him when he leaves. Jake entered the care system too young to remember his parents, before he was old enough to know what terrible things had occurred. But they still leave a mark. Social services, no doubt trying their best, guided him through more irreparable experiences with people who should not have been within a hundred metres of any child. Until he'd had enough. He dropped out of sight and joined the faceless, anonymous section of society it's too late to save.

You can't take anything from Jake. He has nothing to give. You can only hurt someone if they have something they value. Perhaps that's the only way people like him can feel in control. Individuals such as these who will do anything, literally anything, to save face and gain position are what makes jail such a dangerous place. Life has battered him so hard that he's become desensitised to it. The only way he knows he's alive is by undergoing extremes of emotions. Today serves that purpose. Fear, hatred, pain, anger and no doubt finally, regret, will shortly be in this room.

At twenty-one, we're now too old to go to a young offender institution. If you ever have the misfortune to meet a forty-year-old career prisoner, you'll see a considerable difference. Jake and I are tall and strong, but bigger, harder, more violent men than us live here. So today sends a message: we fight, even if we have no chance. We are not to be underestimated. We are untouchable.

Despite Jake's icy, hostile outlook on life, he's the only friend I have in this soulless place. Sticking together gives us the best chance of survival.

To conclude, Jake doesn't care, Donny doesn't understand, and me, I'm angry It's a sad indictment of human nature that, in the ensuing madness, our stock in the prison will rise by our efforts to hurt as many prison officers as possible. So that's part of it. The main reason I have gone along with this reckless plan is that I'm furious. I'm livid with life in general, with God, with my father for dying, with my useless mother, but mostly with myself. Yes, I received a poor hand, but I've played it badly.

What do you do if you're angry? Go to the gym, see your friends, take a walk, drive, shop, Xbox, drink? Here, these things are taken from you and, lacking the courage to hurt myself, I want to vent my fury on someone else. The prison staff will do.

I have a toothache too and that's never a good time to make important decisions. Whatever your imagination pictures a prison dentist to be, it's probably correct. That's if you get an appointment with the tooth-removing fiend.

I'm in Jake's debt too. It feels bizarre to say it, but he sacrificed himself to save me. Even though he failed, he saw my need was greater. It meant he'd go back to prison, but he did it anyway. You don't make many friends like that, so I had little choice when he suggested this foolishness. Although, perhaps, if I hadn't met Jake, none of this would've happened. The horrible thought I'd had enough warnings and near misses to know who was to blame ricochets around in my brain. I'm interrupted by the door vibrating with the sound of someone's leisurely knocks. Three times the door shakes. I stare at Jake.

'Your chum's here.'

'Don't worry. I'll talk to him.' Jake's face is stern.

As we wait for the man to speak, we hear a metal squeak and both see the metal plug in the centre of the cell door being unscrewed. A moment of panic hits me as I realise they can just stick the hose in here. That's what it's there for: flood the cell with high-powered foam and the fire, or our protest in this case, is over.

Clearly inhumane and not permitted, but I have heard it done. Ever the mad men, Jake and I crouch down and stare at an angry blood-shot eye that fills the hole.

'Out now, you little pricks.'

Jake recovers fast. 'No way. We have a hostage, and if you don't do what we say, he'll get hurt.'

'Any requests?' the officer asks quietly.

'We're hungry. I'd like chips.'

'Chinese sound good? I believe we've got them on speed dial.'

Some prisons occasionally give food like this if it avoids a violent incident, even though it encourages demonstrations such as ours. There's no way Cave would fall for that.

'Hmm, I prefer Mexican. They could include a massive cactus. It'll be for you. You can spin on it.' Jake smiles.

That leaves us with a pause. Long seconds pass, with the only sound the drip from the broken sink that Jake kicked off the wall at the start of this journey. The drops become a torrent, surely a bad sign.

'That goes without saying,' Cave finally says. 'I should ask. How is our poor, innocent hostage? Alive, I hope?'

'Only just.' Jake laughs now, but his face is the same; determined.

I see the evil eye squint into a glare as it processes the fact they need to rapidly enter the cell. Failure to do so and there may be a corpse. Any chance we have of a McDonald's or pizza disappears with the eye.

Just before he screws the plug back in the door, he whispers through the hole. 'You are both dead men. I hope that's clear.'

3

The wing explodes again as the SO leaves. More doors are kicked and shouts of 'bastards' and 'scum' echo around the high ceilings. He'll be on his way to his superiors to inform them of the urgency that they'll need to control the situation.

'A cactus?'

'Not bad, eh? Thinking on the spot.'

'No Big Mac?'

'Nope, Ben, don't look like it. I can almost taste one too.'

'Game on, then.'

'Blaze of glory, man.'

'Are you ready?'

'Almost.'

Jake returns to the remains of our eating area, which he's dismantling for weapons. He lights a roll-up. I hope it isn't spice; this definitely isn't a one-man job. He takes a big pull, exhales, and the room fills with marijuana smoke. A smell of hazy memories. He walks over to Donny's CD player and flips through the CDs. I shake my head at his proffered joint. It never did much for me. Paranoia, apathy and hunger will definitely not benefit my current situation.

As for Jake, I don't think it affects him the same way as it does normal people. Before he was diagnosed, he said he was so manic and hyper he knew he was going to end up killing someone. After they put him on Ritalin, he was sure he'd kill himself. In a weird way, marijuana saved him. On the other hand, living your life in a fog of deadened emotion doesn't lead to a productive life in society either.

I'm not convinced by this ADHD and dyslexia thing. From my experience, particularly in here, it doesn't seem that different from naughty boys and poor teaching. Give people, especially kids, an excuse for poor behaviour or lack of effort, and they'll seize it. I think the experts will disagree with me though. After all, look where I am. I know nothing.

The cell fills with the sound of Pharrell Williams' 'Happy' and I laugh in spite of things. As I watch Jake flick the dog-end, the lights go out except for the emergency ones at the sides and the music dies. The cigarette sizzles on the wet floor, the sound firing my nerves. So, maintenance finally got here and cut the power. In the half-light and smoke, Jake still smiles. He strips to his boxer shorts and picks up the bottle of baby oil he somehow acquired this morning. I would bet someone gave it to him just for the entertainment factor.

I forgot about that. Jail is boring. Any entertaining distraction from the misery of your own existence is welcomed. Forget what you've seen on TV with prisoners wandering around. It's no wonder inmates cause mischief or worse. 'The devil makes work for idle hands,' my mum often quoted, and here it applies. Give a criminal mind nothing to do all day and it will think of criminal things. Are we such a modern society that we incarcerate people like this? If you aren't crazy and violent when you arrive here, being locked up for most of the day for months on end with nothing to do is a good way of ensuring you finish up that way by the time you leave.

The idea behind being naked and covered in baby oil is so that, when they send in the MUFTI squad – Minimum Use of Force Tactical Intervention – you're too slippery for them to grab. I like his confidence – unfounded, but admirable nonetheless. I know exactly what's going to transpire as a prison officer told me the procedure on a slow Sunday the last time I was here. He was leaving the next day from what he said was the worst job he'd ever had. I assume that's why he told me as I'm sure it was all hush-hush. Or was he just as fed up as me?

If a cell is barricaded, or a hostage taken, both in our case, they will lock the prison down and try to get the miscreants to give in peacefully. Failing that, they'll ask for volunteers to suit up. Those that do will wear blue boiler suits, leather gloves, shin and elbow guards, boots, a stab vest, and the riot-squad equivalent of a motorbike helmet. They'll form into groups of three per inmate; yes, three on one. It's no wonder they don't struggle for participants. An oiled-up Jake will wait for them in his pants. I believe half the officers here would give their left nut to have a one-sided pop at Jake. He is not a model prisoner. One-sided it is too, as even though Donny is sparko they'll send in three for him. You can imagine what they'll do when they see he is away with the fairies. Not only are we outnumbered and outmatched, they will have reserves if anyone should fall in battle. So yes, we have no chance, but, as I said, it's not about that.

They will find the biggest officer on duty and give him a large Perspex shield. The door will open, he'll enter first, and then they will all storm in.

I remember a long time ago, in a different existence, going to a family friend's farm in the country. We used to sleep in a caravan near the main house. I loved going there. The fresh air, quiet, and animals chilled our minds. My parents seemed so happy without the distractions of modern life. The farmer had about six chickens in a coop and we used to collect the eggs in the morning. Something had been trying to burrow in under the frame to get at the chickens. A mink, my uncle explained. He set a malevolent metal-sprung trap near its most successful burrowing point to catch it. The trap was a rusty old thing and didn't work.

The next morning I encountered a horrendous scene. The predator had got in and ripped all the chickens to pieces. I struggled to imagine the terror for the chickens as the vicious creature crawled in and chased them around the pen. There would have been no escape as exhaustion finally conquered the first one. Then, as it was devoured, the others would have watched, waiting for their turn.

Despite Jake's bravado, I am a realist and our fate will be a similar one. However, I don't care. I've so much pent up rage, I must expel it. Here, this is as good a way as any. I'm royally fucked.

Not everything is lost, but I will be here for so long, it's only a matter of time. I've seen others break down as their children forgot them. Heard stories of how their missus had been banged by a so-called mate. One who went round to 'comfort' her in her time of need as her partner had been locked away. I hadn't cared; indeed I had laughed. Life teaches you lessons like that.

According to that officer they'd have a final briefing now. 'Go in fast. Hit them hard,' they would say. They'll be nervous too, but pumped full of energy and confidence as the odds are so stacked in their favour. Control and restraint is the phrase nowadays, not MUFTI. It's more or less the same thing. Control us by any means necessary and restrain us on the floor. They'll need to be careful. There's so much water in here a man could drown. It's lucky Donny is lying on his back or he would already be dead. As I look at his inert figure, a floating toilet roll pecks at his head, like an evil duck from a disused fairground.

I'm not scared. Apprehensive perhaps, so I perform. Certainly not how I was on the drive home from that football match. Fear of the unknown is a terrifying thing. Nothing can scare you like your own imagination. I know what will happen here and I am ready.

4

When I'm sad, scared, lonely, or want to distract myself, I often think of Jonty, even though he is long gone. I will do that now. Thinking of him is something I save for myself. That football game is a lifetime ago. Our lives were simple then. Simple for a child is just being and not being aware of it. The unknown joy of not worrying about your future, money, your home, or health. That was my life, before that day.

I remember looking at my dad in shock after he uttered those words and felt my veins coursing with a strange, unknown emotion that cooled my body. I had never known fear prior to that moment in my life, not real fear. We were to become regular bedfellows. Although I'm still not sure if, since then, I have ever felt it as I did at that moment. It was as though if I looked behind at my shadow, it would be cracked.

It was then that Jonty jumped out of his seat and cheered in his strange voice, 'Go on, go on.' We didn't even have the ball. Inexplicably, something strange happened. Their player gave it away, and for one quick minute we were Barcelona. Rapid passes and sprinting players bearing down on their goal. Jonty's enthusiasm was infectious, think Ebola with wings, and soon the stand was roaring. I loved him for that, his total immersion and joy in being. His life now seems sad and special at the same time.

Jonty loved few things in life – the three fs – food, females and football. And me. Perhaps in that order too, but I didn't mind. When we went out for the day we'd always ask him what he wanted to do. He used to reply at the top of his voice, 'Three things, three things, f-f-f-f-f-f-f,' and burst out laughing, too excited to get the words away. I think I was sixteen when I realised why that had amused my dad so much. I feel now I let Jonty down, that I should have looked out for him more, even though I'm not sure why because I was only a boy. I'm not much more than that now. I was about to discover that I was unable to control my own life, never mind someone else's.

As the crowd leapt to their feet to see the inevitable goal, just my dad and I remained in our seats, staring at each other. There was a strange expression on his face as the roars of approval turned to oohs of disappointment. He must have known that moment was life-altering. Why choose then to drop the bombshell on me? Destroy football for me? Why not explain things properly? Whenever I see a game on the TV now, I'm instantly back at that match and can't help feeling sad and nostalgic. Then it makes me feel angry and insignificant and I turn away. He should have told me when picking me up from school, since I never liked it there anyway.

I immediately thought my mum's illness didn't affect me. I was wrong, but as a kid you don't know any better. It's just normal family life. I hadn't seen a change in my dad at that point, but would I have noticed anyway? Who really looks at their parents? Who really sees anything?

I recognised that I should feel afraid, and I was. I remember Jonty sitting down at half-time, face slick with excitement. That was the point things started to go wrong for him too. This isn't a tale about Jonty though, or it would have a happier ending. This is about the mess I made of things. Events forced me to look down this path, but I walked it.

* * *

The wing flares up again and I nod at Jake. He hands me a pool cue that went missing on association earlier. That's the hour you get to play games after dinner. He's snapped it in half and tied it together with a ripped-up pillowcase. It's lightweight, but better than nothing. Other than Cave, the staff on tonight are new. When they asked where the vanished pool cue was, the guilty person, Jake, said it broke and had been thrown away. An experienced officer would have seen straight through that, would have known something was up. Spend enough time in a place like this and you develop jail craft. You can almost sense the atmosphere. Tonight was too quiet. That only leads to trouble.

'Afterwards, blame it on me,' Jake says. A gentleman to the end.

As big shadows of boiler-suited men pass outside the metal door, interrupting the light coming through the sides, Jake removes his underwear. I steal a peek through the observation panel and see a long line of helmeted figures queuing up the stairs. I step back out of the way as Jake pours the rest of the baby oil on the floor behind the door.

My other 'weapon', which is just the small tabletop we use to eat our meals on, feels flimsy. A shield and a sword. A gladiator for the modern age. Jake picks up the heavy TV and holds it in his hands as though he's a biblical wise man presenting his gift. The banging by the other inmates on their walls, doors and beds is louder than I have ever heard. It's faster than New Year's Eve when the bell tolls and more intense than when England score. They know it's too late to stop things now. They scream their support, their defiance, as our cell door is pushed open.

An enormous man bends his head to get inside the room and hard eyes survey the scene in front of him, narrowing as he sees Jake holding the TV behind his head. Jake's a naked footballer now, about to take a throw-in. A huge jack-booted foot smashes through the chair and towels, comes over the piled-up mattresses and squelches into the oil and water, like a tyre from a Formula 1 car cutting through the greasy-surfaced liquid. He drags in the shield, and as his visor steams up, he bellows, 'Advance!'

We roar our war cries in turn, and he leans into hell.

PART II

YOUNG

5

16TH DECEMBER 2006

Peterborough United lose 2-0 to Chester City. Jonty leaves his scarf under his seat and I leave my innocence under mine. He is, as usual, over-excited on the way home. So my dad's attention is on him, but I can feel him stealing glances over at me in the front passenger seat as he drives. The journey back is usually the funniest part of the day too, with Jonty shout-ordering the food at the McDonald's drive-thru intercom, but I can't enjoy it today.

As we sit in the car and eat in a companionable silence, I have a thousand thoughts firing through my mind. I don't want to ask the obvious ones in case it makes it more real. Is she going to die? What does it mean? Still, a strawberry milkshake tastes good, whatever the news, and I try to focus on dinner. I tune into the news to hear that 'The Suffolk Strangler' is still at large and move it onto a light pop channel. James Blunt's 'You're Beautiful' is depressing, but better than hearing about death.

The traffic is bad out of the industrial estate, but for understandable reasons I'm not looking forward to getting home. Obviously, my dad drives like he's in *The Fast And the Furious* and as we arrive it feels as though we've teleported back, arriving there instantly. My dad's weary Fiesta turns into Sheepmore, Paston, where we live, and bumps into the empty parking space with a screech. Booze is calling him like no mistress could. We are one of the few families with a car, so you can tell what kind of place it is. I've lived here for as long as I can remember, maybe since my birth, but we don't talk much about the past. I like it here. A few friends live nearby and we don't venture too close to the rougher parts near the Chadburn shopping centre. There doesn't seem to be any trouble and the neighbours look out for each other.

We live in a block that holds four spacious two-bedroom flats. We're on the first floor with just my parents and me in it. The flat underneath us is where Jonty and his mum, Sally, live. In the same way that there's something special about Jonty, there is about his mum too. Sally is so sweet-natured and happy, despite how things have turned out, that it's always nice to be in her company. She is pretty too, having done modelling in the past. I bet she didn't expect to end up here. Jonty's dad left not long after he was born; apparently, he couldn't handle it. That's confusing. I can't see someone like Jonty being much trouble when he was a baby. He's only difficult when he gets scared and can lash out. Still, I didn't know him when he was small.

Anyway, we used to 'Jontysit' so she could get out and my dad was often round there doing jobs. In the past, I've slept over at their place so my parents could go to the cinema, but it's been so long since that happened I wonder now whether I made it up.

The flat along from them has a whore in it. That's what my mum calls her. This tickles my dad, who likes to wind her up, saying it's 'Neighbours' Free Friday' at Michelle's. She has a daughter called Kirsty, who is in the year below me at school. Admittedly, Michelle enjoys dressing in what my mum calls provocative clothing, but she often shouts, 'Yoo hoo, boys' whenever she sees Jonty and me playing in the street. She is always flirting with my dad though, but he never takes the bait. If you told me she was an alcoholic, it would not be news. Her music is louder than her clothes, and she often wakes me up at the weekend, laughing and staggering around in the street as she comes in at 3 a.m. I once saw an old lady doing the washing up at her window and nearly shat myself when she shouted out, 'Yoo hoo, boys.' It was Michelle, with no make-up on.

She's friendlier with the guy who lives above her and along from us. Now this guy is a weird-looking bloke. Dad calls him Shaky after some dude called 'Shakin' Stevens' from way back. I could see the resemblance in a Google image my dad showed me. There's something about Shaky though that makes the hairs on my neck stand on end. He's the only person Jonty won't talk to, despite the man's best efforts. He whispers that 'The Roach' is coming. Sure enough, Vincent Roach and his receding quiff will come over, asking us if we want an ice cream or a lift – he's the only other person I know with a car. Typically, it's also a knackered Ford. My dad and I used to help fix his car for him for nothing, so perhaps that's why he's so friendly.

He lives with his wife, but I've never seen her, which is odd. Kirsty was round there all the time though. They used to babysit her so Michelle could go 'out on the lash' as she called it. Kirsty loved it there and used to joke that Jabba had the best chocolate bars. Vincent has never been fat, so even I understood that one. I'm not sure I would leave my daughter in a house like that, but Michelle wanted to party. They seemed to be the only option she had. In summary, we rub along together.

As my dad opens the entrance door, he says he'll drop Jonty off at his place. So I wander up the stairs alone with as much enthusiasm as a man climbing the steps to the gallows. I notice the smell for the first time in what seems forever. It's musty, but not especially unpleasant. One of my friends lives in a block of flats that honks like the urinals at school.

The paintwork is faded in our communal hallway with trainer prints all over the stairwells. My trainer prints. However, the carpet is clean. We keep our key in the electricity cupboard, between Shaky's door and ours, in case anyone gets locked out. Not safe, I suspect, but we have nothing worth nicking. Few do here.

The weekly shop happens on a Friday so by Monday we don't even have anything worth eating. My mum is in and comes to meet me. That's not a surprise as she likes to be locked in on a Saturday afternoon so she can catch up on her soaps.

'Hi, Benny. How was the game? Did you win?'

After everything my dad said, I was expecting anything but this normality and my puzzled look must have thrown her. It's as though I've received a fresh set of eyes and am seeing everything anew. She kisses me on the cheek.

'You all right, love? You look like you've seen a ghost.'

She smells as she always does: an unusual mint smell and cheap perfume. I only assume it's cheap as I don't think expensive stuff would sting your eyes like this. She toddles off to the lounge and I look at our flat, perhaps for the first time.

It's clean and recently painted. I suspect my dad got the paint 'off the back of a lorry' as I doubt anyone would have bought this weird custardy colour. It gives the place a fresh look though.

When I get to the kitchen, it's obvious all our appliances have seen better days. I yank open the fridge door and see it's packed in there. As mentioned, Friday is food shopping day, so this was to be expected, today being a Saturday. As per usual, it's stuffed with beer and wine bottles. I see full-fat colas in there for me too. We all have our poison.

Before I can shut the door, my dad comes charging in with a sweat on, grabs a can of Kestrel Super, takes a big swig, burps, and leaves. He hands me one of my cans and ruffles my hair on the way out, so I take it and sneak off into my room.

I fire up my laptop, thinking the best thing to do is look for symptoms online. When I say my laptop, I mean Davina Collins' laptop, whoever she is, as it's her name written on the back of it. I'm not sure whose Wi-Fi I'm using either, because we certainly don't have it. Some of the time, we don't even have electricity. After a simple search, I write six giveaway signs of my mum's condition on a pad and go out to play before dinner.

I know where Jonty is as I can hear the familiar grinding sound, so I head out to see him. There's a small grass play area next to our homes with an old, heavy, creaking roundabout in it. Jonty loves to push it like a Roman galley slave at his oar and will do so for ages. Kirsty and I often sit on it until we're giddy and he'll weep with laughter.

I stop when I arrive as a tall gangly lad is on it. He has a mischievous face. He's familiar, possibly the year above me at school. As he goes round each time, he urges his worker on with shouts of, 'Faster, retard.' Jonty is sweating profusely and looks scared. I don't even think about it.

'He's had enough.'

'I'll be the judge of that.'

I pull Jonty away from the roundabout and say, 'Your dinner's ready. Go and get it.' He runs off with a confused expression I know will make me cringe when I remember it, many years from now. The guy climbs off the roundabout and stands in front of me, too close for comfort. I've never had a fight. My body is telling me that this is about to change. He will hit me. Part of me instinctively tells me to do it to him first.

I take a step back and throw a straight punch at his throat. I don't know why I aimed there. Maybe if he weren't so tall I would have punched him on the nose. It works, and even though he reacts and catches some of the blow on his chin, he still goes down on one knee. As I relax he dives at my waist, and we scrap in the muddy wet grass.

It turns out I can hold my own. My dad and I loved to play-fight and I use every dirty trick he showed me. I know where to hit for the best effect even if you can't get much back swing. We end up filthy, exhausted, and clinging to each other like angry lovers.

We look up as a suspicious round face rises over us.

'My dinner wasn't ready.'

It's the catalyst that melts the ice and we laugh. My opponent is first to his feet and helps me up.

'I'm Jake.'

'Ben. This is Jonty.'

Jake shakes Jonty's outstretched hand.

'You are dirty boys.' Jonty laughs at us.

'Nice fighting.' Jake smiles at me.

'You too.'

We survey each other's faces, not realising that our futures will be so entwined.

6

I sneak us back into the house, and we slip into the bathroom and take a shower before anyone notices. Oddly, I don't feel uncomfortable. Jake waits for me to finish, then hauls off his dirty clothes and gets in himself. I edge the bathroom door open. My parents, as usual, are ensconced in the lounge. They will only leave for more grog and snacks. Sniggering, we run into my bedroom and I throw Jake some of my clothes. As we get changed, I notice for the first time how thin he is.

'Like a whippet,' was how my mum used to describe me. Next to Jake, I'm more like a greyhound bus. His ribs resemble a xylophone and are almost painful to see. It's cold and dark outside now so I look in my dad's wardrobe and lift a coat from the back. His wardrobe is a source of wonder for me as it's always full. More 'back of a lorry' stuff, no doubt. Peterborough must have more than its fair share of bad truck drivers.

When I return, Jake is reading the piece of paper with the bullet points on, that I wrote earlier. He gives me a strange look, then shrugs as he puts the massive jacket on.

With the pair of us chuckling, I guide Jake into the kitchen. My dinner is waiting for me on the small counter at the side of the room. There's an anaemic-looking pie, oven chips, and the usual vegetables that my mum insists on putting on my plate and that I never eat. I'm still full of my super-sized milkshake, so tell Jake to tuck in. As I stuff all our clothes in the washing machine, Jake pokes the pie with his finger as though it might be alive.

'Come back tomorrow afternoon and all this'll be ready, OK?'

'Yeah? Sweet.'

I like the way he talks: gangsterish but not too much. Even though he's cool and tough-looking, he has a vulnerable side to him. It could be because my dad's coat and hood are so big it looks as if a large black bear is attacking him from behind. My tracksuit bottoms are short on him too. So it's probably for the best if I don't show him a mirror. Even though his clothes were grimy, it's obvious they're brand new and in way better condition than mine. Jake must have watched the lorries like my dad does. As I choose the right programme, I ponder the fact I never bother what clothes I wear. Trainers yes, but no one round here has much money for clothes, except perhaps the Sky-installation guy.

'You like football?'

'Nah, not really.'

'Cooking programmes?'

He leans back and gives me a raised eyebrow. This time I laugh out loud. He looks just like The Rock. Perhaps if The Rock had fallen on bad times and had been in a concentration camp in Siberia for five years.

'Movies?'

He grins and nods.

'Cool, we've got Sky. We can watch a bit of Dwayne Johnson kicking arse. You got Sky?'

'Nah, just terrestrial, but you can never just chill and watch at mine.'

'OK. We've got all the channels.'

We don't pay for Sky. I don't know anyone else who does round here, yet we all have it. God knows how they make any money.

The lounge door opens and my mum comes staggering out with her head back laughing and tears streaming down her face.

'Ah, here you are, sweetie. I see you've eaten your dinner, and, wow, all your veg. Who's Mummy's good boy?' She makes a 'Mwah' sound as she kisses me on the forehead. 'Hi. Who is this tall, hand-some stranger?' She bursts into laughter again. She's steaming.

'This is my mum, erm, Angela.'

Jake smiles a sheepish grin full of pastry and holds out his hand. My mum is on a mission though and she wouldn't have noticed if he had the kettle in his mouth, like a St Bernard for the teetotal.

She drags a bottle of wine from the fridge and waves it in the air as if she's just won top prize in a raffle. Then she grabs Jake's arm and pumps it like an old-fashioned fruit machine. She staggers back down the hallway, bouncing off the walls. We hear the blare from the TV as she yanks open the door. Muffled laughter follows as she disappears into the lounge and then silence as they're closed in.

I give Jake a look that says 'parents'.

'I'm going to go, Ben. We'll do the movie another time.'

At the door he puts his hand on my shoulder and gives me a serious look. He nods towards the lounge. 'At least you got some.'

7

With that statement ringing in my ears, I grab the list from my room and go into the lounge. It's a big room with two three-seater sofas, one for me and one for them. Perfect. I sit opposite them with my note hidden behind my English book *Cider with Rosie*. The book has been infuriating me. I can't absorb it. It's as though there's too much information. Still, they've seen me battling with it and won't think twice about seeing it now. The advert break finishes for the X Factor and the show resumes. Then, for the first time in my entire life, I study my parents.

They look comfortable together, both sharing flushed, happy, red faces. They are holding hands too, something I realise they do a lot on the sofa. The main difference is my dad is smartly dressed whereas my mother is in leggings and a well-worn jumper. It shows off a bit of shoulder and makes me see, for the first time, again, that she's an attractive lady. Not in the same league as Sally perhaps, but appealing. I got all my looks and features from my mum as I, too, am slim and dark, with a sharp nose and piercing eyes. My dad is almost the opposite with a beefy, amiable presence. It's obvious they like each other and she looks content. She whispers in his ear, and he wearily rolls his eyes. My dad has trouble standing and knocks over his wine glass.

'Oops, your mother wants choc-choc, Ben. We don't get in the way of that, now, do we?' He looks at the spillage and decides to leave it.

'Remember when you were young? You could hear a sweet wrapper rustle from fifty feet even if a Concorde was taking off behind you.'

As I wonder what a Concorde is, my mum springs up like a cricket. As she runs out, I notice a hole in the side of her leggings near her hip. She returns with a tea towel, and then my dad comes in and throws me two lines of Dairy Milk. We resume the good-natured bickering that's part of family life. I check my list again and it doesn't seem to make any sense.

You may be an alcoholic if you:

Feel guilty or ashamed about your drinking.
Lie to others or hide your drinking habits.
Have friends or family members worried about your drinking.
Need to drink to relax or feel better.
Blackout or forget what happened after drinking.
Regularly drink more than you intended.

None of these seem to fit the bill. The best way to describe my mother is slightly absent and mildly dizzy. I can't seem to remember anything different. This is our normal Saturday night and it is fine. She doesn't work but the house is always clean. Something happened in the past, which I've never been told about, and she's on Disability Living Allowance. She goes to the newsagent's to get the paper every morning, returns, and does the housework. In the afternoon, she watches shit telly. That is her life.

My dad works late most nights and isn't home, so it's just the pair of us in the evening. We've always been early risers so I go to bed about nine, listen to music and go to sleep. She often drops off on the sofa before that. Then, I pull the throw over her we keep in the lounge for that sole reason. She likes to wait up for my dad to come home. I'm sure that's what she told me once, and now it's just one of our little daily routines.

Tonight, my parents go to bed early and I know for what sickening reason. Shrugging to myself, I turn off the lamp next to the TV and look through our lounge window. I can see down to the gardens. Only the bottom flats have one, which my dad says makes him happy. He often likes to joke, 'I haven't got time to flatulate, never mind propagate.' I don't even think that's a word, but he's always very pleased with himself afterwards.

Jonty and Sally's garden is spotless and the mown lawn pristine. Next to hers, Michelle and Kirsty's looks like all the Last Night of the Proms' marching bands have gone through. Then a bomb has gone off in a Chinese toy factory. We have all sorts here.

I tidy away the glasses and as I go through to my room I can hear the squeak of my parents' bed. Wrinkling my nose, I put my headphones on to block out any unwelcome sounds, and consider what my dad told me at the game. None of the descriptions seem to apply to my mother.

As I drift off, I also conclude that if my mum is an alcoholic, and alcoholism is an illness, then my dad is infected too.

8

5TH DECEMBER 2007

We stand at the front for the funeral. There's only my mum and me on our pew. A lot of other people are here, although I don't know most of them. My mum is different today, kind of raw and vivid. She's shaking a bit as she stares up at the cross. Her chin is defiant and there's a small light in her eyes I haven't seen in a while. We hardly spoke this morning. Not even in the posh car as we followed the hearse to the crematorium at Marholm. I feel alone, even though I can sense a hundred eyes on the back of my neck.

The bottom of my coat is being tugged and I turn round to see Jonty and his mum. Jonty gives me a doleful look. He clearly feels the gloom of the occasion and I reach over and give his hand a hard squeeze to let him know everything will be OK. His mother has a white blouse on and a striking silver necklace with a big blue crystal resting on her bosom. My eyes slide to her breasts and I chastise myself. What is wrong with me? At my father's funeral, for God's sake.

I catch a few commiserating smiles and recognise some of the neighbours. Jake was invited but said he doesn't do funerals. Instead, there's a sea of unknown, pinched faces. It's weird though.

My dad knew he was dying, and we all knew it would be soon. Yet here, at the funeral, we look shocked.

It turns out my dad took out a policy years earlier that is paying for all this. 'That's typical of your father's vanity,' my mother said. I didn't know what that meant then and she hasn't enlightened me since. It has been a strange year. I suspected something was up as my dad missed work and slept a lot.

He finally told me after I found a load of hair in the shower. We had one good chat near the end. He told me to never give up. He stressed that if I made any mistakes, I should try to rectify them. That we can always do good. Our Macmillan nurse was awesome, but eventually the pain got so bad he went into Thorpe Hall Hospice. I still thought he could beat it at that point. Someone should have explained what a hospice was. The people who leave Thorpe Hall are generally those who specifically want to die at home. My dad didn't.

I only saw him there once when it was time to say goodbye. I had been avoiding going there, thinking I could talk to him when he got out. You would think it depressing, a place like that, full of death. It wasn't though. It was peaceful and almost beautiful. We have to die and we must do it somewhere. Better to do it in a converted mansion in picturesque grounds than in a filthy, understaffed hospital.

I thought he was asleep the last time I saw him. When my mum left to go to the toilet, he moved his hand over to mine, ever so slowly, and gently held it. He looked at me. 'Take care of your mother. She's put up with a lot.' That was it – no 'I love you, son', or the passing on of any wisdom. Maybe he was aware I knew he loved me. Perhaps he had already told me what was important. I think that just saying those words was such an enormous effort for him he could manage no more. He was asleep again before my mum came back, and died the next day.

So here we are. I hear little of the service, as though it's happening in a world next to mine. My mum stands proudly beside me like a statue. I can hear sobs from behind and I wonder whose they are. We don't really have any family as my parents are only children, and both sets of grandparents died when I was too small to know them. It's nice that someone is capable of crying though, as it is beyond my mum and me.

9

The wake is held in a pub on the other side of town in Woodston called the Swiss Cottage. It's a small Irish pub and heaving for a Wednesday lunchtime. We are sitting on the right of the bar as you walk in, so we have a full view of the room. I can't help thinking the landlord must be pleased with all the business. Years ago, when my dad still brought me here, I'd see a different side to him. He said the accents reminded him of the old country and made him feel alive. I suspect the whiskey he used to drink helped with that too. He used to dance with women in the bar and sing with the old men playing dominoes. I got a glass of real Coke and a packet of Walker's crisps, so I liked it here too.

None of our neighbours have come so I recognise no one. It's left me feeling weird. They don't know me and they don't appear to know my mum either. We've become bit parts in the film of our own lives. Everyone else seems to be having a good time though. It's perfectly clear everyone loves a funeral. After you've paid your respects, you can drink as much as you want and no one will judge you. That beer or slice of cake tastes nicer today. Perhaps for these, the working class, it's a while since they savoured anything but the bitter taste of disappointment. They are still here though, still fighting. My mother hasn't touched a drop. She looks pale and I worry it might be too much for her.

We have visitors to the table. They all say the same kind of thing. 'He was the life and soul.' 'We will all miss him.' 'I can't believe he's gone.' 'An amazing bricklayer, your dad.' A man with tears in his eyes comes over, gives my mum a whiskey, and leaves without saying anything. A woman in a dress more suited to a summer wedding comes over, freely crying, and ruffles my hair. She smells wonderful. I watch her as she returns to her seat at the bar and drinks a large glass of wine as though it's a medicinal brandy. For someone who worked all hours and came home late, my dad seemed to have found the time to cultivate many strong friendships as he was clearly bloody popular here.

My stomach tells me we didn't have breakfast and I remember seeing food when we arrived. 'Do you want something to eat, Mum?'

'Not for me, love.'

I squeeze my way through the, by now, boisterous crowd to a table on the far side of the pub. There's a small buffet on it. It looks as if a plague of fussy locusts has beaten me to it. As I sift through the detritus, a tall man stands next to me. He gives me the same look everyone has been giving me today.

'A good man, your dad.'

I look up at the man and nod. I almost mumble 'thank you' but I can see he has something else to say.

'No one's happy he's gone, although not everyone is sad for the same reason.' He inclines his head towards a red-faced man who's making his way to my mother's side of the pub. 'Yes, I'll really miss him, but I stopped lending him money a long time ago.'

I finally say, 'Thank you,' and weave back to my seat. As I arrive, the guy is leaning over my mother, whose face is slack with fear. I stand behind him and clear my throat. For the second time in my life, my body tells me a fight is near. I have a strong urge to go to the toilet and my fingers tingle. I'm not as scared this time. My dad's just died. What's the worst that can happen?

I inhale long and deep through my nose. Even though the man must be fifty years old, he's much shorter than I am. I'm still only fourteen but I'm already over six feet tall. I'm not sure what stops him. Is it the size differential, the fact I'm so young, or because he's at a wake? He brushes past me and disappears into the throng.

'What did he want?'

Mum looks like she's about to speak, then shakes her head. I'm missing something.

'Come on, Mum, it's just you and me now. We must be honest with each other.'

She opens her mouth, but the jukebox sparks into life and 'The Wild Rover' by The Dubliners blares out to a raucous cheer. My dad's favourite song and my mum can't take another minute. She gets up and walks round her side of the table and leaves. No one notices. I get up and follow her and I know no one cares.

10

Taxis cost money, so we walk home from the pub. It's a long way and we have to walk through some of the rougher parts of town in the drizzle. Nobody bothers us though. I think the look on my mother's face is enough to scare off the most desperate of street robbers.

We take over an hour, and my mum doesn't say a word the whole way.

When we get to Paston, I can't face going back to our flat.

'Mum, I'm nipping downstairs. I'll catch you in a bit!' I shout to her back as she lets herself in. She doesn't reply and I conclude it'll take more than words to penetrate the carapace against the world that's forming there. I can hear singing, music and laughter from behind Jonty's door. I wonder whether I can handle the other side of the happiness coin, but I don't have many appealing options. I knock and he opens the door, pulls me into a hug, then drags me down to their lounge. His mother is red-faced, sweating and dishev- elled. Jonty grabs her and pulls her into a clumsy jive.

'That's enough now, Jonty. We have visitors.'

She isn't getting out of it that easily.

As he swings her round like a giggling rag doll, I realise just how big Jonty has grown. She seems tiny in his arms in comparison. Dancing is not Jonty's forte. It is 'strictly come stumbling' but very amusing. I can't remember who said, 'Dance like no one is watching,' but they were talking about the joy on Jonty's face right now.

'It's OK!' I shout above the racket. 'It's just what I need.'

I settle back and watch the show. Everything is changing. It's felt as if my life has been on hold for the past year, but obviously, the rest of the world has continued to spin. Jonty is a few years older than me and in some respects a man. We had played together since we were so young it wasn't until I was about eight when I realised he was different. I didn't even know what a person with Down's was. His mum was always explaining things to me about it, often after my dad had put his foot in it. He couldn't stop himself using terms such as 'mongol' and 'high functioning', but it was me she used to explain it to. She'd look at me and say, 'He is a person with a condition. Down's does not define him,' and, 'There are no degrees of Down's – you either have it or you don't.' She'd be slightly fervent when she told me this, and it sometimes scared me, as though at some point I would be responsible for him and I would need to be up to speed.

He was the best friend a boy could have. I know that sounds cheesy, but it's true. He was always happy to see you and never had a hidden agenda. How he felt was clear on his face. People with Down's develop slower than other children, but Sally used every spare hour helping him. Due to the age gap, we spent most of our childhood at the same level. Things are changing now he has hit adolescence. The big difference is he attends a special school. Sally thinks he will find it beneficial to be with other people with disabilities at this challenging time. 'To find the understanding and mutual support that comes from shared situations,' was what she said. I can remember the phrase because I kept repeating it in my head, trying to work out what it meant. Maybe I need that too.

I miss walking to school with Jonty but I seem to spend more and more of my time with Jake. He's good fun and doesn't give a shit about anything or anyone. Occasionally we meet up and he has marks and bruises on his face or is limping. I was shocked at first, but he is stoical about it and just admits to having wound up the wrong person.

* * *

Jonty's mother eventually extricates herself from the Yeti's crush and goes to get us a glass of squash. She also brings us back a mini Mars bar and a happy smile slips out of me for the first time that day. I suppose some things don't change. Once, she left two full-sized Mars bars in reach when we were young and we ate them when she nipped out. She said the sugar rush made us go mental, and I laughed so much I actually pissed myself. Sally was cool about that and sent me home in a pair of Jonty's trousers. They hung off me like a maternity dress on a supermodel.

The Macmillan nurse had told my mum and me about the five stages of grieving: denial, anger, bargaining, depression and acceptance. Dying of cancer often takes a long time. Could that be why I don't feel too bad? Perhaps my mum and I have already been through these stages and have come out the other side.

Jonty – it's actually Jonathan Thacker. It's one of his mum's favourite stories. One for adults only. When he was little, he always introduced himself to people with his full name. I think a lot of kids do it. Thacker is not an easy one for any young boy to say. He always used to shout it too, the words slowly bellowed in the recipient's face. It sounded like, 'Hi, I'm John, Fucker.' So his mum said, 'Just say, "My name is John T"', and it stuck. She says having a child like

Jonty is a burden and a gift, but as the years go by the burden becomes lighter and the gift gets bigger.

The doorbell rings and startles me. I can't remember ours ever working. Jonty bounces off to answer it.

He returns to the room holding the hand of an older man. He's good-looking, how Sally is. They kiss and look at each other in a way I don't quite yet understand. They're all in high spirits. I can't help thinking of my dad, just burnt up in the crematorium, and the fact he is already forgotten. Have they also been through the five stages? They're bustling around in the kitchen and I feel like a spare part, so I retreat and shut the front door behind me. As I do, I realise that's the second time today I've left and nobody's noticed. I need to work on my exits.

I get interrupted on the stairs.

'Ben.'

I turn to face Sally and give her a smile.

'He was a good man, your father. He did so much for me over the years. Sometimes the only person that kept things ticking over here was him. Those nights out and the occasional brief respite helped keep me sane. You played your part too, you know, so thank you.'

I return to her door, hug her, and then trudge up the stairs to my mum.

11

My mum is in the lounge when I get back. Surprisingly, the TV is off. The house is so quiet I can hear the fridge even though the kitchen door is shut. Mum is sitting on the sofa doing the crossword. I sit next to her to see what clues she hasn't done yet. It was one of our evening things, doing the crossword. She is brilliant at them and, through her, I am too. It's why my vocabulary is so good. My mum often corrected my speech if I dropped word endings or used bad grammar. She would joke 'Why use a short word, when you can use a long one?' We played games where we would try and say many different words for the same meaning. Then we discovered Scrabble. I took it to heart. She sometimes called me Rip Ben Winkle as I slept a lot and had such a mature outlook on life. I was an old head on young shoulders. I sometimes think that's why people think I'm cleverer than I am.

As I lean over her I get a strong whiff of cider. Specifically, my dad's cider. It's robust stuff, distinctive smelling, and normally my mum won't bother with it.. It's not an easy drink for the uninitiated. It's been in the cupboard for months because my dad became too ill to imbibe. Jake and I drank it once. Well, we had a swig. It tasted like a heady mix of apple cough syrup and aviation fuel. It gave me a strange feeling in my mouth where I couldn't tell if my teeth were being cleaned or dissolved.

My dad loved it and used to swill it back as if it came from the fountain of youth. I could see, after my dad lifted the curtain at that football game, that both my parents had issues with alcohol. My dad was just able to function on a slightly higher level. It's a fine line. I can see that life is all about small differences. Happy and sad, healthy and sick, rich and poor, alive or dead.

She hasn't started the crossword. Her grip is white on the pen. The light in my mum's eyes has changed now. It reminds me of the Terminator robot's blazing-red eye as it is crushed in the compressor at the end of the film. She's unable to keep her head still either. Before she opens her mouth, I know she is drunker than I've ever seen her.

'He is not the man you think he is.' She slurs, even though her words are chosen with care. 'Sure he was a good person in some respects, but he had the devil in him. I should've left a long time ago.'

I won't sit here in silence and listen to a drunkard badmouth my dad on the day of his funeral. Hot anger spreads through my body like the light creeping over you as the sun dawns. It's good, I welcome it.

'I hope you were going to leave me here. He worked hard for a living. He took us to places and paid for everything. You sat on your arse and got slaughtered so maybe you shouldn't be the one who judges.'

Her head swivels back towards me and her eyes follow after. I can see them fade.

'Did you know bricklayers are paid brilliant money? If you're the best. Your father was.'

She gestures her hand around our lounge in a dramatic swirl and I look at our shabby furniture and battered TV.

'You aren't like him. You're a good person. Much better than him.'

She looks like she'll say something else, something terrible. I can see the internal fight raging, but she gives up, as if she has given up on life.

'You don't know. You know nothing.' She weeps as I stare her down. 'How can you? You're so young.'

My rage is complete and the detonation approaches. For once, I don't have the words. I leave, before I say something I can't take back, slamming the door behind me, and go to look for Jake. I still have control but the foundations I built myself on are liquefying. If I'm not careful I will wash away.

12

1ST MARCH 2008 (FIFTEENTH BIRTHDAY)

I slide into crime in the same way you sink into a hot bath – gently, with a little trepidation. Then enthusiastically, with a smile, and without thinking about the consequences. I guess that's how everyone starts: the thief taking a pen from the office store cupboard, the lingering hug by a weakening paedophile, or the first wing idly plucked from an injured butterfly by a psychopathic killer. Once you're on that slippery slope, it's just a matter of how far and how fast you go down. It's very hard to get off once you're in motion. Obviously, Jake is involved.

He lives in a children's home about a five-minute walk from my house. He says, as these types of home go, it isn't a bad one. When we first met I used to question him about his past, his parents and the other places where he'd lived. However, he was always reluctant to talk about them.

As our friendship progressed, I realised Jake doesn't have many happy stories. Eventually I stopped asking. Occasionally he would volunteer things, but we lived in the present. The more time rolled on, the more I realised my past has not been as normal as I thought it had. Compared to his though, it was great. However, I never appreciated it and took things for granted.

Even though we are in different years, we began to associate together at school as well as outside. Jake was a loner. I think a lot of the teachers had given up on him. He was disruptive and aggressive. If he didn't turn up for their lesson, they wouldn't go out of their way to find him to get him back into it.

I was more law-abiding but had always struggled with school. My last teacher described me as being like a far-off bright star. Intelligent, but distant. I struggled to see the importance or the relevance of it all. My dad had never helped in this regard. Parents should never say to their children, 'I dropped out of school and it didn't do me any harm,' and, 'Don't worry about exams, learn a trade, that's where the money is.' I persevered as my mum encouraged me. You would have thought Dad dying would swing the pendulum her way. It didn't. My mum withdrew from life and, along with everyone else, except Jake, she retreated from me.

Jake seemed to understand. He never said as much but life seemed more comfortable when I was with him. It shouldn't have been, it just was. Conversations became downright cringe-worthy with some people. Most people in fact. Of these, the most damaging were the children I used to be friends with before I became different. After a death, few know how to talk to you. The answer is, the same as before. Although I didn't know that either, until it happened to me. I don't blame them. Death is scary. Who wants to think about that, especially when you're young?

Some kids wouldn't speak of it, but it was as if they used up all their brainpower in trying to avoid the topic and therefore had nothing left to say about anything else. Others couldn't avoid it and would ask questions as though the subject were the sum total of my existence. As I answered, they'd listen with a look on their faces as though they were trying to solve a complicated maths conundrum. A look of concentration and confusion concerning something they couldn't, or didn't want to, understand. I can assure you it isn't contagious... not this type anyway. It is clear, even to me, that I'm becoming isolated.

* * *

I'm staring at my alarm clock, when it goes off. It's my dad's old clock. Neither he nor my mother have any need for it now. It's my birthday and my dad used to come in with a present first thing, but that won't be happening this year.

I have a job as a paperboy at the local shops, so I struggle into my jeans and sneak through my bedroom doorway. Mum sleeps later these days but I bump into her carrying a tray of bacon sandwiches. I catch the plate to stop it sliding onto the floor.

'Hi, honey. Ah, I'm sorry you're up. I was trying to catch you in bed, like, you know.'

I feel guilty for doubting her and kiss her on the forehead. I'm not sure if she has shrunk or I've grown but I have to lean down to do so. We're both aware that this is the first bit of physical contact since the funeral.

I take a big bite of one of the sandwiches, carry the tray into the lounge, and pick up a small gift box next to the plate. I raise an eyebrow at her excited eyes, anything to distract me from the cloying taste in my mouth. Expectations of the present aren't high either. She simply doesn't go out any more. Of course, she goes to the local off-licence most mornings, as I hear the clink of the bottles when she returns. Sometimes I smile if I can hear her cursing as a bottle gets away from her, and I imagine her hands shaking as she desperately tries to silence them, like someone going through cold turkey and playing whack-a-mole. I stop myself laughing – I'm not sure what kind of person would find that funny. Jake springs to mind.

The bacon is cold and so greasy that the bread is sodden and I realise she must have fried it last night. No wonder I couldn't smell it. She's never cooked first thing in the morning. I wish I hadn't caught it and the carpet was gagging on it instead.

'Good sandwich, Mum.'

'I'm glad you like it. Go on, then, open it.'

I put the sandwich down, wondering if I can leave without finishing it, and look for a way into the package. I imagine cocaine smugglers would use less tape. With my dad gone, I suspected we'd live off discount white bread and value beans. Things have changed; they have improved. My dad was a big bugger and once he got going, he could inhale food like one of those whales that just drifts along with its mouth open. My mum used to buy treats, like a four-pack of KitKats. We would have to hide them or he'd eat all of them in one go. One day he washed his own work shirt, which was unusual. He said he had a mark on the collar. It was the last time he did it because when he pulled it out it was covered in chocolate. Consequently, that was the last time we hid stuff in the washing machine. He took it in good humour and used to laugh and check in there when we looked suspicious about something.

The present is a watch. One I wanted two years ago but didn't get as it was too expensive. I can feel tears well up so I just stare at it. It will have taken a lot of effort for her to get this. She hates the crowds in town, never mind the slow bus to Queensgate shopping centre. I understand that it's not just the gift she wants me to have. It's the knowing she had to put herself out to buy it and that she still cares. I look up and she is crying.

'Thank you, Mum. That means a lot.'

I grab my beanie and depart.

* * *

I walk to the shop with a smile that turns into a frown. One present and no cards. I got loads last year. Sally will get me something, but she likes me to open it with them. As I strain to think of who sent the other cards, I remember one of the last things my dad said. He was in a drug-induced haze at the time so I didn't analyse it. 'I'm the glue that stops your mum's life turning to chaos.' I thought it the rantings of the miracle that is morphine, but it's starting to make sense. Even though he was hardly ever at home, he pulled his weight on the cleaning and the organising. She's drinking more now, the house is getting messier and as time goes by there is a strong sense of having climbed on a roller coaster. The ride edges forward, then picks up speed, until you are holding on for dear life and the screaming starts.

* * *

'All right, mate.'

I look up in shock at Jake standing behind the counter in the newsagent's. I forgot that, as some kind of favour to the children's home, they offered him a Saturday job. He did tell me, but I just assumed he'd turn it down with a sneer.

'Hello, sir. First day, is it?' I smile, but I'm curious.

'First and last.'

The strange look I receive in exchange is unsettling. I go to the back of the shop where the owner, Mr Patel, is waiting. He's a short, kindly man with a big beard who always reminds me of an Asian Robin Williams. Saturday is payday for the paperboys and, by virtue of that, my favourite day. I have a big round and receive twenty pounds a week. Jake worked the hourly rate out for me once and told me I could make better money in a Bangladeshi sweatshop. Odd, then, that I always feel rich. I think I value it by the amount of sweets I can buy, which is a lot. Normally, I chew until my jaw hurts, and read all the comics for free prior to doing my round. Mr Patel will chase me out of the shop around eight-thirty when the old folk have the hump and ring the shop wondering where their paper is.

After returning to the counter, I browse the sweet display for my favourites. I select a variety including Drumstick lollies, despite them playing havoc with my teeth, and give them to Jake. He rings the items through the till as if he's worked there all his life. I pass over the note and he wedges the change in my palm. As he does, his eyes narrow, and he whispers, 'Happy Birthday.'

At that point, Mr Patel wanders over and asks if everything is OK.

I mumble and daren't examine the scrunched notes in my grip. Stuffing my hand in my pocket, I return to my comics. I eat my sweets as usual, flicking through the comics with blank eyes. I find I can't concentrate so when I hear the phone ring out the back, I put my bag on my shoulder and stand up to leave. I'm the last paperboy left anyway and the shop is empty. Jake calls me over and I wander towards him with my ears straining to hear if the newsagent is still talking.

'Here.' Jake puts down five packets of cigarettes.

'I don't smoke.'

'That's right. We know people who do though.'

Obviously, I have options, but do I really? I won't rat on Jake, but could just leave them on the counter. Guilt makes my face hot as I stuff them in my paper bag and leave the shop at a canter. I run as though a rabid dog is after me. Although, when I reach Paston Ridings and leave everything behind, I smile. I'm buzzing. For the first time since that football match, everything else is forgotten. I feel alive.

13

It's not until the end of my round that I dare look at the change Jake gave me. All those sweets and I have thirty-two pounds in change. Very suspicious. Even *his* adding up is not that bad. I know it's wrong but I can't help wondering why I've been paying for things. I have everything I wanted, yet I still have my money. Realisation is like a drug as it flows through me.

I decide to drop in on Jonty first thing. My feet hurt from walking my round. I can feel a big stone as I tread on it due to how thin the sole is, but my battered favourite trainers make me grin. Thirty quid gets you some new ones. Perhaps I won't have to pay for them either.

* * *

As I get back to the turning for our road, I see some of the other paper boys glide past on their bikes. I've never had a bike. Mr Patel was aware of this and gave me my round within walking distance of the shop so it didn't matter, but these lads show me freedom. To be fair, I had scooters, but I'm too old for them now. However, we don't have a shed to put a bike in anyway. Would the neighbours mind me keeping one in the corridor? I have a little internal debate as to whether it would last five minutes until some git nicked it. I smile again, twice in a minute. A thieving rascal like me perhaps.

As I knock on Jonty's door, I consider that my mum wouldn't notice if I kept it in the lounge. Especially if I hung washing on it.

'Hi, Ben.'

'Hi, Sally. Is Jonty in?'

'Erm, sure, come in.'

My legs almost don't respond to my urgings. It's the coolest response I've ever had at their door. Am I unwanted?

Jonty's bedroom is on the left as you walk in. The door is half open so I can hear his voice reading to someone. It's the same guy I met here before. Sally's special friend, as Jonty calls him. He works at the school Jonty attended after puberty and, apparently, he and Sally have been seeing each other for years. I doubt that's true as I haven't seen much of him, but as I listen to the interaction between them there is a strong familiarity. There is real warmth in the way that he encourages and corrects, and almost cajoles Jonty along.

We used to read children's books together, lying on the lounge carpet as his mum watched quiz shows on the TV. He seems to have progressed somewhat under this man's watchful gaze. I've no idea what he's reading but I would struggle with some of the words he is speedily reeling off. Sally is nearby. I realise I'm looking down at the carpet divider as I listen. It's like some kind of force field stopping me entering the room. Every nuance of Sally's face tells me not to go in when I glance at her.

'We're going out in a minute. He's taking us to Burghley House.'

At my blank face, she continues.

'It's a beautiful old house near Stamford, just down the road. Like a stately home with deer. Michael thought it would be nice for Jonty to get fresh air and history at the same time.'

'Sounds nice.' For a happy moment I think she'll invite me, but she doesn't.

There is an awful silence while we stare at each other. As my eyes drop to the same blue-stone necklace she wore at the funeral, it sinks in that I have to leave.

'OK, cool. Have fun.' I scrabble around in my brain looking for something to save face, like a desperate kid trying to bob an apple at Halloween before his time's up.

'Would you mind if I kept my bike in your back yard?'

'I didn't know you had one.'

'Yeah, well, not yet. We just wanted to check if I could leave it in your garden.'

'I think that'd be fine, Ben.'

'Great. I'll let you know.'

'Ben, before you go, can I ask you something?'

So I was definitely not invited to their lovely day out. 'Sure.'

'You know I, we, are very fond of you.'

Not fond enough to take me on your fucking walk. 'Yes, I know.' I manage to smile.

'Will you be careful who you're friends with?'

'I'm sorry. I'm not sure what you mean.'

'That boy you've been hanging around with. Michael knows him. He might be a bad influence on you.'

I can't stop myself letting out a curse. So I'm not welcome on their educational ramble but I also shouldn't hang around with Jake either. Does she recommend I sit on the roundabout on my own?

'OK, I'll bear it in mind.' Incredible.

As I stamp out of the flats and let the door slam behind me, which I know winds Sally up, I realise she hasn't given me a present either.

* * *

I lie on the roundabout, on my own, rotating it with my foot when it slows. As I spin, I grasp what a non-event my birthday is. What happened to being unable to sleep the night before, due to the excitement? I miss the mysterious pile of presents on the sofa. At least I got my watch, although I can't face going upstairs to my mum again. I feel like that a lot. We used to be close, so it is hard to see her disintegrating in front of my eyes. It's as though she's turned into grey sand and the grains are slipping off. One day soon a foul wind will come and blow her away.

I can't stop thinking my dad is in the kitchen when I'm on the sofa watching TV. It stops me relaxing. I don't know what to do with myself. The day ahead stretches out in front of me like a featureless motorway.

It's fresh outside so I put my hand in my pocket and find my 'unpaid for' bounty from earlier. I remember the money too and things suddenly don't seem that bad. As if he was waiting for that moment to make his entrance, Jake appears with a wry smile. I make a big show of checking my new watch for the time, which Jake notices with an exaggerated, 'Wow.'

'Early break?'

'My career in retail was a short one.'

'That's a shame. There seemed to be benefits, especially for your friends.'

'Yes. In hindsight I think we may have missed an opportunity there.'

'As Mother says, hindsight is a wonderful thing. I take it he sacked you.'

Jake laughed out loud. 'He caught me eating the penny sweets. Twice. Said he couldn't trust me.'

'What? A few sweets?'

'Yes, I know. He said, and I quote, "It's not the monetary value, it's the principle."'

'Weird. Ah, well. It was good while it lasted.'

'How much did we make?'

There was no question of not sharing. As we split the money and sweets – the ones I hadn't eaten anyway – a bond was forming, which I knew would link us for the rest of our lives.

'Who do we know who smokes?'

'Everyone. That's not the question though, is it?'

'It isn't?'

'Nope. It's who can we get the most money off for these top-of-the-range, finely blended cigarettes.' He flares his eyes at me as he looks up from the packet.

'The Roach!' we shout in unison.

Vincent Roach is an odd one all right. He works on the production line at Perkins Engines so we often see him driving to and from work. A few weeks back, he upgraded his car and bought himself a black Porsche. It isn't a new one, but it still looks remarkably out of place where we live. Jake, who knows a lot more than I do about cars, assured me it was only about ten grand's worth. Despite that, he and I spend a lot of time looking at it. Vincent keeps it gleaming clean and shiny. He used to offer us lifts in his old banger but never had takers due to his unusualness. However, we now badger him every time we see him to take us for a spin. Such is the way with children. Anyway, ten thousand pounds seems a lot to me, and he has better clothes. Luckily for us budding entrepreneurs, he smokes a lot. I suspect his wife doesn't like it as he blazes away out at the front of the building. Anyway, that all adds up to him having the need and the money.

We knock on Vincent's door and giggle as Jake tries to make himself look like a serious door-to-door salesman. I don't think they have tracksuits, or dodgy bum fluff, but it's better than me running the show.

Vincent answers the door in a weird light-blue dressing gown and leather slippers. He looks like *The Hills Have Eyes*' version of Hugh Hefner and I almost choke on the Polo I'm eating. A strange cabbage-like smell wafts out after him that sobers me up fast.

'Good morning,' Jake says with a straight face. 'We have some reasonably priced cigarettes for sale.'

Vincent looks at Jake suspiciously. 'A little young to be selling ciggies, aren't we?'

That has me stumped. Jake, though, is primed.

'My mum's packed it in. You know how expensive fags are, so we thought we'd get her some money back by selling the ones she had left.'

Vincent looks at me for the first time. 'How's your mother?'

The question confuses me for a minute. 'Fine, you know, as well as can be expected.'

He waits for too many seconds and adds, 'Life's been hard for her.'

'Yeah?'

He'd shut up if he could read my mind and see the irritation that is building there.

'Yes, well, your dad, he seemed to calm her down. He was a good influence.'

'OK?'

'He's gone now, isn't he?'

Jake and I look at each other. I'm not sure where Vincent's going with this line of questioning. I don't want to know either.

'Look, mister, you can have these for two pounds a pack, or you can miss out.' I prefer the direct approach.

They both look at me with respect. I don't know how much fags cost to buy from the shop, but, judging by the slimy grin that arises, that is a bargain.

'I'll get my wallet.'

As Vincent scuttles off, Jake and I exchange expressions of victory but he grabs my arm and hauls me into the flat.

'I want to see her,' he whispers.

Before I know it, he's manoeuvred me into the lounge. I don't know who's most surprised, The Roach, us, or the enormous being that is rectally absorbing the sofa. I didn't know people could get so fat.

Jake recovers first. 'Sorry. I thought you said follow me.'

The stench of rotting vegetables is intense, and it's more that, than the horrified look from the two inhabitants, that sends us into reverse. Vincent herds us out and puts a ten-pound note in Jake's hand. Vincent looks embarrassed and sad. I realise, at that moment, I've never thought of Vincent as a human being. He must have the same hopes and fears we all have and I'm sorry for him. All I can offer is, 'Thank you.'

With a tired grin, he pushes the door.

Just as it shuts, Jake whispers, but is audible, 'Pervert.' The door stops closing for a few seconds and then snecks.

As we walk down the stairs, I stare at Jake's back and wonder what made him do that. It was unnecessary, mean, and malevolent. Jake is whistling. We are unalike, he and I.

'Man, did you see how big she was?' I say.

'Yep. Just think, we worried if we went in there we'd get interfered with. We should have been worrying about getting eaten.'

As I crease with laughter I realise that we aren't so different.

14

I'm nervous as we walk towards the shops at the Bretton Centre and our ultimate destination that afternoon, Sportsland, so I chatter like a chaffinch.

'So anyway, I want a bike. You know, for getting about.'

'Bikes are easy.'

'Easy what?'

'To steal.'

'Oh. I'm saving up.'

Jake looks at me as if I have just told him I'm partial to looking at naked old people.

'Don't you worry about getting into trouble with the police?'

'When was the last time you saw a pig? They have better things to worry about than a bit of petty thieving.'

I suspect I would consider it more than petty thieving if it were my bike that had been stolen.

As we arrive, my nerves increase; however, so does my excitement. I can almost feel those new trainers on my feet.

'Right, you go in. Find which pair you like. They only keep the left trainer on display so we need to get them to go out the back and get the right one so we have a pair. Unless you're a mutant.'

'Are you not coming in?'

'Not together, birdbrain, or we'll get clocked.'

I walk in the shop and it feels as if I have a chorus line of girls from the Moulin Rouge behind me, all waving placards with 'Thief' on them. I know the shoes I want as I've looked at them so many times before. Nike Air Max 360, in blue. My chest feels tight, so I walk back out to Jake, who is talking to a girl from my class called Lily. She's with Kirsty from my block of flats. As I approach them, Jake says something to them and they disappear.

'What were you talking to them for?'

'I've got us some dates for later.'

'Really? With them?'

'Yes, doughnut, with them.'

'Dates for what?'

He looks at me askance for the second time that day.

Lily is the girl in class who nobody knows. She has been in my year for as long as I can remember – junior school and senior school – but I don't think I've ever spoken two words to her. Some of the other lads take the piss out of her as she smells musty; in fact I think kids called her 'Smellily' at our last school. Oddly, though, if someone had put a gun to my head and asked me to name someone I would like to kiss, I would have said her.

She is plump and a little spotty, but she has the most haunting eyes that always feel like they can see my heart beating when they settle on me. Many years ago, we had country dancing at school. It was horrific and embarrassing for us boys, especially when you had to find a partner. Every time, she would come straight over and I would always be thankful someone wanted me. We never talked, just skipped around together. It's a combination of all those things which makes me like her, so I really want some new trainers.

'OK, what do we do?'

'What are they and what size are you?' he asks. I tell him.

'Very nice, like mine. Right, I'm going to go in and ask for the other foot. You wait five minutes and then you come in. They're always short-staffed so wait until the assistant is a bit away from me and ask him about something further down the shop. I'll do the rest. You just leave nice and slow or if you want to be super cool go and buy something for nothing.'

'What about the security guard?'

'Him? I'm fifteen. He's fifteen stone. He's about as much chance of catching me as Daddy Pig.'

'Who?'

'A fat, slow thing. Now, chill. This is easy. Well, easy for you.' Without a backward glance, he strolls into the shop as though he owns it.

* * *

Time drags in situations like these and I'm glad of my new watch. My mum would be ecstatic if she found out how useful it has been.

After the time is up, I walk in and see a young, fit-looking lad in a tracksuit hand Jake a box. I realise now why he wants him distracted. He looks like he could catch us both at the same time, even if we ran off in separate directions. I'm not sure whether to be annoyed that Jake didn't mention this, or pleased that I didn't know because I might have wimped out. The security guard has his belly resting on a table of T-shirts. It's an effort to stifle a snigger. A right dodgy-looking pair on the female side of the shop have his attention. They look as if couldn't afford any laces in here, never mind the actual items themselves. Yes, it's Lily and Kirsty.

Jake catches my eye and gives me an almost imperceptible nod. I walk past the assistant and there in front of me, like a nest of jewelled eggs, is a basket of small assorted footballs, the kind you play with during break in the playground, with no price tag on them.

'Excuse me. How much are these balls?' I mumble.

'Sorry, could you say that again?' His tired smile indicates a shortage of staff, but it has genuine warmth. Harry, his name badge proudly declares.

'These balls. How much are they?'

'Two pounds.'

'For all of them?'

'No, each.' He gives my joke the small grin it deserves.

'OK, I'll have one.' Picking up a small yellow one, I hold it aloft.

'Come over here, then, please. I'll put it through the till for you.'

As he walks past, I steal a glance down the shop and find it to be empty. There has been no beep from an alarm or concerned shout. The perfect crime.

As I leave the shop, I see the security guard searching Lily's handbag. Kirsty is giving him some shit. I wonder if Harry will get in trouble for the stolen stock, or even lose his job. I wonder if I care.

* * *

It's a long walk home. Next time we should agree on a meeting place nearby.

After a few minutes, I hear running footsteps behind me and I'm about to bolt when a female shouts my name. I recognise Kirsty's voice.

'Ben, wait for us.'

'Shit,' Kirsty says. 'I thought that fucker was going to strip-search me.'

'You would've liked that,' Lily says.

'I take it he didn't find anything, then.'

'No, I hadn't touched anything. Jake just told us to go and fool around in there.' Daft, but not stupid.

We get back to Paston and I ask where Lily lives.

'I'm back with my mother for the moment. Now she's been released. I shouldn't think it will be long until I'm back with Jake, unless my aunt will have me. Although she was inside last year as well.'

I stop walking as she carries on, leaving me stunned. Kirsty comes back, links arms with me, and breezily declares, 'Her mum's a junkie.'

* * *

Jake is waiting outside, next to my dad's car. It hasn't moved since he became too ill to drive it. It's covered in dust and leaves and the tyres are flat. I suppose we should have sold it but it's a bit late for that now. Jake is bouncing a golf ball as he looks up the road at us. At his feet is a shiny looking Nike box.

'Is your mum out all day, Kirsty?'

'Yep. She's gone shopping in town, which means she'll walk through the market and then go straight to the Wortley for some reasonably priced booze. She won't be back for ages.'

He stops bouncing the ball and looks up to the top flat. We all follow his gaze and then smile. The Roachs' flat. One window to the lounge is open. Jake cocks his leg like an American pitcher, pulls his arm back and throws it hard. I imagine it landing in a huge plate of spaghetti bolognese that Mrs Roach is about to inhale in one mighty breath. Instead, there is a high-pitched tinkle as it flies through the pane of glass next to his intended target, and we run inside.

* * *

Jake remembers to pick up my new trainers, but I don't have time to put them on. I'm not sure why I want Lily to see me wearing them. As I'm the last to arrive at her flat, I'm the only one who doesn't trip over something on the floor, as their hasty cursing has forewarned me. I'm not shocked by the ravaged look of the place. It is foul though. There are beer cans all over the place and containers of half-eaten food on the floor, all enveloped in a smoky atmosphere. With a sinking feeling, I realise if it weren't for the smell of cigarettes, I could be in my own flat. Lily and Kirsty disappear giggling into a bedroom. I follow Jake into the kitchen and we laugh at the stack of plates next to the sink. Like in Pisa, we are impressed it hasn't fallen over. He picks up a bottle of wine, which is half full, and we look for some clean glasses. It's a futile task. Instead he drinks from the bottle and passes it. I take a tiny sip, but hope it looks as if I've taken a big one. Even so, it's a Herculean effort to swallow the foul liquid.

We chuck the piles of clothes off the sofa onto the floor and sit down.

'Lily's mine. You can have Kirsty.'

It's clear by the look on my face that I'm about to protest, even though I'm not sure what we will be doing with them, but he cuts me off at the pass.

'You got some nice new footwear. It's only fair. Put them on.'

As I do, I can see just how filthy my old pair are, and I feel like a scumbag. The new ones look dazzling, but out of place above my ill-fitting, dirty jeans. I think I must get some new clothes and then ponder whether that means paying for or 'borrowing' them.

Lily and Kirsty reappear. They've got dressed up and put some make-up on. The clothes look as though they've come straight from Michelle's party range, the face paint from the clown shop. I know nothing about cosmetics, but I know that this looks wrong. I don't care. My feet sweat in my new footwear.

'Where we going, then?' Kirsty asks.

'Nowhere. We don't need to go anywhere to have a good time.'

'You said you would take us somewhere.' Whining doesn't suit her.

Jake grabs Lily's hand and they disappear into the bedroom that the girls just exited. Kirsty turns to me with a big grin. She grabs the wine bottle out of my hand and takes a big swig. She doesn't grimace, just smiles.

'Looks like it's you and me, then.'

Then she is kissing me. I expect it to taste foul but perhaps two wrongs make a right in this instance. I've never kissed a girl. Not a proper snog, so I'm unsure what to expect. We bump teeth on occasion but we seem to fit together and it's not unpleasant. Kirsty grabs my wrist and places my hand over one of her breasts. I squeeze as though I'm checking an orange for ripeness. Also not unpleasant.

She casually descends from our embrace and kneels at my feet. She pulls my jeans and boxers down in one quick, practised movement, and suddenly my penis is in her warm mouth. Now, that does feel good. I'm glad I had a shower this morning.

Without knowing where to look, I eventually peek downwards. It's Kirsty. I've known her all my life and now everything feels weird. It's like doing it with your sister. I'm about to pull away when something changes. I can feel my temperature go through the roof and I grab her head with both hands.

We lie on the carpet afterwards. It's sticky, but not with fresh liquid. I try not to think where that went. Kirsty has her head on my shoulder and is looking up at me with a kind of mad devoted expression. I'm very aware she is fourteen. I want to leave.

'Did you like that?'

'Yes,' is all I can come up with. I think I would rather have had an ice cream, but I don't say it.

'Lily showed me what to do.'

Before I can absorb and process that titbit, Jake exits the bedroom and comes back in and grabs his coat.

'We've got to shoot, pick that stuff up, Ben.'

I almost run to the door. I pull my coat on and turn to Kirsty, who isn't pleased. 'See you later,' doesn't seem appropriate, but I say it anyway.

When we get outside and hasten from the flats, I ask the obvious question. 'What have we got to pick up?'

He keeps walking, says nothing, just wears a small grin. There is nothing to pick up. He knows me better than I know myself.

15

15TH MAY 2008

I'm already late for school when I go into the kitchen. This isn't unusual. There is a strange feel or smell in the flat that catches in my throat. My first thought is that we've been burgled. I relax when my brain reminds me I wouldn't care. Someone has tidied away the rubbish. Our carpet is brown. Fancy that. I wander into the lounge and note the lack of clutter. My mum is on her hands and knees cleaning the back of the toilet. She looks pale as her gaze focuses on me. That's not surprising, it would be a nasty job.

'I'm off to school.'

'Doesn't the watch work still?'

I'm stunned. I'm not used to her questioning my stories and I've stopped burning energy on making them believable.

'Yes. I'm just late.'

'It's lucky then some people from the school are coming here.'

'Really? What for?' My mind enters creative mode and searches for something terrible.

'The letter says to have a chat at this hard time and see how they can help. We don't want them seeing us living like a pair of skunks, now, do we?'

I can't help smiling and she does too. If she's putting the effort in, then so will I. I'll need to find my school uniform for starters.

'Can you take down that rubbish bag? They'll be here in half an hour.'

I grab it and see my mum's room is now spotless. If there were a few seagulls in it, mine would look exactly like a rubbish tip. So what? I am a boy. I drag the black sack combining speed with care. It popping on the stairs would hamper our efforts to present a clean home life. I almost have a heart attack as I step outside and see the flashing blue lights of a police van arrive. They must be here for me. Another van and a car appear. Everything I'm wearing, down to the ring on my finger, was shoplifted.

Before I can answer the adrenalin rush that swamps me and tells me to flee, three men get out and jog past. A gnarled-looking police officer holds the entrance door open.

'Do you live here?'

'Yes.' I suffocate the sarcastic remark about the sack in my hand.

'Throw that away and go back to your property.'

* * *

Typically, all the bins are nearly full. The only one with enough space has a dead cat in it and smells accordingly. I empty some of our foul waste on top. Another nasty job. I cross the road and lob the last bit in the bin for the house opposite. The owner yanks his front door open to curse me but is distracted by the sight of a cuffed Vincent Roach getting dragged out of the flats. They aren't being as careful as I was with the rubbish. Vincent stares at me as he passes as if I can help. He shakes his head as he gets his spine bent and is shoved in the back of the closest van. Then they are gone.

The bins are in a row next to the two car spaces and are now being looked in by other officers. My dad's old car is now parked next to a smashed-up black Porsche. That is weird. The police make me nervous, but I can't resist.

'That one has something dodgy in it.' An unpleasant surprise.

I slide back inside, and run up the stairs and through our doorway as fast as I can.

'Vincent's been arrested.'

My mum nods, grabs a towel out of the airing cupboard, and shuts the bathroom door. I turn on the TV and don't give him another thought.

* * *

I let in the visitors. I also give them the huge smile my doting parent has instructed me to. Jake calls people like these 'do-gooders'. They're looking to give you an excuse for your behaviour, any behaviour, so act contrite and they will let you get away with murder.

'So, Ben, we notice that you missed a few days' school and didn't follow the absence procedure.' They both look the same; grey and helpful. They wasted their time telling me their names.

'Yes. It's been a tricky time, with all that's happened.'

'I'm sure it has. You've been very brave.'

I nod.

'I can't imagine what it must have been like for you both.'

My mum shakes her head.

'Is there anything we can do to help?'

I'm sure my mum also wants to tell them to fuck off. She bites her lip, and Jake has taught me well.

'Sometimes it overwhelms me and I just need to be on my own. Nothing else will stay in my mind. I go to his grave and remember.' I don't think he has a grave, just some kind of plaque, but I say it anyway.

The pair look at each other. 'If that happens, just come and see us the next day. It's only a few weeks now until the end of term.'

'Thank you.' I steal a quick look at my mother, who is sweating as though the Gestapo have come round for brunch. The lies roll off my tongue like bowling balls down a lane. One after the other, smooth and fast. Strike after strike.

My mum shows them out and flops back onto her sofa opposite me. We share a conspiratorial smile.

'I'm going to the shop,' she says. My face falls. 'Just for a few, to take the edge off.' She leaves the room and I hear her banging drawers in the kitchen.

I can't say I blame her, although I am disappointed. The school doesn't come around for nothing. She did what was necessary to avoid any conflict. Surely, a normal parent would ask for some more details, want to know what days have been missed, even put me on the spot, there and then, say, 'Funny, you always left the house on time?' Maybe I should give her credit for supporting me. I get up and put on my coat.

'OK, I'm off out with Jake,' I say to no one. She was in a rush.

I look around at the flat as I leave. Would it be too much trouble for us to keep it like this?

16

Jake's pretence of attending school is now over. We hang around down a park in Woodston, just off Oundle Road. Opposite the halfway house. It's nearly summer, so there are quite a few of us. Jake knows them all well. He says they disappear in the winter, but he doesn't know to where. I only tend to see them at the weekend so I'm just on nodding terms with most. They are the underclass. Some of them sleep at the back of the Key Theatre, or nearby, under the railway arches. A lot of them pass out on the spot, depending on what level and type of substance they've ingested. We are a teen crime wave.

It turns out stealing a bike is not as easy as Jake said.

As I arrive at the park, he's his usual over-confident self. The problem is, I want a decent bike, and people don't leave those lying around. I have told him I'm happy to pay for one but he won't have it.

'Today is the day, my friend.'

'You reckon? OK. No crazy shit though.'

When I say we're a teen crime wave, I should qualify that by saying not a cunning one. There are about twelve of us who hang around here but it's a revolving dozen. I didn't think you could go to prison until you were eighteen but I was wrong. They don't call them prisons but if the doors are locked that's what they are. However, you have to be extremely naughty to end up in one of those. Jake, who seems to be the expert on this topic, assures me they're expensive to run and the public have little appetite for locking up children. However, after exposure to kids like these, people would queue up to throw away the key.

Jake and I discuss the topic all the time. We agree that you aren't born bad, but we differ on rehabilitation. I say there's hope and we can still offer something as we are only young. Jake says it's too late. His favourite analogy is that we are broken, like an expensive vase dropped from a height. Yes, you can fix it, but it's incredibly time-consuming and expensive. Afterwards, the end result is still going to be weak and worth less. Society would be better off spending the effort and money protecting the really young, before they end up like us. It's a depressing point of view but not without merit. When Jake talks like this, I see glimpses of a bright person who never had a chance.

If you don't go to school, you have plenty of spare time. I found that if I turned up, registered, and then cleared off, no one was liable to say anything. I would just lie about being upset about my father, feeling angry and violent. That usually did the trick. They mentioned me seeing a school psychiatrist. The more I thought about it, the more I concluded it might be a good idea. My normal emotional state is irate.

Lily comes down here too, often with Jake. I don't discuss whether they are boyfriend and girlfriend as they don't act like it. They are close though. I think it's something to do with finding the understanding and mutual support that comes from shared situations that Sally used to bang on about. It's the one thing we three don't discuss. I don't see Lily at school either, not even in the morning. We chat but she's distant, for want of a better word.

She's back in the children's home as her mum got some serious time for sticking a needle in the arresting officer. Lily has also lost a lot of weight, which endears her to me. I want to ask her out but I can't think of anywhere to go. Also, I don't feel I have much to offer. Lily, Jake, and I are the only ones who haven't done any custodial time. Lily and I are late to the party and Jake is the smartest thief.

The police arrive. They don't bother moving us on as I think they like to know where we are. Solving crimes this way must be like shooting fish in a barrel. When they come, Jake and I put up our hoodies and walk away, run if necessary. Driving around in a squad car drinking coffee will not hone you to catch a razor-thin youth in the latest athletic footwear. The other kids hang around. They have given up already.

I suspect Jake is going that way as he's getting more reckless with his stealing. He's had close escapes and any goodwill is gone. A lot of shopkeepers will let you off if they don't know you and you have a good story. Jake has used up all the understanding in that regard.

We walk over Town Bridge, past the magistrates' court. Jake is a regular visitor there, and I consider if he realises he speeded up for that part of the journey. Jake is walking funny, as if he has a false leg.

'Did you donate your leg to medical science?'

'I tried to, but it was too muscular. Pets At Home took it instead. They were running out of meat for the animals.'

'Yeah? You have a spare. How much did you get?'

'Twenty quid?'

'Not bad.'

'They gave me a hundred for my dick.'

We walk to the bicycle racks outside Boots to do the equivalent of window shopping. As we subtly peruse the range, Jake gives me a little whistle. The problem we've found is that those D-Locks that people use nowadays are fiendishly hard to break open. Trust me, we've tried everything.

Freezing compressed air works. The hardest materials in the world become brittle when they're dramatically cooled. If you then hit them with a hammer, they will shatter. That's the science. Jake and I are not scientists but we are optimists. Last week we found a suitable prize D-locked to the green railings of the market in town. Jake used the spray while I kept watch. My nervousness was ascending as the spray was a lot louder than I expected and Jake kept cursing that his thumb was freezing. (Jake said this caused his thumbnail to later fall off.)

So why aren't bicycle thieves using cans of compressed air and making off with every bike they see on the street? Because, even though this trick can break the lock, it still takes quite a bit of hammering. At 2 p.m. on a busy, warm, spring Saturday afternoon this is not subtle. Jake almost had it off when some little shit shouted, 'Thief,' causing Jake to hit his thumb (the most likely reason for his nail to fall off). We had to leg it, losing our lovely claw hammer in the process, and then we had a big argument over whether he should go to A&E or not as the police would check. (He didn't.)

Anyway, this fine-looking conveyance today has the type of three-digit combination lock on it that a strong man could pull apart. Today, we will be winners. Admittedly there are two locks, front and back. I imagine Jake has hand-held cable cutters to do the job. As I said, he has become brazen. With a flourish and the sound of sticky tape coming away from skin, he presents me with an enormous bolt cropper. It is a metre long and screams 'bike thief' in a way that oily hands declare one to be a mechanic. Incredibly, as my brain stops, my body coolly clips off the locks like I'm cutting through two rubber bands. I swear someone raises the alarm by shouting 'Rape'. Everyone in a fifty metre circle turns and stares at us.

Jake and I share a look but we know the score. It's every man for himself. I'm not leaving the bike either. Jake is off on his toes like Usain Bolt on his way to the toilet with the trots. I yank the bike out of the stand, run with it until I'm up to speed, and then jump on. Jake is already out of sight. I go through Cathedral Square and then career past the town hall. As people dodge out of my way, I head, ironically, towards the police station on the corner of the bridge. As I hit the traffic lights, I have to stop for the steady stream of fast-moving cars. I look behind me as I do. I wish I hadn't. There's a bloke running after me. A big one and he looks cross. I curse as I pump the pedals through the now-stopped traffic.

It has slipped into a stupidly low gear and the crank spins round with hip-juddering speed. I get it to change gear just as I hit the rise of the bridge and have to lean forward out of the seat to keep up the pace. Heavy footsteps are almost on me as I accelerate.

I grunt as a hand grabs my coat but I've reached a pivotal speed. Fear lends strength to my legs and I fly over the town bridge and pass Jake, who is throwing the bolt croppers over the side into the river. The drivers gawp as I blast through another set of red lights. Jake flies down the slope towards Charters car park and the footpath out of town. I power down London Road and am away.

I scan the air, knowing Jake will be doing the same. We live in fear of the police helicopter. It is elsewhere.

17

13TH NOVEMBER 2008

Jake has disappeared. He's been missing two months. I asked at the home, but they didn't know as he hadn't lived there for a while. I wasn't aware of that. We saw each other a lot over the summer holidays. However, he got caught stealing from Marks & Spencer. He blamed me for not going with him, which was unfair. Whoever's fault it was, I haven't seen him since he went to court.

Our thievery had evolved with my new set of wheels. Natural progression, you could call it. Jake was already saying, 'Think what we could do with a car.' In some ways it was still a game to me. I got caught a few times, apologised, and escaped further punishment. By now, Jake's face should be over every billboard in the city.

That day, I told him I couldn't help as I was busy tidying. Every now and again, my mum experienced a moment of clarity and we blitzed the flat. We would wash all the bed sheets, throw away the rubbish and clean the bathroom. It was nice afterwards, when it was respectable. Although I didn't seem to notice the mess most of the time so it felt like maximum effort for minimal reward. I would rather sit in the park and have a laugh. I enjoyed watching my mum sneaking the empties in someone else's recycling bin.

The crazy thing is, no one round here cares. Certainly not The Roach as I never saw him again after the police incident. Michelle and Kirsty have moved out too. In fact, they left without even saying goodbye. Is that normal after all those years? As I watched the Asian family move in, it felt strangely unsettling, like another piece of my stability had slid out from underneath me.

Anyway, on the day in question, Jake borrowed my bike, without asking, and cycled into town. His favourite scam was to park the bike outside the shop, saunter in and grab something expensive. Occasionally we took items we'd received requests for. Yes, Jake was so well known that people would ask him to steal to order. It was a good way to make money with a guaranteed sell-on price and it also meant you didn't have the goods for long. I kept my name out of it; if anyone got caught with the goods they named you immediately. There's no honour amongst thieves and even less amongst their recipients. The usual routine was I would wait outside near the bike. That way no slippery little shits like us stole it while it was unlocked, and Lily, if she was with us, would distract the staff, or security guard, to give Jake his chance.

There was a high degree of success as long as you stuck to two things: one, do not do it in big department stores as the size and class of the shop is directly proportional to the quality of its security. CCTV is to be feared. If you go in with a huge furry trapper hat on to conceal your face, it kind of gives the game away. Therefore, John Lewis, M & S, Next, and so on are to be avoided. Two, don't do it on your own. It would be pertinent to say drugs had a hold of Jake by then.

He hadn't been able to locate Lily, so he went by himself. Michelle had asked for a two hundred quid coat, so easy money at Jake's usual 50 per cent. He'd have got away with it if Lady Luck hadn't intervened. As Jake scampered out of the store, he found someone stealing his bike, or so he thought. It was the bike's previous rugby-playing owner. How unlucky was that? The wasted seconds of push-me pull-me with the enraged man allowed the security guard to get out and shout for help.

After a desperate footrace Jake was never likely to win, it was the aggrieved proprietor who brought him down with a classy tackle straight out of the textbook. Jake said he'd made it as far as the Guildhall before the man pinned him to the steps. After that, it took the police ten minutes to turn up, and he had to lie on the floor in Cathedral Square all that time while hordes of shoppers swarmed round him. The security guard, who sat on him, even took off Jake's hat, he swears, so people could take photos. Big stores are also more likely to prosecute. He only has himself to blame.

Therefore I know Jake won't be there as I hop off the bus next to Woolworths.

As I walk to the park, I remember my reclaimed bike with a smile and a shrug. Easy come, easy go. The thought that just buying a new one is the way to go, then that sort of thing would not occur, appears in my mind and evaporates. I am only on the periphery of the thieving group so never make much money and I spend all mine on clothes and phones, so I suspect it will be a while until I get another form of transport. Unusually, for us lot, I like to look good, and I also enjoy paying for things, especially if they are convinced I'm about to sprint out of the shop. With Jake off the scene, I stay at school during the day. The teachers have been helpful and, while I will never catch up in some subjects, they are hopeful I will pass most of the exams.

Today is an exception because Lily has texted to say she wants to meet up as she has something important to tell me.

She is the only person at the park. She looks beautiful. Thin, but striking. Lily always seems to have money but has never spoken of getting caught or what she's been up to. She and Jake have a strange relationship. They care for each other, that's obvious. More in a protective way for him, and she treats Jake like a naughty older brother. Maybe it's because they have been through similar experiences, but I will never know as neither will discuss it with me. That history is theirs alone. She and I are closer though, after Jake's vanishing act.

'On your own?' I ask.

'Yep. Although I have some exciting news.'

'You won the lottery?'

'Kind of.'

That gets my attention. She's smoking a joint, which she passes to me. I take a quick puff and half choke on it. Her look of affectionate disdain disarms me. I shake my head at her and she continues.

'You know that uncle who used to let me stay with him?'

'Yes.' By uncle, you are most likely picturing some compassionate gentleman doing his bit as opposed to the shaven-headed, over-friendly hobgoblin she is actually referring to.

'He's in prison.'

'That's a shock.'

'Quite. Someone attacked him and as he fought back, the person fell over and ended up in a coma. Self-defence, like.'

I look at her to see if she is joking but she doesn't appear to be.

'Anyway, his solicitor says because it's a violent offence and he has some previous, he won't be out until he's cleared at the trial, which is about six months away.'

'OK. It's clearly a good thing that the streets will be free from that lunatic for a while, but hardly lottery-winning news.'

She elbows me in the ribs with a giggle. 'It's his mum's house. She's in a home for dementia and it's all paid off. So he lives there for free.'

Lily is enjoying this. I nearly tune out before the punchline.

'So who do you think he's asked to look after it while he's inside?'

'No way. That's brilliant news.'

'Yep, I moved all of my stuff out of the home yesterday. They don't know where I'm going either so nobody can grass me to the truancy officer.' The pleasure she takes in saying that has alarm bells ringing in my head, the kind I have come to ignore.

'What are we still sitting here for, then?'

* * *

The house is a terrace down Palmerston Road. I have never been in it prior to this, as her uncle's presence made me uncomfortable. He sometimes came to the park to look for her and everyone could pick up on his instability. One wrong word and he would fly into a rage.

The house appears small from the front, then, as she shows me through it seems to go on forever. It looks as if a bachelor lived in it though, as the furniture is basic to say the least and it smells stale. It must be grimy if I've noticed that fact. The windows are smeared and dirty fingers have smudged the light switches, although it is undoubtedly the countless old newspapers and over-flowing ashtrays that are ruining the general impression.

Lily gets us a beer each from the fridge. There is something wrong with the scene. She is fifteen years old, yet it seems so natural that I wonder if she's used to doing it for herself or another. I clear some space on the sofa for us, which is a big task. We sit down next to each other in a companionable fashion. I take a swig out of the bottle to show willing, but I still can't see what all the fuss is about. It reminds me of my parents. I realise my mum will be doing the same thing, even though it's mid-morning. Lily's deft fingers roll another joint. Practice makes perfect.

'Let's tidy up,' she says.

'What? I hate tidying my own house.'

'Come on. It won't take long. I've already done upstairs.'

I watch her fondly as she pulls hard and blows a heavy cloud of smoke across the room. She was the girl who turned up in uniform on dress-down day, the child whose family never came to parents' day or sports day. The one whose clothes never looked clean, and whose shoes looked as if they were hand-me-downs from River-dance. I have a recollection of her from infant school. It was our first day and is one of my earliest. I can see the teacher handing her a book and her holding it as though something strange would happen. She flicked through the first few pages and looked up in wonderment. One day I will share this memory with her. I hope it's a gift.

Nowadays it feels like I look at the past through a film, as though the images are in a dirty pool of oily water. I remember my childhood story-time. My giggling parents sat next to me in bed as we flicked through a battered favourite. I know now they were pissed. However, that's still a different world from it not happening at all.

That mixture of pity and attraction means I would do anything Lily asked. Her eyes are glazed but she seems perfectly normal. It must be tolerance. She used to roll spliffs almost entirely of weed. Just the smallest amount of tobacco necessary to ensure it didn't keep going out. I don't know how she functions. I take a quick toke and drop it on a pile of butts in a saucer. No more of that or she'll need to peel me off the ceiling like a sticker.

'Come on, then, before I change my mind.'

She holds out her hand and I haul her out of the seat. She stumbles and falls into me. As I hold her, I am aware this is the closest we have ever been. Her long dark hair is loose, my nose has ended up buried in it, and I can't resist slowly breathing it in. I didn't do that at country dancing. The smell is intoxicating, even more so as it is unexpected. A mixture of smoke and woman. She pulls away and, still holding my hand, draws me out of the lounge.

As I follow her into the dining room, my eyes are fixed on her rear. For a wonderful moment, I think she is going to take me upstairs. Instead, we enter the kitchen, which doesn't have a single inch of clear worktop. She turns on the tap and throws me a tea towel.

'You're drying.'

* * *

The time passes in a blur. We laugh and joke and clean like Trojans. We can't find a hoover so Lily goes round the neighbours' and asks them for one. She comes back with the woman who answered the door. She insists on doing it for us. I'm not sure if she's being helpful or doesn't trust us not to break it as we're chuckling as though we are off our faces. We're not though, or, at least, I'm not. It's fun, doing something positive and doing it with someone you like. The neighbour is delighted when she hears the uncle is out of the picture for a while.

Eventually, it's done. It looks like a different house. I go round to the mini-mart, buy a thirty-pence packet of own-brand custard creams, and steal a tin of fabric freshener.

When I get back, she closes the windows and, after using half the tin on the sofa, curtains and carpets – while squealing at each other - we stand in the lounge and look around.

We turn to each other and smile. As we do, I feel our hands touch and she gently reaches up and brushes her lips against mine. I kiss her back. I have kissed other girls but not like this. The house is freezing but that is forgotten. We kiss until my back becomes sore from leaning down to her. I don't want to let go in case it breaks the spell we are under. I needn't have worried. She takes my hand and this time she does guide me up the stairs.

A single dim bulb without a shade lights the landing. It's bare of anything, but the carpet is clean. She takes me into the first bedroom, which has a single bed in it, and flicks the light switch. We laugh as nothing happens and I relax. She takes off her jumper and T-shirt quickly, showing she isn't wearing a bra. I do the same and we press our bodies together. It feels as though our skin is on fire. I can feel her hipbones as I press her into me. I drag my trousers and pants down and she follows suit, then we fall onto the bed. She pulls me on top of her and I glide inside her. Our faces are centimetres apart.

'Shouldn't I use something?'

'Chill. It's taken care of.'

Then, we are moving. I actually gasp in pleasure. The musty sheets and the sound of arguing outside barely register. It's just us, and perfect.

* * *

Afterwards, as the sweat dries on my forehead, we lie together for hours. She sleeps as if she hasn't slept for days, which is fine by me; all I want is to be next to her and alone with my thoughts. I can now see what all the fuss is about, definitely better than ice cream. Even a Magnum.

I wonder what I will remember afterwards when I think back to the day I lost my virginity. Surprisingly wet and warm will be one thing. I hope I have found something solid, something to anchor myself to. I feel I know Lily and I understand my feelings for her. Perhaps the foundations of my life can be rebuilt on this small, yet perfect, beginning.

18

13TH FEBRUARY 2009

I finally feel normal as I meander back from school. Lily still occupies my head, but as an echo as opposed to a constant. She pops in when I least expect it. I shout, 'See you later,' to Tom and Gary. They are two lads I've been hanging around with. Normal boys, who don't do drugs, steal things or get drunk. They have done the odd bit of all that, but only the necessary experiences that are an essential part of growing up.

I showed them the sleeve trick: you wear the biggest coat you can, with the tightest cuffs, and enter a busy shop. Then pick up bars of chocolate or whatever else is about, and wait for the shop assistant to look elsewhere. Then slide it up your sleeve. So easy. I still wonder why anyone pays. Too much Jake, I expect. I realise that within reason you can do anything and people will avoid confrontation. I showed Tom and Gary this in a shop by pushing a display over. While the guy was picking up the stuff, I stuffed my pockets full of Cadbury's Dairy Milk, not even bothering to use the sleeves. I paid for a Chomp bar and left.

When we got round the corner I split up our gains but Tom said he didn't want his. He said, 'It doesn't feel right.' Gary's gluttony got the better of him. He told me afterwards he hadn't enjoyed them. He knew he had done wrong. Those feelings – guilt, remorse, regret and shame – I'd had them before, but somewhere along the way I'd learnt not to think about them. Jake deleted his emotions a long time ago. I hope I'm not beyond redemption. So I stopped robbing and, for the first time since my dad died, experienced some peace.

I haven't seen Jake for over six months and Lily for three. I haven't looked very hard for Jake, but I have for her. She hasn't been to school since that special day and never answers her phone. I get the odd text off her but she doesn't respond to requests to meet up and she's never in when I call round. Let's say she never answers her door, as I see her curtains twitch. There's a bench at the end of her street so, once, I sat and waited for her to come out.

After only a few minutes, the door opened and a young man left. They knew each other well as they chatted in a familiar fashion. When he departed, she looked up the road and our eyes met. My brain scrambled for what I would say to her but she didn't even wave. She closed the door.

I didn't sleep well for a long time after that. I'm not sure what kind of person that makes me. One who loses more sleep from a girl not calling than the tragic early demise of his own flesh and blood.

* * *

As I approach our block of flats, I hear a police siren approaching. I'm not sure why but I jog. I bump into Jake, who's running in the opposite direction. Our lack of contact is instantly forgotten.

'What happened?'

'He's gone mad.'

'Who has?'

'Jonty.'

'Why?'

Jake looks shifty. He shoves a magazine into my hand. It's a porno mag called *Anal Nasties*. I give Jake a puzzled look.

'Look at page thirteen.'

The police car screeches past me as I stare at a picture of a naked woman. She's surrounded by men and literally every hole is filled. She chokes at the camera with an open-eyed shocked expression. I too have that same look. It's Sally, Jonty's mum. I blink at Jake in surprise.

'I know, it looks just like her.' He doesn't laugh.

My gaze is drawn back to the picture and as I flick through the gruesome and graphic collection, I see it isn't Sally. There are slight differences, not discounting the age gap, but she is uncannily similar.

'I showed it to Jonty,' says Jake.

I drop the magazine and sprint.

There are two police cars outside the front of our building. A big policeman sits on the grass with a stunned expression and blood on his face. The woman who moved into Michelle's flat is coming out of the entrance with a tea towel so I race past to find Jonty's door open. I can hear shouts from the lounge.

'Calm down! Calm down!'

Jonty is backed up in the far corner of the room looking petrified. There's a white-faced policeman opposite him, grimacing and holding his arm, who tells me to 'Get out now.' This leaves one more presence, a thickset black man, who is crouching in front of Jonty. I'm not sure who looks most terrified. Jonty is holding a solid-looking chair by the leg and swirling it around like it's a flag at a home-coming parade.

'It's OK,' I say. 'I know him.'

The policeman with the injury backs out of the room with

relief. In the doorway I see an understated lady, whom I don't recognise, has arrived. She carries herself with importance.

'Jonty, Jonty, please. It's OK. It wasn't your mum.'

As soon as the words are out of my mouth, I regret saying them. It's as though he is scared but has forgotten the reason why. He runs straight through the policeman and me as if we're digital projections. A heavy elbow catches my stomach and I spin over an armchair.

Struggling to my feet, I hear Jonty powering up the stairs. He will leave footprints in the concrete. Then I hear the lighter sounds of pursuit.

For a few seconds, I flex my aching hip and then I comprehend, with abject horror, where he is going. My mum's not daft. There is no way she'll open the door in the afternoon. She'll be off her face by now and in all likelihood asleep. The sinking feeling returns as I recall Jonty knows where the key is.

As I limp up the stairs, I try to recollect what state the flat is in. We've had no tidy-up days for quite some time. I picture the kitchen, and the mouse, with a cringe. He was on the floor this morning under the small breakfast bar. Dead and oddly flat as if steamrollered. My mother's cookery will always be a lottery. I left him there, wondering in a perverse way whether my mother would bother to move him. We have been playing brinkmanship with the washing up too, waiting for the other's resolve to weaken and get it done. We have both won, or lost, depending on which way you look at it. Recently, I avoided the lounge for weeks, flitting in and out of the kitchen, bathroom, and bedroom on my brief stays. The last time I was in there was to look for a long-lost schoolbook. I have vague memories of tripping over empties and debris. The sound that cannons down is not one of dodging and weaving through an alcoholic's obstacle course. In fact, it sounds like an elephant falling from a great height into a bottle bank.

When I get to our flat, there is silence. Then, just the sound of one glass vessel rolling off the lounge laminate floor into the hall, where it rests against a large heaped collection of miscellaneous footwear. I walk into the lounge and feel my face flush with humiliation. Jonty is sitting in a huge pile of what can only be described as rubbish, traumatised by the sight of my mother. She is lying on the sofa with her hands under her chin as though laid out for burial, butt naked except for my dad's old New York Yankees baseball cap, which is perched sideways on her head. I absently wonder why this vivid sight didn't set him off. Maybe his porn receptors have become overloaded and burnt out. She is snoring. How long has she been this thin? It's like looking at a starved shipwreck survivor three weeks too late. The smell of urine stings my eyes. A pair of jogging bottoms with a wet crotch dries on the radiator.

More footsteps approach from behind and I am barged out of the way by Jonty's mother, who pulls him into a hug.

The policeman, who is as stunned as Jonty, looks at me in astonishment.

'Who are you?'

'I live here.'

'You live here?'

Before I have a chance to reply, the lady comes out of the kitchen holding her nose.

She flashes a badge at me. Carrie Longfoot, Social Worker. 'How old are you?' she asks.

As Sally walks past, somehow supporting the hulking presence of her son, she shoots me a look that would cause a great oak tree to wilt.

'Fifteen?' Carrie asks. She knows.

The social worker and the policeman exchange a look I don't like one bit.

19

'He's brown.'

Carrie, as she insisted I call her, examines my face for racism.

'Is that going to be a problem?'

'I guess not, as long as he doesn't try to radicalise me.'

'That's an interesting phrase. Do you know what it means?'

'Yes.'

I get another long glare.

'He's a Sikh. Non-practising, I believe.'

'Hmm.' He still has a turban on.

'Are you a Christian?'

'My mum likes to think so.'

A vision of her necking the sacramental wine, then shouting, 'Same again,' pops into my mind.

'That might make you a non-practising Christian. You could have a lot in common.'

I return the stare to her. Eventually I look back at the man. He's reached the end of his long driveway and leans back onto his expensive car. He appears relaxed and seems happy just to stand there as though this is a perfectly normal turn of events. 'So why have I got to stay here?'

'Whatever you may think, you're still a minor. We have a duty of care not to leave you in a toxic situation like that.'

'I'm fine with my mother. We get on OK. It's not been easy for her after my dad died.'

'Yes, you, your mother and the rodents are all struggling.' Carrie smiles and I can't help grinning back.

'So how long do I have to stay with Gandhi here?'

'That's enough of that.'

'Sorry.' I know I'm being a dick and mentally chastise myself.

'I want to go back home though.'

'You won't be here long. Mr Singh and his wife are emergency foster carers, so you'll only stay here for a few days. Your mother will be given some help and we will assess whether you can go home or not. I suspect that's unlikely in the short term but not impossible.'

'She'll starve to death.'

'We'll help her.'

'Then what happens?'

'You'll go to a longer-term foster-care family.'

'You know I'm sixteen in a few weeks.'

'This is the best option for you right now, Ben. Yes, you can do what you want at sixteen, but it doesn't mean you should.'

As I get out of the car, I recall Jake not being very complimentary about such places. Mr Singh, though, doesn't look as if he means me any harm. In fact, as I shake his hand, he has a gentle manner, not to mention I have a foot in height on him. I follow him towards his house, eyeing the other mansions and spread-eagled bungalows. We're in a place called Stonebridge. It's clearly not a rough area of town but I always thought it was. Perhaps I don't know everything.

We walk into a large lounge with an unusual smell. Not unpleasant, but not familiar. Something tells me it's furniture polish but I don't know how I would know that.

Carrie and the couple have a cup of tea and I have water. Mr Singh gives me it in a cold bottle and it tastes incredibly refreshing. My nervousness dissipates. I'm like an angry dog unable to stay in that heightened state for long. They chat and I let the drone of the conversation wash over me. Carrie assures me she will come back tomorrow. Mrs Singh lets her out, leaving me and her husband alone.

'We'll be having dinner shortly.'

'OK.'

'Do you like vegetable curry?'

I remember to be polite but my face says it all.

Mr Singh smiles. 'Every white child who comes to us thinks we are going to serve them curry. Society makes me laugh sometimes. I was born in this country, as was my wife. We are very much western Sikhs. We usually have a takeaway when we have the gift of looking after someone for a few days. We usually let the guest decide what sort.'

I look suspiciously at him, but he seems genuine.

'Pizza would be nice,' I suggest.

'Domino's?'

My family never order Domino's. We've been getting them from Jimbo's Jumbo Pizza. I'm sure Albania is not renowned for pizza, but they are cheap and filling, which counts round our way. I had a Domino's once, at a friend's party. The avalanche of flavour was like a new experience. If he wants to bribe me into having a good time, this will work.

It's nice to chat. I realise I don't do this any more with an older man. There are no male role models left in my existence. What am I missing out on? Some of the male teachers show an interest but there are over thirty kids in our class and some of them don't speak English. The staff have no time for life lessons.

I stand and pick up a photo. It's a family snap, taken many years ago, judging by the slim Mr Singh staring back at me. There are three children, two girls and a boy, all seemingly in their late teens.

'Have your children left home?'

'The girls are happily married although they shun giving us the joy of grandchildren.' He smiles as he says this, pride all over his face.

'Seema is a doctor now, very busy. Sarna runs her own business. They want to make their mark in the world.'

I wait for him to tell me what his son does. Instead, he walks over to me and takes the photo. I can see the shadow arrive.

'My son, Yuvraj, has left us. He liked heroin, a lot. And other things. That was a very hard time for us. We thought we had it under control. We fought together. Then he had a stroke. He was in hospital for a long time. It took... a long time.'

His gaze returns to me, strong and determined. 'I am in a state of shock in some ways, one I suspect I will never fully leave. However, I still have much to offer. Most importantly, understanding. There is no judgement in this house, just acceptance.'

'Is that why you don't practise your religion, because your son was taken from you?'

'Who says I don't? I believe Sikhism still has a lot to offer. Religion is a very personal thing. It is different for every one of us. When you lose a family member before their time, it is only natural to ask many questions, not only of religion but of yourself.'

He isn't angry. That makes me feel it for him. What kind of world is it where people, good people like him, suffer? His wife comes in and interrupts the stillness. She eases his fingers off the photo frame.

'Are we having this pizza, then?' she asks him. She smiles at me. 'Am I right? Everyone asks for pizza.'

'Come on.' He grins at her. 'I'll order it and you get out the plates.'

They leave me in the room. There's something between them that's ever so slightly different from how my parents interacted. I suspect it is respect. I absently play with a gold ornament of a horse, which is on the mantelpiece, and slip it into my pocket.

Mr Singh comes back and turns on the TV for me. He puts on the football and gives me a smile. I appreciate the gesture and don't correct him. The pizza takes a while to arrive. When it does, Mrs Singh calls me into the dining room. It's a little weird eating pizza so formally and the first slice doesn't taste how I expect. I can feel the horse in my pocket. As heavy as if it were real. Excusing myself, I return to the lounge, where I place it back.

At the table, I look from face to face and they smile warmly. He passes me another slice. It tastes just right.

* * *

I lie in bed afterwards and analyse what a mad day it's been. These people didn't even know I existed before today and yet here I am. They told me to take a shower, the best in town, they said. I explained that I didn't have a towel. Mrs Singh gave me such a look it brought a tear to my eye.

The shower was so powerful it almost knocked me over. The blast was cleansing on many levels – a whole new experience. Their towel was soft and didn't smell like any I'd ever used before. It seemed a crime to put on my dirty clothes. They said there were pyjamas on the back of the door. I haven't worn any for years but they smelt the same as the towel. I crept out of the bathroom wearing them, my clothes balled up under my arm. I wasfeeling shifty and embarrassed. As if I had done wrong. Mr Singh was at the far end of the upstairs landing, near the stairs. He pointed towards a door and told me, 'That's your room,' and, 'I'll see you in the morning.' Then he was gone.

So here I am. The bed is soft and inviting and the duvet just the right thickness for the warm room. There's another bottle of water on the side-table.

I had to thump the pillow to dent it. I think of my mother. Where is she now? Treachery lowers my eyelids. Is it money that buys these things? Or would these fine people be the same whatever they had? I want it too: clean sheets, normality, sharing, caring. Feeling like I haven't in a long time, safe and comfortable, I drift into a deep sleep.

20

Jake answers Lily's door, looking as if he's about to go to work for the Highways Agency.

'Interesting look,' I say as I appraise his fluorescent, high-vis, waterproof jacket and trousers.

'These are going to make me a fortune, my friend. Come on in.'

I follow him into the lounge that Lily and I tidied all those months ago with a small pang of longing for that happy day. Jake moved straight in with her after his release from what he affectionately calls 'the slammer'. They stay in different rooms so I'm still unsure how they interact alone.

I stayed at the Singhs' for three nights. It was a pleasant time. As it was the weekend, there was no mention of school and they let me be. Obviously, they had cable and I watched no end of movies. Carrie came to see me and told me my mum was kept in hospital. She seemed to have a case of malnutrition, but no mention was made of her other, more obvious issues.

The Singhs ordered a taxi on the Sunday and took me out to a real restaurant down Cowgate called Prezzo, which was awesome. I had more pizza, different from Domino's, but also tasty. I could barely breathe by the time I left, I was so full. We walked home along the river, beside the rowing lake, and I almost forgot that I had any problems.

Monday came round all too soon and Carrie picked me up. It was like in the movies when people are saying goodbye to relatives after a lovely weekend. Mr Singh shook my hand and squeezed my shoulder, and his wife gave me a teary hug. I put my stuff in the back of Carrie's car and we drove to my next home. This was in Bretton, a similar estate to mine. They were nice enough, but it seemed I'd had the best and they were never going to measure up. So I left and went back home, just before dawn. My mum was released from hospital a week later.

* * *

'Sit down, my friend. I've got something that's going to blow your mind,' Jake says.

'What's with the get-up?'

'I had community service. All part of my order. Today was litter picking.'

Despite Jake assuring me young people rarely get custody, that is exactly what he was given. He was up in front of the Youth Court. It's like a magistrates' court but less formal. The public can't go in these courts and they mostly deal with burglary and drug offences (which Jake hadn't progressed to yet), and anti-social behaviour and theft cases (which he most definitely had). In brief, the district judge had seen Jake on so many occasions he said he spent more time with him than his wife. This little joke didn't stop Jake getting a twelve-month detention and training order. The first half is served in custody. The second in the community doing civic service, repairing damage and generally trying to make up for the harm caused. Jake said he was in no rush to go back to a 'secure unit for children' as he was the only sane one. It doesn't take a genius to work out there are troubled children in these places. He saidall that, but it doesn't seem to have tempered his behaviour. Get your head round that if you will.

'I thought you said only fools did their community service.'

'That's true. It's possible you can be sent back to custody for failing to attend, but unlikely. I wanted to go because I wanted this gear. I got all dressed up and waited for the supervisor's back to be turned as we picked litter opposite Orton Longueville school. Then, I ran into Ferry Meadows and hid amongst the anglers.'

'You don't strike me as the type for fishing.'

'Fishing for what, though?'

'Jake. Put me out of my misery, please.'

'What people in shops see when you're dressed like this is railway worker, road maintenance, or something like that. Not a mucky junkie shoplifter, so they're less vigilant. You put bicycle clips around your ankles, strong ones too, and then walk into the shop all full of busy bluster. As soon as their backs are turned, you pop open your elasticated waistband and fill your trousers, whistling as you do so.'

'This works, does it?'

'We'll be finding out today. You'll be the distraction, I'll bag up. Someone in the slammer told me about this. That and a whole load of other scams and tricks. That's what a custodial sentence taught me. Crazy, uh?

'First, though, we have some fun,' he adds.

I move a load of papers and magazines off the sofa so I can sit down. I don't know where all these materialise from because I've never seen either of them read anything. Jake gets out a small bag that contains some small yellowy-white rocks. He takes a small glass pipe off the table.

'This is mine. You smoke it. I'm going to inject.'

I know I'll shortly do something stupid unless I'm really careful. I think of reasons for not doing it. All I can come up with is it's bad for you. Alcohol is bad for you, yet everyone still seems to drink it.

'What is it?'

'Crack.'

'What's crack?'

'Crack is incredible.'

'OK, but what's it made of?'

'Crack is cocaine.'

'I thought you snorted coke?'

'That's the powder form that tired rich people have, so they have the energy to go out at night. That shit is expensive because it's a lot purer. This is rock. Crack is called crack as that's the sound it makes when it burns. We don't have the money for the good stuff. This, however, will do the job, but you need to smoke or inject it to get that special feeling.'

I can't help noticing the cold sore Jake has at the side of his mouth.

'No offence, but if I use your pipe won't I catch your salad accessory?'

'What?'

'Your coleslaw.'

He looks confused and then disdainful.

'Very amusing, Mr Fussy. You can use Lily's pipe.' He gets out of his seat and picks it up from the fireplace as I'm too stunned to move. As I watch him place some rocks in the pipe's bowl, my brain wobbles unhappily. I am surprised and I am not. Sad, but as I search my feelings I consider if that's more because I didn't know. She had a secret from me, but told Jake. Jake shows me the method of inhaling it while I seek confirmation.

'So Lily does crack, then?'

Jake chokes as he looks up. 'She's the original crack fiend.'

He hands me the pipe and I smoke it almost without thinking. The smoke is no worse than a joint although the pipe burns my lips. It takes a few seconds for me to realise what the fuss is about.

As the vapour fills my lungs, a strange feeling creeps up my legs. Butterflies fill my stomach and then boom, euphoria explodes in my veins. I am alive. I could rule the world. Jake is smiling at me and I feel a lot of love for him. I have a lot of love for everything. They are the same sensations I had that day with Lily.

I sit in contented silence and watch Jake pour white vinegar onto a rock that he's put in a bottle top. He grinds it with the top of the syringe in a twisting motion while saying something about less wastage. I can't follow the conversation because my brain is in the clouds.

'So where is Lily?' I ask when I'm near earth again.

'She's working.'

'Really?'

'Yes. This stuff's not free, you know, and she's got a ferocious heroin habit to service at the same time.'

'I can't believe she has a job.'

Jake shoots me an odd look. He drops a small piece of cotton wool in the lid, reconstructs his syringe, and draws up the fluid through it. The penny drops as he inserts the needle into his arm, lowers the angle, and slowly injects.

'She's a prostitute?'

Jake roars with laughter. His eyes dance as he replies. 'I'm not sure that's the word she would use as her job title, but yes, she's a whore. I thought you knew. How else would she have the money to pay for everything?'

I didn't know, not at all. I don't admit it, although I suspect the fact glows from my stricken face like a thousand-watt bulb. My mind stretches back into the past and it becomes clear. The weight loss, the distant gaze, the nice clothes, the departing men, keeping her distance, and the horrifying fact I lost my virginity to a filthy hooker. I crash back down so hard I can barely breathe.

'Her mum got her on it when she was young, the drugs and the whoring. That's why her mum kept going in and out of jail. She wasn't allowed to go to the red-light district and every time she breached that order, she got sent to jail. She was too disorganised to claim benefits and sign on at the right time so if she couldn't sell herself, she stole. When she got caught, and the desperate do, she was sent back to prison. Her mum's dead now. Killed by a client, they think, but not before she got Lily on the game to pay for her habit. Her looks had faded and she was a foul smack-rat who only the desperate, sick, and violent would fuck. Whereas Lily was only twelve.

'Here, have another bang. You'll be coming down by now.'

A bigger understatement there has never been.

I pull long and hard on the short pipe, and as the glass burns I do not stop. As I fly again, I suddenly wonder what nastiness Lily's pipe has on it, but my concerns are soon left behind. The pipe slips out of my hand in shock at how good it feels.

'How long do you think you'll be allowed to stay in the house?' I ask. The feeling doesn't last as long this time.

'Good news for us, not so for the owner.'

'How so?'

'He's looking at twelve years.'

'I'm pretty sure you don't get twelve years for an accident.'

'She's dead now. Accident might not wash. The judges tend to be less forgiving when there's a body.'

'I thought it was a fight. What actually happened?'

'He pushed her, and she fell down the stairs.'

'You mean he pushed her down the stairs.'

'I guess it depends on your point of view. He'd prefer the first version.'

'Oh dear. He is such a nice guy too.'

'Yes, with his history of domestic violence, he'll be advised to plead guilty to manslaughter. Take ten years, out in five.'

I laugh. 'You know things are fucked up when you think getting ten years is a result.'

* * *

Jake eventually drags me from my happy, chatty daydream by waving an empty, dusty bag in my face. I have no idea how long we've been sitting on the sofa.

'We need money,' he states. 'Soon we'll sell Lily ourselves to get more, but we'll be paranoid and lethargic, so let's get on it now, or it'll be harder later.'

I already know what he means. I'll never tire of that feeling immediately.

It always seems to come down to cash. I never have any. My second foster carers were working class. They had little money. It shouldn't have mattered, but it did. I remember the things I want. I have so little but want to experience a better life. Was it Coolio in 'Gangsta's Paradise' who sang, 'Too much television watching got me chasing dreams'? Money will buy me my dreams but, like Lily, I have little to offer the world in exchange. For people like me there is only one way I can get what I need, and that is to take it from somebody else.

21

1ST OCTOBER 2010

Lily opens the door after about ten minutes of me knocking. At least I think it's her. She looks so frail and white she could be mistaken for a ghost of her former self. She doesn't even bother to acknowledge me. Instead, she leaves the door open and goes back into the lounge.

Jake is on the sofa and also looks dead. I refrain from ringing for an ambulance as his eyes followed my entrance. There's a rancid, burnt-plastic smell in the room and the hint of urine. Human, I think. I'm not sure if the recent smoking of cocaine is responsible for these smells directly or indirectly. I look at my watch: 5 p.m. They could've been doing this all day, maybe yesterday too. They are brilliant at it.

I haven't been round for a few months as Jake has been in prison and any semblance of control in the house has gone. It is the proverbial crack house. The water and electric have been turned off a long time ago so it smells accordingly and it's absolutely disgusting. Grimy mattresses have appeared downstairs and at any time of day, you will find unconscious people on them. When Jake is here, there's a thin element of order despite him only being eighteen.

When he isn't, the cat is away and Peterborough's vermin crawl in. You would think no one would want to sleep here, but if the alternative is outside, round the back of the Key Theatre, then I guess it's all relative.

I've given up caring about what Lily, and Jake for that matter, are doing to themselves. If they don't care, then why should I? Unexpectedly, it's my parents' crazy addiction to alcohol that has stopped me falling into the self-destructive pit of drug-soaked insanity into which these two have dived head first.

I was wary to start with and if ever there was a salutary example of what lies ahead, then it's my mother. She is doing well at the moment, comparatively. After her spell in hospital and mine in foster care we are more mindful of each other. We had a talk one morning, first thing of course, and we've reached an agreement. We keep on top of the house and we look out for each other. It was strange being the adult in the parent-child conversation but if that's where you are, you need to embrace it. She doesn't mention my father, her drinking, or the fact that, with all the boxes and bags of stolen goods in it, my room looks like a distribution centre for Amazon Her self-abuse seems different from Jake and Lily's, more medicinal than recreational. All three of them are cocooned in their own bubbles though.

'Ben, my boy. How's things? You been working?' Jake asks.

Jake likes to call stealing stuff 'working'. I understand now. Anything you have to do feels like work. They are driven to satisfy insatiable urges. They need to feed the monster inside themselves. It seemingly has no limits.

'Yes, bits and bobs as usual.'

To be honest I haven't. I've been seeing a fairly normal girl called Isla, whom I met when I was out stealing. We clocked each other across the aisle in an independent shop called Shoe Shake. That's the thing about our 'work', you can spot another 'worker' a mile off. Instead of 'gaydar' we had 'shopliftdar'. That phrase came from the first night we, as a couple, spent with Lily and Jake. I made them agree to no hard drugs, which they did, although Jake later whispered in my ear that Peterborough was 'dry'. Just beers and weed, then. How civilised. We must have spent hours coming up with names on the radar theme: taxdar, robdar, cabbagedar, doinkdar, teefdar, boostdar, rolldar, blagdar, deebodar (my favourite). Jake again showed his intelligence with an impressive variety, many with an American theme.

Isla refused to have anything to do with them after that night, which should have set alarm bells ringing, especially seeing as neither of them were on anything. I'm not sure of a way out though. I can't be the first person to realise he's in a business relationship with a madman. Anyway, Shoe Shake had two shops in town and had made an error. One had the left shoe on display and the other shop had the right out. An expensive mistake. Trust Jake to notice. Isla's issue, and it seems everyone has one, is shoe hoarding.. By mistake, she had taken a pair back to the wrong shop and had also noticed. Shoe hoarding, as any good shoe hoarder will know, is an extremely expensive hobby. So seeing as she is still doing her A levels and has limited funds, she looks for other avenues to satisfy her urges, rather than paying for them. It's weird how compulsions can override a normally strong moral compass. The shop assistants were relaxed, thinking no one would steal one shoe, but, unbeknownst to them, we were dead keen, taking its companion from their other establishment.

Anyway, I waited for her outside until she scuttled from the shop and then whispered in her ear, 'Have you paid for that shoe?' The rest, as they say, is history, because apart from the footwear thing she is normal and ergo makes me feel the same way. As for crime, I've been stealing for the same reason a wild animal kills its prey. Only when hungry, hence less time spent with Jake.

I've come round to talk him out of his latest business idea and to remind him not to text me. It's no wonder I have little money as I keep having to throw my mobile phone away. When he's high, he imagines criminal acts I have neither the experience nor the appetite for. If the police ever catch me, all they will need to do at court is read a transcript out of my phone. They will pin no end of shit on me. Even if I haven't done it. You can get an acceptable mobile for about fifteen quid and, even though you can just change the SIM card, most data is stored on the phone. It's a ball-ache to delete it and I'm paranoid it might be like storage on your computer and can be recalled by an expert.

So we just throw them away. It all adds up. Americans call them burners. I picked that up from watching *The Wire* with Jake. It was his favourite show and we would often have it ticking along in the background. That was until Lily sold the Blu-ray player for a fiver, desperate one Tuesday morning for a bag of coke that turned out to be just Tate & Lyle's. Jake was livid as the player contained the last disc of his favourite series.

'The answer is no, Jake.'

'Come on, man. The house is empty. It's been empty for months.'

'I'm not burgling a house.'

'It'll be a big score. Dan said it's full of hardware.'

I roll my eyes. More Americanisms, and from Dan too. He is the most despairing, hopeless, unreliable junkie I have come across so far. We call him Desperate Dan for obvious reasons.

'Jake, this is a line you don't want to cross. Where are most of our friends?'

Jake looks away. I hit a nerve and he knows it. After your habit gets a grip on you, shoplifting can't pay the bills as it works best as an opportunistic crime. Like Isla's. Take your wins when they present themselves. If you must do it, and are barely functioning, you lose. By definition, most drug addicts don't need to let people know what they are. Looking like a thief gets you noticed and your success rate drops. Desperation leads many a man to a reckless move and the prisons are full of such people.

It was Jake who told me this, but he seems to have conveniently forgotten it. Junkies chat about doing a big job, not so they can move away, get a fresh start, or get out of this line of work. Their dream is sitting on their arses and doing loads of drugs without having to worry where their next hit is coming from. Burglary is the next step up. The underclass is full of stories of finding twenty k under a pensioner's mattress, or a drawer full of gold.

'How are you, Lily?'

She doesn't look good. Slick hair and pallid skin don't do it for me. So much for heroin chic. I used to bring food round but it went to waste. Jake interrupts, although I was waiting for an answer that would likely never have arrived.

'She needs to get spruced up. Her first trick is going to be here soon. You won't get a tip looking like you just crawled out of Fletton cemetery you know.' He directs the last statement at her with venom.

'You know they don't give a shit, Jake, so why bother?'

Horrifyingly, Lily told me that most of her punters don't care about what state she is in. It seems men who sleep with prostitutes enjoy the power, the money changing hands, and the general sleaze of it all as much as the actual act itself. For some, the grubbier the better. Few last longer than a couple of minutes. It's a constant source of friction between boss and employee. Yes, you heard correctly. I suppose it was only a matter of time. It's funny what becomes normal.

'Go!' he shouts at her. She gets up, farts, and then walks past me with vacant eyes and no change in her expression. Jake and me look at each other and laugh.

'Come on, I need something big.'

'No. If you get caught for a dwelling – a burglary – you're looking at eighteen months minimum. Why do you need so much money? You work Lily hard.'

'Things aren't cheap, Ben.'

I see he is scratching his arms. Again, it was him who told me the name for it in a matter-of-fact kind of way – formication, the sensation of insects crawling on or just under the skin. It's a common side effect of drug abuse and withdrawal. You would think if he knew the cause of something so uncomfortable, he'd be interested in addressing the issues in an attempt at resolution, but that isn't the case. As I wince and feel a strong urge to rub some kind of soothing cream into his bleeding arms, the door opens and a big, hairy man in his fifties walks in as though he owns the place. He gives me a look that makes me nervous and then points at Jake.

'Back room,' he says. Jake scuttles after him.

I sit in my seat and listen to them argue for a few minutes. It's clear Jake owes him money, but I can't ascertain what for, due to the loud music thrumming through the ceiling from Lily's 'office'. No doubt she's trying to get herself in the mood, I think with a grimace. The doorbell makes a weird buzzing sound. Sadly, it's the last thing in the house that even remotely works. No one will admit to selling the microwave, which also used to function. A confident knock follows. I open it to an Asian man standing next to a taxi. As I wonder who's ordered one, he triggers the remote locking on the car and simply says, 'Lily.' I step out of the doorway to let him by. I pull the door shut behind him and stride down the street, dropping my latest phone down a drain on the way.

PART III

YOUNG OFFENDER

22

20TH JUNE 2011

My lifestyle dictated that prison was inevitable, so it shouldn't have been a surprise to be finally sent here. It is, though, a nasty one. Jake and I are in the holding cell at Reception, waiting to go to the wings. I wonder whether I should be angry, as it's his fault I'm here, but he paints such a wretched image that it's hard to stay too irate with him. The phrase 'finally in here' sums it up though and I know I can only blame myself. There was no gun to my head. I had also begun to get caught for my misdemeanours and the police were involved. So I had seen my fair share of the Youth Court too. Naturally, I used all the reasons that got me out of serious trouble at school. The triple-pronged excuse-fork of poverty, death and addiction had kept me away from any custodial stay, but it was as if my face had been beamed to the skies; like the deaths in *The Hunger Games* I was known, both to the police and to security guards alike.

We had been going to other towns to rob. However, that brought its own problems as well as rewards. You didn't know where was safe to run to, and I strangely found the whole 'not buying a ticket to travel' stressful. It was easy enough to just give a false name as we had stolen IDs galore, but I hated being on edge, waiting for the inevitable argument with the guards.

Jake's misery was threefold too. First, he'd only been out of jail a few months. It turned out, not altogether surprisingly knowing Desperate Dan, that the vacant house he tipped us off about wasn't empty. It had a frail black lady in it who lived in the back room to save on heating costs. Not too frail to use the phone to ring the police though, or too weak to bounce a can of baked beans off Jake's surprised head either. As his luck would have it, there was a canine unit on duty that night and, even though he outran the police, the dog near gave him a heart attack as he tried to hide behind a shed. A strike one burglary charge resulted, earning Jake a ten-month sentence. It could easily have been much more.

Second, Lily's uncle got wind of what was happening at his lovely house the week before Jake got out, and he acted on the information. No lengthy delays with eviction procedures at County Court for him. Three heavies turned up one morning and dragged all the sleepy occupants out into the garden. Lily texted me after, as I queried her rights, and she said no one complained. They all knew the score: leave of your own free will, or get a battering and then go. Courts weren't for the likes of them. Due to their illegal occupations, or lack of one, they all had a natural anxiety about such places anyway.

Jake's things were still in there though and, as it was now boarded up, he hadn't been able to get to them. Lily had also disappeared in that period. No doubt another budding entrepreneur had spotted an opportunity with her and stepped into the void. I had advised him to let them both go, but he obsessed on getting them back. He knew that by the time he got out, the trail would be cold on Lily, and the house would be empty of his things.

Third, Jake was rattling. He had consumed an ever-growing range of mind-altering substances over the last few years and the lack of those in the recent past was causing his body to wake up to itself. He plugged drugs up his arse before he came in, but the screws knew him of old. As he crouched during the routine strip search, some cling-film was showing. His stash was withdrawn by, no doubt tentative, gloved fingers. I was in the next cubicle undergoing the same demeaning charade and noted neither the screws nor Jake said anything through the whole event. Not a new experience for either party.

In a way, we were unlucky, although I'm now beginning to see you make your own luck. Jake and I were walking through the outer gate to the cathedral grounds, on our way to the market car park where Jake reckoned one in ten owners left their car unlocked. Jake stopped and whispered, 'Motherfucker.'

'What?' I said, looking for the police.

He pointed to some skinny bloke sitting on the grass. It was Desperate Dan incurring the wrath of God by drinking cider in the shade of one of the country's finest places of worship.

'He's got my trainers on.'

We ran across the forecourt with Dan seeing us too late to make good his escape. As he got up and tried to scramble away, Jake booted him up the arse. Painfully for all of us, Dan, at that moment, and us later, his legs were open and the toecap of the incoming footwear landed squarely onto his poor plums. He jumped into the air like a grasshopper and screamed like a chorister. Jake knocked him off his feet and sat on him. I playfully cuffed him round the head and pulled the stolen items off his feet, laughing as I did. We left him clutching his groin and writhing on the grass. Typically, unbeknown to us, some students had been filming in the grounds and a public-minded do-gooder had recorded the incident. That got into the hands of plod. It did not make nice viewing and a guilty plea was the only answer when questioned. I suspect I might not have gone down if it were just me. However, the judge had seen entirely too much of Jake and felt it only fair to impose a custodial sentence on the pair of us.

Court was confusing. I wasn't sure whether we'd been done for common assault or street robbery. It was mentioned somewhere along the way that I was guilty by association. It was like the getaway driver getting the same as the bank robbers in a daring raid despite only driving the van. Although obviously much less cool. Probation and, to be fair, our solicitor fought our corner well, but we got four months, do two. So here we are.

There's only one other man in the holding cell and he appears to be insane. He keeps jumping out of his seat and banging his head against the Perspex glass and shouting in what might be a Scottish accent. Jake just sits next to me with his head in his hands and lets me worry about it. I hoped I would be more relaxed than this. Inside I am terrified. We are boys amongst men. Most of the prison officers seem huge, but it's their indifference to my plight that's unsettling me. They are neither rude nor unprofessional. I'm just a number. We saw a connection worker. These are trustees who are there to help with settling in. Jake bombarded him with questions about where was best to get drugs. I suppose you could say he was good at his job as he provided Jake with some very detailed answers.

Finally, we get taken to the wing. Thankfully, the lunatic is left behind. The prison is quiet even though it's 6 p.m. and I wonder where everyone is. All we have is a bag with some prison clothes in, our free tobacco pouch and a set of grey plastic cutlery.

'This is the work area. Everyone will be back on the house-blocks,' Jake explains. At my confused expression, he adds, 'You'll see.'

We walk outside and I stare at what looks like an ugly hotel with barred windows. We approach double doors and I can hear people. Loud voices. A lot of angry shouting. The officer unlocks the first solid door to another barred one, and the sound hits me like a blast from a shotgun. The smell hits me too. Body odour and bad language engulf me as if I'm opening a fridge that packed in the day after I left to go on a two-week holiday. I can't slam the door shut now though, even if every part of me yearns to.

I can hear roaring voices. 'Meds. Bravo 1. Guv. Last call Alpha 1.' We're let onto B1 wing. It's an Integrated Drug Treatment Service (IDTS) wing. Jake said to make up the fact I had issues with drink and drugs at Reception. I told them the truth, that was enough. Therefore, we were put on an IDTS wing.

We arrive; it is unbelievable. Jake said it's easier on this wing. There would be fewer 'big fish', as they'd be too embarrassed to be classified as drug addicts.

They, the junkies, are queuing up for medication and we have to barge past them. It's like infiltrating the undead in Michael Jackson's 'Thriller' video. I feel like grabbing Jake's hand like a child with its parent in a busy shop. We're left outside an open office door. The first officer throws two files on a desk and leaves. The seated, visibly harassed man takes one look at us.

'Jake, you know the rules. Cell twenty, both of you. You've missed dinner. Bang up is in fifteen minutes. No questions now. Talk to staff tomorrow morning.'

He looks down at his paperwork, finished with us.

I follow Jake, my stare on the floor, although I can feel eyes upon me, weighing the catch. All I can think is 'fresh fish' from *The Shawshank Redemption*. I can hear the odd shout though of 'Yo, Jake' and 'Jake, bruv', and that stiffens my spine.

When we arrive at cell twenty the door is shut, but only pulled to. Jake gingerly pushes it open. He turns with a big grin.

'Bagsy bottom bunk.' He laughs, as though it is indeed a hotel, and fiddles with a TV that's in better condition than the one my mother and I have at home.

'OK, it works. Right, man, I'm off to score. We've only got a few minutes. Fill those two up.' He gestures to two silver battered flasks on the side next to the telly and vanishes, as purpose has lent him wings. The cell is tiny. Two beds bolted to the left-hand wall, a low table on the right-hand wall and no space to dance between. The toilet on my right, judging by the stench in the room, is not in great condition. The noise is deafening outside, and I don't want to go back out there. I turn as the din blares louder and a pale fervent-eyed man walks into the cell. His broad shoulders naturally block the light from my exit.

'First time, is it?'

I nod.

'I'm number one on this wing. It'll do you well to remember that.'

'OK, I will.'

'Don't look so nervous. It's pretty easy on here. Don't be a dick, help out. I'll look after you.'

'OK, cheers.' I feel I'm missing something.

'When I saw you walk in, you seemed so scared it reminded me of my first time. Fifteen years ago now. Hard to believe.'

He still doesn't leave. I silently pray for Jake to return.

'Look, come see me tomorrow. I'll get you some toiletries. Bit of coffee maybe, help you settle in.' He nods, smiles and finally departs. I wipe the acidic sweat out of my eyes. I'm not leaving the room, ever.

Jake comes back to the bellow of, 'Behind your doors,' which I assume means it is bang up. He looks relieved.

'Right, we're sorted. Did you get hot water?'

'Sorry, mate, no.'

'To be honest, I only had time to get the important stuff, so it doesn't matter anyway. All they had was a bit of brown and I could only get my hands on a pin. Sorry, I know you aren't keen on that but we aren't in Boots here.'

I want strong drugs. It must be five minutes since my 'visit', but my heart is still going like a trip hammer. The chances of me injecting myself with heroin from a prison syringe, however, is zero.

'Mate, you cannot be serious about using that.'

He dismantles the syringe and runs a lighter over the needle.

'It's new,' is all he says.

That's Russian Roulette, with a cannon.

'So we have nothing to drink, then, or eat?'

'Nope.'

As he replies our door is closed and locked. I sit there quietly. Jake doesn't say anything, but is waiting for something. I hear a door being slammed. Then another. Each one being opened and a number shouted as it echoes around the wing.

'What was that guy doing in here?'

'He was being friendly.'

'Over-friendly?'

'Yeah, I guess.'

Our door opens, an impassive officer looks in and shouts, 'Two.' The door shuts and Jake's eyes narrow.

'We'll sort that out in the morning.' He gets back to the task in hand.

I get up and pour myself water from the tap on the small sink. I hate drinking from plastic cups, but it's all we have. The water is warm and tastes metallic. I push the button to flush the toilet and am gobsmacked when it flushes. I try the door. It's heavy and clanks but is very secure. It goes against all your humanity to be locked in, unable to exercise your free will. Unable to go to the fridge to get a cold thirst-quenching beverage. I look at Jake and think of the wasted souls we walked past at the wing gates.

The first time most teenagers come to prison they must arrive like Jake, full of fire and rage. With the strength, endurance and persistence that only the young possess. No doubt imagining the glory of going down in a hail of bullets if it all goes wrong after experiencing money, girls, and infamy. The reality has already stared at me from the wing gates, through jellied eyes. Years of poor diet, absent dental care, and no exercise has left the inhabitants here slack-faced and haggard. The lack of love, support, and planning left them no future at all. The living dead.

Jake finishes and is now 'on the nod'. He doesn't even seem to get the big, initial, euphoric buzz any more, just slips into this sleepy dreamlike state with a smirk. I leave him slumped in the small plastic seat and lie down on the fusty bedcovers. If I sleep, I hope he is still alive when I wake.

23

21ST JUNE 2011

Jake is in the same position when I open my eyes in the morning after a fitful night. It's still early but I can hear coughing and quiet talking on the wing. He opens his eyes and looks at me.

'Ughh.'

'I bet you wish you got coffee and milk instead now.'

As usual, he pulls himself together quickly and pees like a scattergun sprinkler in the corner. The room fills with a foul, acrid smell. I guess I'll have to get used to that. He gets on the bottom bunk with a groan.

'So that bloke last night, he was a bacon?' he quietly enquires.

'What's a bacon?'

'A faggot. He offered you stuff, I take it?'

'Yeah, in a circular kind of way.'

'I bet he seemed all reasonable. A nice guy.'

I say nothing.

'Screw you nice and easy, plenty of lube.' Jake's voice hardens.

'Prison is full of predators like him, hoping to prey on the young like us!' he shouts. 'He will ass-rape you and inject his poison into you the first chance he gets. I know these...'

His eyes shift from me to the floor and back as he searches for the word. He settles on 'reptiles'.

'You have to go and fuck him up. Take the initiative. I'll get you a tool.'

He lies back down and leaves me thinking of my mum.

* * *

Shortly after breakfast, we're released to go to the med hatch. The wing is locked down. As we walk to join the line, it's strange to imagine there are people living their lives behind the long expanse of metal doors. We're queuing up to receive medicine. At least that's the general impression I have.

'So what is this stuff?'

'Methadone. It's a heroin substitute – 80 per cent of this wing will be on it.'

Sure enough there's a big queue of skeletons waiting at the gate. One of these worthless beings looks directly at me.

'All right, Ben.'

I drag my eyes away from his startlingly yellow teeth and look at his vacant face.

'You don't remember me, do you?'

He doesn't even look vaguely familiar. I can see the exact shape of his skull through his flaccid skin.

'It's Barry.' I get a blast of breath so foul I'm surprised I know who I am, never mind him.

'You remember! Barry and Terry. The twins from across the road.'

My brain pulls an image from the darkest recesses of my brain as though a dentist is easing out a stubborn tooth. Two chubby lads, playing in the street. Terry got killed playing chicken on the A47 and the family, what was left of it, moved away after. The being in front of me can't weigh more than eight stone, but the eyes that peer expectantly out of his crumpled visage pick at the memory like a vulture at its dinner.

'Shit, Fat Barry.' I actually gasp.

'Yes, bro. You know it. Good to see you. You OK?'

An odd question considering we're queuing in a prison for some heroin replacement with a load of freaks.

I'm almost too stunned to respond. He is twenty but could pass for forty.

'Yeah, good mate,' I reply. 'You?'

'Sound.'

I'm saved from any more small-talk by the officer blocking the gate shouting, 'Next,' into the face of a bloke who looks so absent-minded Barry must have breathed on him too.

'Come on, mate. Go get your jungle juice!' Jake shouts at him.

I notice Jake's grey orange-peel-like complexion is not so different from poor Barry's, although Jake at least knows what a toothbrush is for. His eyes connect to mine but he misreads my concern.

'Jungle juice, the methadone is green. Sweet too, I quite like it. Gives me a mellow vibe all day, so why not?' Jake winks at me.

'Filthy stuff though. It's more addictive than actual heroin. I wish I'd never started taking it,' Barry says as an afterthought, as though we're discussing the relative merits of filter over instant.

'True, dat,' Jake sagely adds.

We get to the hatch and I watch Barry knock back a flimsy plastic cupful of a thick viscous dark-green liquid. As though he's in a high-brow Mexican restaurant, sampling their tequilas. After an argument, he's made to drink the same quantity again of water by a young officer who looks as though he could cry any minute. Jake whispers in my ear.

'If you can get away with not drinking the water, then don't. Not all the screws are that diligent. You can then spit it out back in your cell and sell it on the wing. Some of them make themselves sick afterwards and sell it anyway. There's a market for everything here.'

I watch Jake sip his as if it's a fine whisky, and he too, argues with the officer about the water. When I stand at the hatch a very cheerful nurse gets me to sign a form and then hands me a cup with about a tenth the amount the others had. I pause and then hand it back to her. To the man behind's shout of, 'I'll have his,' I walk back to my cell, overwhelmed that this is my life.

Jake is pleading with the officer locking him up.

'Guv, I need to make a phone call.'

'Ring at lunchtime.'

'I can't. It's my solicitor. He'll be at lunch.'

'If you can spell solicitor you can ring him now.'

'Fuck you.'

'Ride your bang-up, you.'

Jake is smiling as we're locked in, having been told to do our time like men

'I like him. He does actually do stuff for you. Some won't. It's all a game in here. Cat and mouse.'

'I take it we're the latter?'

'Yep, although sometimes the new screws are afraid of some of the bigger rodents.'

'Don't you get put on report or something? I thought everyone would be subservient.'

'I'm not sure what that means but there are eighty of us, two of them. If they put everyone who's rude to them on report, they'd never go home. Vent your fury on them, it's what they're paid for. What can they do to us? We're already in jail.'

As I ponder this strange view of human interaction, I think at least we weren't violent towards them. That would come later.

* * *

So much for keeping my head down. That was the advice every person I ever met gave me about prison. It is evening association by the time Jake gives me a burnt-black toothbrush with two razor blades melted into it where the brush part should be. There are two blades in parallel so it's difficult to stitch the skin back together after you're cut. A double slash-up. He assures me it will leave a gruesome scar. He also tells me to say the man touched my dick if I get caught. I dodge between the pool table and the arguing table-tennis players and make my way up to his cell in the top corner of the wing. For fleeting seconds, I wonder if it wouldn't be so bad to suck him off for an easy time, but I recall Jake's warning. Now I understand. How many other young boys before me must have accepted his proposals for a safer life. I grit my teeth and continue.

Sure enough, as Jake said it would be, the CCTV camera is broken and hanging off the ceiling of the top landing, pointing to the floor. So I just need a clean getaway. I don't think my heart has stopped pounding since I walked through the entrance to this foul place. Now it has reached ramming speed, desperate to get out of my chest. I push open the door to his cell and he turns to face me with a serene but savage expression. Time drags out and the din on the wing becomes muffled. Is this the last moment of my life? Surely it can't have begun.

'I won't invite you in,' he finally says after studying my face. 'I've heard who you came in with and no doubt he'll have talked you into coming here. Tooled up, are we?'

My brain is pounding so much I'm surprised I can still hear. In fact, perhaps I can't and I'm just lip-reading.

'Look at me,' he continues. 'How hard do you think it would be for me to take whatever you're concealing and use it on you instead?'

He is naked from the waist up and, unless he has a nasty case of alopecia, shaves his muscular chest. He must weigh double what I do. My laughable shank burns a hole in my pocket. I am his to command. He walks towards me; my body becomes numb. He stops inches away.

'It's different here, this is my house. It's survival of the strongest. There's no valour here. Only the most ruthless survive and I make the rules. You remind me of me, son. Even what you're doing now has shown balls, even if it meant you losing your own. Homosexuality isn't a crime, but, even if it were, I'm in control. Forget what you think you know about a place like this and make sure you never come back. Next time the person like me, and there always is one, may not be so understanding.'

How I stop myself running back to my cell I'll never know. Even as it is, I stumble and catch strange looks. I am a child and I shouldn't be here. I'm more afraid now than I was before, when just recently I would have denied that was possible. I don't know the rules. Jake doesn't. No one does as they are a sea of quicksand, constantly changing and sucking people under. Maybe there are no rules. You fight first and forget the questions, as there are no answers.

I get back to the cell and Jake stops me going in by blocking the door with a mop handle. Incredibly, he's been cleaning it. 'It's not dry yet,' he says. More unsettling madness, but he is all I have. I nod.

'Did you get him?'

'We talked. It's fine.'

Jake gives me a tough look and I think I could have done with that countenance standing next to me a few minutes ago. 'Go in,' he says.

I walk past him and look outside. I know this isn't a place for tears and I choke them back. How much more of my life will I waste staring through barred windows? I turn to Jake, who's admiring our shiny living space. Jake, who lives like a tramp in a pigsty on the out. Suddenly it becomes clear. It's something he can control here. This is our home. He can focus on it, take pride in it, and use it to burn time.

'Coffee?' He smiles at me.

'You're a good friend, Jake.'

I'm adrift, but without Jake I am drowned.

PART IV

A FREE YOUTH?

24

17TH AUGUST 2011

The train journey back from the prison to Peterborough on the day we're released is surreal. The countryside looks uneven and unbelievably green after such a grey place of hard angles. We were moved to Glen Parva, a prison solely for eighteen-to-twenty-one-year-olds near Leicester, after a week, and it's from here they let us go. No one asked where we were going. I mean, they asked us where they needed to write out the travel warrant for, but no one seemed to care whether it was to a park bench or a hotel. You would think a place for youngsters would be better, but in some respects it was worse. It was a place with no hope and no optimism, just anger, despair and violence. Jake however, was known and, whereas in an adult jail he was a mouse in a cattery, here he was King Mustafa. In those few weeks I learnt more about thieving, violence, drugs and survival than I had in the previous eighteen years and through that time Jake had my back.

He says little on the journey home, his mind on other things. We walk to Asda when we arrive at Peterborough and buy the cheapest mobile phones they have. Fifteen pounds may not seem a lot but the prison discharge grant is less than fifty quid and, after working in the prison for two pounds a day, the price, frankly, seems outrageous. We swap numbers outside and he gives me a bear hug, says, 'Laters,' and is gone. If I want to get hold of him he'll be at the park at times but I have no desire to do drugs or see Lily. That is his plan. I have no urge to see my mother either. She sent no money or letters, despite me writing to her asking for both. I wander round town and eat a Mars bar. If I'm hungry I don't notice. I'm used to partitioning that feeling now. And others.

As the afternoon wanes, I have few options: my mother's flat or the possibility of a few flop-houses around the city that may or may not be usable. Typically, it rains. Almost warm summer rain but heavy nonetheless. I decide to give the one safe place I know a try. I dash through Queensgate shopping centre to the bus station and jump on the Orton bus to Mr Singh's house.

It's Mrs Singh who answers the door. She's visibly shocked.

'Ben,' is all she can say. It's nice to see her, but she closes the door on me.

I'm still standing there, open-mouthed, when Mr Singh appears. As usual, he is coolness personified.

'This is a pleasant surprise, Ben. Come in.'

He takes me into his kitchen, which is warm and smells of toast. I haven't eaten since the chocolate bar earlier and a small bowl of cereal at the prison prior to that.

'Cup of tea?'

'Please.'

'How have you been?'

The only answer is dreadful. My thoughts bounce around my head like a violent pinball game, each memory firing the projectile into another shocking experience. Drink, drugs, stealing, and prison.

'Not the best,' I finally say.

'How can I help?'

'I was wondering if I could stay?' When I say the words out loud, I see how pathetic and ridiculous the idea is. They barely know me. 'Just for a few days.'

He stays quiet.

'Sorry, I shouldn't have come.' I smile, one of defeat.

I wouldn't let someone like me stay in my house if they randomly knocked on my door. Why should he?

'Ben,' he begins. 'As much as we like you and felt an immediate bond to you, you can't just arrive here unexpectedly. We often have very vulnerable teenagers and young children here, at the slightest notice.'

'I'm sorry, I shouldn't have come. I'll go.'

He puts his hand on mine. It feels alien.

'Stay tonight. It's late and we don't have anyone here. You came for a reason. Will you have somewhere to go tomorrow?'

'Yes, thank you.' I want to say no, but he doesn't deserve my problems.

'Shall we get a takeaway? Chinese this time, broaden your horizons.'

I nod. I would have eaten a breeze block with a wooden spoon as long as he let me stay.

We eat the Chinese in the lounge on plates on our laps – strange food but delicious. Afterwards I stand up to stretch, full to bursting. I find myself holding the golden horse again. Was that really only just over two years ago? Mr Singh takes out the plates and Mrs Singh stands next to me. She gently takes the horse out of my hand and hefts its weight.

'It's iron, not gold. We get through a lot of them. It gives us an idea of what we're dealing with, but we don't condemn. The fact you put it back last time is the reason we let you in today. Remember that.'

Realisation causes something to snap inside me and I laugh, but it's high pitched and doesn't sound like me. She takes me in her arms and I sob.

It's strange that I open up to her. She, who asks no questions. I tell her everything, all the time searching her face for judgement, but I find none.

'Life is a journey,' she whispers. 'It can't be a never-ending succession of ever-better experiences. There are ups and downs. It is how you respond to those that matters. We didn't always live in this house. We planned and saved, won and lost, but eventually we got here. That is the passage of life. Try to enjoy yourself along the way too. Take risks, as you don't want to arrive at your death having not lived, but be sensitive to others as well.'

It seems easy when she says it like that.

I still have my mother and somewhere to live. God only knows where Jake will be staying. I'm looking at life the wrong way. Hopefully, together we can create something, or failing that I will do it myself. I think of the things I have stolen and the money I've wasted. All that effort and nothing to show for it. I resolve to make sure I will not be in this position again. This time I will save something from my criminal activities. I don't think she has that in mind when we have our little talk, but I'm only eighteen. I'm still an idiot.

* * *

For once, I don't slip out with the dawn. We have a normal breakfast – cereal and small-talk, although I'm keen to leave. I want to see my mother and get started on my new life. For that, I'll need Jake too, so I'll have to hunt him down. I get the bus back into town and do some light shoplifting to prove I've still got it. I employ the techniques that my new acquaintances at Parva taught me. There are many. Big supermarket workers are on minimum wage so don't want the hassle of challenging people, so they are easy pickings.

Prison tip number one: The best techniques usually involve paying for something, while stealing other stuff at the same time. I pay for a can of Coke in one place, go outside and drink it, then go back in and pick another one up and walk out with it. If they ask, I have a receipt and was going back in as I'd forgotten something. There is an unusual thought nagging at the back of my mind though. I hate to admit it, but I think it's the Singhs. Weird how my own conscience doesn't bother me, but I don't want to let them down.

I walk back to Paston and, even though it has only been a few months, it feels as if I haven't been here for years. That feeling is heightened when I knock on Jonty's door and it's opened by a small smiley lady who doesn't speak English. I let myself in quietly and find my mum asleep on the sofa. She has either been there since last night or she had wine for breakfast. The house, though, is spotless and the fridge surprisingly full. There's a letter with my name on it on the stand, where my dad used to put his car and house keys before his demise. I open it up and find a twenty-pound note in it with a small letter saying, 'I miss you, looking forward to when you come home.' I feel pleased. That money would have gone a long way in jail but at least she didn't forget about me, which was what I thought.

'Welcome back, son.'

She is standing at the door to the lounge. Older somehow and drained. She gives me a hug, which feels stiff but still nice.

'Thanks for the money,' I say. I squeeze her hand to let her know it's fine.

'I'm sorry. I wasn't sure of the address and before I knew it you were due to leave.'

'How many prisons do you think there are here?' I shrug and add, 'It's the thought that counts, Mum. I'm home now.'

'Do you want a drink?'

'I picked up some nice coffee earlier. Use that.' Prison tip number two. Steal coffee. It generally isn't security tagged, is surprisingly expensive, has a long shelf life and is easy to sell on.

'You still getting out, I see?' I gesture to the stack of empty bottles in the corner.

'Yes, the Portuguese lady from downstairs has been taking me with her when she goes. Everything is much cheaper at the supermarket.'

You can say that again, I think. 'When did Jonty and Sally leave?'

'Not long after your...' she considers her word choices '... vacation. He came to say goodbye and was sad when you weren't here.'

'Bollocks.'

'He was a sweet boy... man, I suppose. I hope it works out for him. Her not so much.'

I open my eyes wide in surprise.

'I thought you liked her.'

'It was your dad who liked her.'

That statement lingers in the air like a juicy apple on a low-hanging branch, but my mind is elsewhere. For the first time since being released I feel bad. Losing touch with people is one of the many downsides of going to prison.

* * *

Later, on my bed, my mind flicks through my Jonty memories. There is nothing bad in them. Kind, fun, happy reminiscences. The friend I lost. I feel as though I'm at a picnic, resting on a blanket, having a great time, then the sun goes behind a cloud. I miss him and know my life will have less joy without him in it.

PART V

YOUNG OFFENDER

25

26TH JANUARY 2012

As the officer walks me to the induction wing, I consider that the only surprising thing, is that it took six months until I got sent to jail again. He tells me to wait as a long line of big men walk past on their way to evening exercise. One of the few positives of receiving a prison sentence is that, if you behave, you can work out a lot in a great gym. I guess it helps control as I've seen many angry prisoners wind their necks in when they've been threatened with the withdrawal of bodybuilding privileges. I allow myself a small smile as I clock a lot of disproportionately thin legs. You only get an hour and it seems biceps and pecs take precedence over calves and thighs. Still, you wouldn't go looking for trouble with some of these as quite a few look as if they could bench-press me and the tired-looking officer I'm with. A few people I remember from my previous stint are amongst the throng. We nod to each other.

I'm trying not to think about the fact I was given a Reception call, but had no one to ring. I guess it's to let your family know where you are. Get someone to go and feed the cat if you live alone. I didn't need mine as they arrested me at home. My mother was slaughtered and didn't even get off the sofa but I'm pretty sure she knew what was going on. The police turned up in the early evening with a search warrant. It was unfortunate that I was in, although I suppose that would have just delayed the inevitable. Someone must have grassed me up, and I couldn't have been more guilty – our flat was an Aladdin's cave of lifted goods. It was plain to see from my mother's addled state she wasn't up to generating such a hoard. Still, I confessed to everything, just in case.

Cuffed, read my rights, taken to the police station, locked up overnight and then put in front of the same magistrate who sent me and Jake down previously. I didn't stand a chance. I was having a cup of tea, wondering what was on TV, and then, less than twenty-four hours later, I am standing in the same clothes waiting to begin my custodial stay at Her Majesty's pleasure. Impressive. There were no probation reports needed this time, no probation worker present at all in fact. I was just sent down. The life of a thief.

It's time for evening meal so the wings are raucous. This time I expect it, so I'm not shocked. I'm also not concerned by my custodial stay. Jake is here. He rang me with his free call three days ago – ironically, to get me to send some clothes and money in for him. If I'd known, I could have just brought them with me. He said he would explain later, but he'd been given twelve weeks for theft. That's rather annoying when I got sixteen weeks for handling his stolen goods. He said he couldn't get on the wing for smackheads and the like, as the prison was full to bursting still with all the London rioters. The judges had been instructed to slam those caught, and the London jails were overwhelmed. So they shift them out and up the line and now Peterborough is overcrowded too.

When I arrived, they asked me if I had any substance issues. I told them 'no' as Jake would still be on the induction wing. The junkie wing, as he called it, was apparently full. It was the truth, though. I can see the drugs eating into Jake and I know there isn't a happy ending waiting for him. We are both under twenty-one so will be moved on within two weeks of arrival to a young offenders' jail like HMP Glen Parva or HMP Littlehey regardless. Maybe prison would be a scarier, more threatening place if Jake weren't here each time. This is the last time though. I won't be coming back.

What the last depressing day has confirmed for me is life-altering. Now I understand why people pay for things. To live your life with your pulse racing as you are constantly looking for the next opportunity will only go one way. I wonder whether I should be pleased that it has only taken me two spells in prison to understand that salient fact.

Jake is leaning against the wing gates with his arms through the bars when I arrive at my new home, arguing with an officer.

'I said get away from the gate.' He looks resigned to the confrontation as this wouldn't be his first argument with Jake.

'No, I'm waiting for someone.'

'I said move back.'

'Why do I have to get away from the gate?'

'There are rules.'

'Not good enough.'

The officer I'm with opens the gates, lets me in, and then shepherds Jake away from the gates with his sheer presence, talking as he does so.

'It's so that nasty little things like you can't pass contraband to each other.'

'Contraband?' Jake asks all innocently.

'Drugs, tobacco, photos of your winkie, that sort of thing.'

They laugh, and the tension evaporates. My escort gives my file to his fellow worker. 'YO. Been here before, no issues.' He nods at me and leaves.

'Put him in with me, guv,' Jake pleads. 'I'll move out of my single and you can stick us in a double together.'

That works for the officer too. They always want single cells freed up. For obvious reasons you can't put a murderer or an arsonist in a double cell. He shakes his head and smiles at the same time, bemused by Jake's belligerent, irritating tone one minute, only to change to a beseeching, compliant one seconds later. As though what went on moments ago doesn't matter in a place like this.

An hour later we're settled into our cell. Jake has acquired all the necessary home comforts in his few days here and doesn't seem upset he's been sent to prison three times in a year.

'I've had enough of this, Jake.'

'I know, me too. We need to get smarter. Move towns.'

'That's not what I mean. No more shoplifting. This place will be like a revolving door for us otherwise.'

'I thought you were all against dwellings.'

'Yes, mate. I'm not going to be robbing old people's houses either.'

'So what you going to do? Get a job?'

I sit in the small plastic chair near the window and put my face in my hands. Why do there seem to be missing choices for people like us? How do you even get a job? We both have records now so would anyone even want to employ us?

'We could get some labouring work.'

As if to confirm my situation is hopeless, the rain intensifies its dance on the plastic window.

'I know, Ben. What else can we do? This is our life now. I'm worse into it than you. I know the drugs got a hold on me. Every time I think of doing crack I'm like a flower turning towards the sun, with my pleasure receptors unfurling like petals.'

I look at him in disgust and surprise.

'Fuck that. This is not my future, and where did you get that petal shit from?'

'Lily told me. I liked it.'

'You found her?' Some good news at last.

'Yes, just before I got pinched again. She's staying at some old guy's house for free. Kind of free, if you know what I mean. She said to say hi.'

'Why can't we all just get a place together? Don't prisons do courses and housing for people like us?'

'Yes, Ben, but you need to get some serious bird to get put on them. You'll be gone in a few weeks, they won't even realise you're here, and it'll be time for you to leave.'

'Until next time.'

'Yes, until next time.'

'Do you have any bright ideas at all? I don't want to spend another second in a shithole like this. Look around you, Jake. All these pathetic blokes in their thirties trying to look hard with missing teeth and shrunken heads. That's us if we don't do something about it. There must be a way out of this trap. We aren't even classified as adults yet. We're too young to have no hope.'

'We might have something more pressing to worry about than your career prospects.'

'Now what?'

'Did you notice it was a bit dark here?'

'What? It's raining, so bound to be gloomy.'

'No, knob-head. Go and look at the people on the wing.'

I poke my head out of the door, look round, and notice instantly that there is a significantly larger population of black people than usual lounging around. Jake isn't racist though; he doesn't like anyone.

'Yeah, so? London gangs aren't interested in the likes of us.'

'No, that's not it. The laundry guy just tipped me off. Turns out that the house I tried to rob with the old lady in it belonged to one of these bloke's sweet grandma.'

'Oh. Shit.'

'Yes, I think he only realised a little while ago. They'll come for us. Tomorrow morning, I would think.'

It feels as though antifreeze has been injected into my circulatory system.

'What are you going to do? Tell the officers. They'll move us off.'

'What? End up on the nonce wing? No way. I'm no bacon. No one has a shank on this wing – I've already asked – but I'll think of something.'

As they lock us in, I lie back on my bed knowing I am in for a sleepless night.

26

27TH JANUARY 2012

I wake from a fitful sleep to find Jake doing press-ups on the cell floor. I've always found his ability to do them one-handed impressive, but he's so emaciated it isn't as though he has much weight to push.

'What time is it?'

'Seven.' He doesn't look up from his exercises as he replies.

The wing-workers are unlocked in fifteen minutes to prepare the breakfast. By that, I mean give us a scoop of cereal and some strange-tasting long-life milk. You get half an hour for breakfast and a shower. Then it's half an hour of exercise in the yard. Neither of which we'll be partaking of. If you're going to get assaulted in prison, then these two places are the most likely. The showers, as there are no cameras and the yard because, in this jail anyway, there can be as many as eighty prisoners walking around in a futile circle being watched over by one uninterested officer. If it kicks off, he will be less than enthusiastic about dealing with a mass altercation on his lonesome. By the time the cavalry arrives, revenge will have been taken.

Jake has switched to sit-ups now, but carries on talking.

'I didn't tell you, did I?'

'Tell me what?'

'How I got sent back here.'

'Let me guess, you were unlucky.'

'How did you know? Unbelievably so.'

'Go on, I could do with the distraction.'

'I'd been chilling with Dan at his place.'

I interrupt. 'When are you ever going to learn that hanging around with him only leads to bad experiences? By chilling, I assume you were off your faces.'

'OK, I agree, but there were different circumstances in this case. Dan had managed to blag a one-bedroom flat in Orton Goldhay when he last got released from prison. You know they say to tell the council you're homeless when you get out and they'll help you?'

'Yes, but it's some kind of urban myth, unless you turn up with one leg and three kids in tow, all of them different colours.'

'Exactly, but that's what he did, and you know what? A few hours later he was given the key to this flat. Just near the Orton Centre. I refused to believe him so he took me there. Admittedly, it was in a rough area but it still had furniture and a TV and stuff. It was sweet, man. I mean, my main complaint was the fridge was noisy. Anyway, I'd just had a touch and got rid of all that stuff from the chemist.'

'Which you still owe me for, by the way.'

Jake had been sleeping with this grubby urchin on and off for the last few months who said she might be pregnant. Obviously, that amused me. I said we should get Daddy a pregnancy test, so he could make sure. Not that I would have taken the piss of course. Who'd have known that these damn things were over a tenner each? We intended to pay for it but the security guard clocked us the moment we walked in anyway. He wasn't even subtle about keeping an eye on us. Sadly, a man collapsed near the till. He looked old and went down fast, like he was now an empty shell. His daughter screamed.

The security guard was in a quandary. I could see the indecision on his face. His humanity won out, and ours failed. We both had the obligatory plastic bag that all thieves carry for such heaven-sent purposes. The security guard started CPR, the pharmacist rang for an ambulance, and we stole all the pregnancy tests, condoms, and creams we could get our hands on. Jake took it too far. He walked to the front counter and took a load of things off the shelf in front of the pharmacist talking to emergency services. He stared at her, knowing she wouldn't defy him, as our hero pumped away. If our place in hell wasn't already secure, I suspect that day's labour would have our names etched on two pitchforks, in preparation for our arrival.

'Yes. That's the nasty part. Word got around we had loads of good stuff and some guy at the market gave me two hundred quid for the lot. Dan had his discharge grant and some hardship money from the council, and suggested a little moving-in spliff to celebrate. I thought that was a great idea, got a few beers, and took round my PlayStation.

'I woke up on the sofa three days later with what felt like a caved-in head. The flat looked like every rock star in history had been round, done their worst and then left because it was too much for them. You couldn't see the floor for crap like empties and fast-food wrappers. Weird rubbish too, like lone female shoes and dog collars. More than one person had done a shit in the bath, but when I saw the state of the toilet, I understood why. The noisy fridge wasn't a problem either as that and the TV were gone. Someone had also taken my Superdry coat and game console. Of course, Dan was nowhere to be seen. All I had on were cargo shorts, which I'm pretty sure Dan was wearing when I met him, and a thin yellow jumper, which was a hint too flamboyant for my liking. I think the only reason the sofa was still there was because I was asleep on it. There was also a noise abatement notice stuck on the lounge door. The weird thing is, I don't remember anyone else being there apart from Dan.

'I just wanted to get out of there. I wandered to the local shops feeling like death warmed up. Hunger attacked and I picked up a Snickers bar. I didn't have any money to pay for it. Not a penny, but I had to have it. I slipped it into the back of my shorts, forgetting I didn't have my coat on to cover it. Now here is the unlucky part. I had huge, violent stomach cramps. You know, real gripes, and it was instantaneous. I had to use every ounce of my being, every single piece of my self-control, to focus on the small muscle that was my ring-piece to stop me shitting myself that very second.

'At that fortuitous moment, the owner came over and asked if he could help. I was straining with everything I had to prevent the download of the day occurring and was unable to answer. It was freezing in there, yet I was sweating like I had the flu. He asked me again. All I could do was stare at him. He asked me to leave. To him I was a wild-eyed loon. I managed to get out a snotty sob and snarled, "Just looking," at him through my gritted teeth. Just that one distraction caused me to lose focus, for the tiniest millisecond. A big plug of shit popped out of my ass like a spider out of a hole before I could shut the trap door. It crept down my inner thigh and hung suspended on my knee like a tear drop on a chin.

'I didn't want to look, but I couldn't help myself. As the horrible smell permeated around us, we peered down and saw it slip off my leg and land with a brown splat on my white trainer. At that moment, a kindly old man shouted out, "He's got a chocolate bar stuffed down the back of his shorts!" The owner grabbed my arm, yelled, "Thief," and my bum exploded.'

My laughter bursts too. Who says doing drugs isn't fun? 'Go on, then what?'

'I had nothing left. I sank to my knees in the foul liquid that was pooling on the floor. It was as if someone had poured two pints of warm Guinness down the back of my legs. I'm not sure if I was crying, or it was the shitty chemical smell that was making my eyes weep. The owner's son came out of the back and gave me such a look of incomprehension. I would have laughed if the old bloke hadn't been prodding me in the kidneys with his walking stick and saying, "You bugger, you." The police came, they were disgusted. It's the first time I got a shower at the police station. So here we are. Unfortunate, eh?'

I'm laughing so hard now, I fear I may suffer the same fate.

27

A minute later, our door is unlocked, and I stop laughing. Jake sprints out of the door. I grab our cereal bowls and get to the front of the queue. I'm served fast so I scuttle back to our cell. As I return, one of the upper single cells opens and a huge black lad comes out and stares at me as I walk down the landing. Just before I step out of sight he draws his thumb across his throat.

I step into the cell and push the door shut. Some cells have a courtesy key that the prisoners can lock so other prisoners can't go in their cell. Obviously, the officers' keys override them. What I would give for one of those now. However, this is the induction wing and in the past I have taken that very key to another wing without bothering to return it. Even thrown it in the bin when I realised it had no use to me as opposed to returning it to the staff. Another way in which I deserve my fate.

Jake comes back and waves a small kettle at me with an earnest look on his face. He fills up the kettle and turns it on. These things suck. They take ages to boil. Someone told me hotel rooms have them and they are the same. Only privileged prisoners are permitted them and they should only be on the enhanced wing. They are another currency though, and therefore commonplace.

'I couldn't get my hands on anything else. The wing is bare. We'll only get one chance with this. There could be loads of them.'

We both know what that means.

'You aren't going to put sugar in it, are you?'

Boiling water and sugar is often called "napalm" in prison as it causes the burning substance to stick to the victim, intensifying the suffering and causing horrific injuries. I heard someone got eight years for doing just that, so I'm not at all keen. I would rather just get a good beating. The problem is, it's unlikely to be just a few well-placed kicks and punches. The gangs from London are ruthless and the chances of them arriving without some kind of blade are small.

'No, if I play this right, we'll still get away with it virtually unscathed.'

'How so, Moriarty?'

'Who's Moriarty?'

'Never mind.' I sigh.

'You stand in their line of sight when they come through the door and, at the last second, duck out of the way onto the bed. The first person in gets it. He squeals, we fight until the screws arrive.'

'A disappointing plan to rely on. Maybe it won't come to that.'

I remember the throat-slitting thumb gesture and know I'm kidding myself. I open the cell door and look down the wing. There's a large congregation of black and white men at the top of the landing. They turn and look at me. Kill someone unknown and no one mentions it, upset a man's mother and it's all a big deal. Madness.

'That thing not boil any quicker?' I almost shout as I jolt myself back into the cell.

Jake is bending down looking at it. 'We've got a few minutes yet.'

'Why do you say that?'

'It's exercise in five minutes. They'll call it and one of the screws will wait on the yard gate outside while the other one lets the nice inmates out for a stroll. The wing will be empty and we'll receive a home visit.'

Shit. I am in so much danger and I'm incapable of solving it. Relying on Jake and a small kettle, percolating like a coffee pot, for my survival. I swear on my dad's memory I will remember this moment and vow I will never be so vulnerable again. If I live, that is.

'Let's just go on the yard. We're trapped in here.' I cringe at the whining sound in my voice. Jake's is steady.

'It'll be worse on the yard. They can surround us. I know how to fight in a cell, many don't.'

Including me. I've experienced some slow times in my life, watching one of my parents die being one of them, but this is on an altogether different scale. Someone once told me to run a film through my head to speed it up. I could have gone through *Titanic* in each one of those lingering seconds, staring at that damn kettle. We sit on the lower bunk together, in silence, waiting and praying.

In unison it finally boils, just as an officer shouts, 'Exercise to the gate!' I hear people walking past our door, so I take another sneaky look out. That old lady's incensed grandson walks towards our cell, swollen with revenge, with four large, determined men. The ringleader also has something in his hand that takes an idle glint off the harsh prison lights. I push the door to, and turn to Jake.

'They're coming.'

'How many?'

'Five.'

'OK,' is all he says.

Strangely, his calmness makes me more nervous. Shitting your pants, though, never helped anyone's predicament. Jake here can testify to that. I take deep breaths. If I'm going to go down, I will do so in flames. The only weapons we have are the metal flasks issued on arrival. They are lightweight, but better than nothing. Jake fills them up with water and passes me one. Why didn't I think of that? I hope they work better as coshes than they do at keeping your water hot. Jake takes the lid off the kettle but keeps his finger on the button so it continues to boil. The water jumps and sizzles. Steam shrouds his face.

I have my back to the door but the shout of 'Last call exercise' is clear, so I know our door has been opened. I look over my shoulder and see an angry, snarling expression, bearing down on me. I jump out of the way onto Jake's bed.

What happens next will stay with me to my dying day, and possibly beyond.

28

The man entering our cell isn't expecting the well-known hot water trick, as kettles aren't allowed on this wing. A rookie mistake. In prison you must always fear the worst. He's imagining us to be tooled up and there are more of them than us. He thinks it will come down to simple mathematics. Instead, it will be physics.

With an almighty yell, Jake launches the contents of the kettle directly into the oncoming face. With his rangy arm extended, the water is barely out of the boiling kettle before it makes contact. Then, the screaming starts.

I have never heard a scream like that, and if there is a God I will never do so again. I instantly know, many years from now, when I am old and can't remember who I am, or why I struggle, I will still recall that terrible cry. It is high and shrill, but as a solid wall of sound, like how a small girl would scream if she had the voice box of an opera singer. It goes straight through me and every other man there and freezes us where we stand.

As he takes a huge breath, his skin slides from his brown face as though someone is removing the wrapper to a much-wanted gift. A livid-red-faced figure of horror stares at us in agony. He screams again, louder and longer and impossibly higher, while his also-burnt friends back out of the cell, nursing stinging splashes and haunted expressions of fear. I have never felt so compelled to action in my life.

I get up and step behind him and put my arms under his armpits and pull him out of the cell past his stunned companions. An officer tries to stop me going past until he sees the gruesome face. He is sick down my leg. I pull the burned man into the wing shower, hit the button, and hold him under the spray.

What happens next is almost as surreal as the incident itself. I'm not sure if he's in shock, or being under the cold water is why he isn't moving, but he doesn't struggle at all. He is heavy though, and I'm relieved when my place is taken by an officer who continues to hold him up. I've never seen so many screws in one place. That cry was never going to be unanswered. 'Behind your doors,' is being bellowed into every face. Traumatised inmates are pushed into their cells as I'm brutally shoved into mine.

Jake is watching TV.

He turns with a wry smile. 'I didn't put sugar in it because then it's premeditated. We were having a cup of tea and they barged in. What else was I supposed to do in the heat of the moment? They can do me for an unauthorised item if they like.'

As I try to calm my pounding heart I can't help wondering if, through the last horrific five minutes, Jake's pulse has risen at all.

29

A strange couple of hours pass by. There's movement on the wing, although we can't tell what's going on. I can sense Jake wanting to talk, but know that if I push he will clam up. So I just lie here, feeling and hearing the air flow in and out of my nose. Eventually, he speaks.

'This is it for me, isn't it?'

I stay silent, knowing he'll continue.

'Same shit, maybe a different hole, the usual pricks.'

He's right. His life will be a continuation of similar events in comparable places with contemptible people. Until it ends.

'You don't hear me saying, "When I've got this" or "When I've got that" it'll be great, because it won't, will it?'

'Jake,' but I've interrupted mid-flow.

'There's not going to be a fancy posh wedding to a pretty girl. My parents aren't going to be there either way. No surprise fancy-dress party on my thirtieth birthday. No mystery beach holiday because of my work promotion. My family won't be all gurning into the camera for my first boy's christening photo. No champagne to celebrate buying my first house, and no fucking weeping crowds at my not-so-distant funeral. I will lurch from one terrible experience to another, desperately trying to grasp some pleasure where I can. When I die, and let's not pretend I'm going to see fifty, apart from the people whose lives I've ruined, no one will even have known I was here.'

Chilling, disturbing, and likely, is all I can think. I thought, when my father died, attaching myself to Jake was a way of saving myself from sinking into depression. In reality, my boat was just listing from shock and would have righted itself in time. Whose job was it to tell me that? Instead, I am the man who climbed back on the *Titanic* as the deckchairs were sliding off. Jake is in the engine room and will go down with the ship. There is no hope for him. I pray there is still time for me to be saved.

'Why don't you give up the drugs, Jake? That's a big part of your problem there.'

Even as I say it, I don't believe it. The words come out thin and reedy, like the conviction in them. Those do-gooders have no idea. It's like the massive fat people when they lose all their weight. It's too late. Their skin is stretched beyond breaking to accommodate something awful and will never go back. It hangs around and gradually drags the person back in, weakening them and sickening them, until they are back where they started. You can't fix Jake. The dawning realisation that I need to cut him loose if I'm to survive, registers like an InterCity train going through a platform on a station where it doesn't stop. My eyes widen as if I'm too close to the edge, but I need to get on. Jake's reply is quiet.

'The drugs have got a hold on me but in some way I need them. A nice rock, some peace and quiet, and I know I'll be happy, at least for a while. Sometimes, though, I keep smoking crack for days, just to avoid the crash. That's the worst, dirtiest feeling in the world. Then it's gone. You smoke a ciggy but don't enjoy it, put on some music and don't hear it. Nothing matters any more. You try to fall asleep, instead you think about doing it again.'

Therein lies the madness and what drives Jake to do some of the insane things he's done. His problem is he has a disease where the emotional and motivational need for drugs outweighs any threat of negative consequences.

'I need people like you around me, Ben. There's something fundamentally good in you. Take that bloke back there. I would've let him burn.'

What do you say to that? He signs his own death warrant. We lie in what he probably thinks is companionable silence for a few minutes.

'You, and Lily, are all that I have. Dan too, incredibly.'

'What? You do not need that noxious weasel in your life.'

'What does noxious mean?'

'Harmful or very unpleasant. Both of which apply to him.'

'That's the thing. My life is so toxic that I need him. He's so fucked up and rotten that at least I know with certainty, and that's the vital point, that I'm not the worst excuse for a human being on the planet.'

To think that wreckage of an existence is what he clings to is a pathetic and harrowing thought. On that sobering note, our cell door is abruptly opened. A huge man stomps into the cell like a seething ogre. I look up, expecting to see something from the *Lord of the Rings* films but the reality is worse. It's Senior Officer Cave from Reception. He has a well-earned reputation for beating people for answers to questions he hasn't even asked yet.

We stand up and he looms in front of us – so close, we have to lean back to stop any physical contact. The size disparity in our chests is incredible. My neck feels like a chicken's opposite the corded tree trunk that's flexing in my eye line. He doesn't say anything at first, just puts a huge hand between us and flicks me towards the door. I lurch violently at the officer there, so inconsequential it's as if I'm made of bamboo. The man there stops me banging my face against the door frame.

'Don't say anything, Ben. They know nothing.'

I hear a bump and a groan that can only be Jake but don't turn round.

'Laters,' he gasps.

I stride from the room without looking back. Something inside me crumbles as I think it, but I know it is the right thing for me to do.

'Not if I see you first,' I whisper under my breath.

There are four officers in a circle outside. I stop and raise my hands as though I'm in an old Wild West movie.

'I'll walk!' I shout.

One of them gives me a pitying look.

'Get out of here and go with Officer Duke. Your things will be brought to you later.'

Confused, I follow the officer out of the wing gates.

As he waits to lock them behind us, I ask him the obvious question. 'Aren't I being taken to the block?'

'Why? Have you done something wrong?'

He isn't interested in my answer. They have their views.

'We saw some lads go to a cell on the CCTV and get hotwatered. There are only two people in that cell. One of them drags the scalded victim to the shower. You wouldn't need a degree in criminology to work out that little conundrum, now, would you?'

'No, I guess not.'

So Jake was correct. I, at least, will get away with it. I feel a small flowering of remorse about the fact I was going to cut him off but smother it with harsh memories before it can blossom.

'Where am I going, then?'

'E1.'

'The remand wing?'

'Yes, it's the only other double in the jail with a free bed and another YO in it.'

Suddenly, I feel incredibly exposed. I've only ever shared a cell with Jake. He has always been there. All too soon, I'm truly on my own. I welcome back my old friend: fear. My mind whirrs at a frantic pace. I also have the worry that the man whose face we took off this morning is likely to have friends. They'll want revenge. My shower manoeuvre will be forgotten in the scheme of things. The prison will want to defuse the situation so they'll rapidly transfer me. That's desirable. Jake will have to rot in solitary while the investigation drags on. It's possible we'll end up at the same jail eventually; however, it's when I'm released that I'm hoping to detach myself from Jake's never-ending swan dive to ruin.

E1 is still locked down because of the disturbance, so the wing is empty. Officer Duke takes me halfway down and opens the door. I walk in and he shuts it behind me. Just like that. No advice proffered. I didn't think to look at the name card on the panel on the way in so it's a mystery who I'm about to be spending some considerable time with.

The bottom bunk is unmade. The messy covers conceal whoever is lying on the top. I clear my throat. Nothing. I edge along towards the window and look out, and then quickly look for a head. With relief I see the bed is empty. He must be at work. I breathe again.

I decide just to sit down and wait. The cell is essentially tidy, which is a good sign. His breakfast bowl and cutlery have been cleaned too, which is a rarity. There is also a small home-made ashtray with a few butts in it. This is also a positive as many chuck them on the floor. I touch nothing. On the surface he could be normal. That means nothing. Jake told me he once shared with a Welsh lad who had OCD. For a whole week, he would shout in his face if he touched anything and would watch Jake as he moved around the cell, to make sure he didn't touch any of his things. Jake beat the shit out of him in the end and got sent to the block. He said it was worth it just to escape the continuous supervision.

There is some paperwork, which I steal a quick peek at to see if I can see a name. I'm careful; if he came back and found me looking through his legal documents he would be most displeased. It's all in a foreign language so I put it back unread. I've never thought about this side of prison life, this horrible feeling of being exposed. If the man who comes back is a psycho, there's not much I can do about it. If he is bigger and stronger than me that makes my situation worse. Nearly 80 per cent of all inmates have mental illness. They are not good odds. We will be locked in together, regardless.

On Saturday night, the door will be shut at 4.30 p.m. and not opened for fifteen hours. That's a long time in anyone's book with someone you've never met before. To sleep, when you are most vulnerable, in the same room as a person you know nothing about except the fact they are in prison, is not easily done. No wonder everyone struggles to sleep, despite having nothing else to do. They are too scared to close their eyes.

I never considered that this is what most people must go through when they first arrive in jail. The only positive is that he must be under twenty-one as it's illegal otherwise. So, if he's a violent rapist of sleeping men, at least he'll be a young one. He may not speak English, have bad feet, snore, or have AIDS. A friend I made in Glen Parva told me he came back from work early to make a legal call one day and found his pad-mate using his toothbrush. They'd been sharing a cell for six months. Apparently, he didn't need a toothbrush afterwards.

The noise of the workers returning focuses my attention and I force myself to inhale and exhale, deep and even. In through my nose, out through my mouth. If there is to be trouble, it will be now.

I don't know whether to sit or stand, be friendly or cool, as until he walks through the door he could literally be anyone.

The door opens and a clearly East European man walks in and eyes me suspiciously. He puts a folder next to me on the table. Casually, his eyes scan the room for his things. He steps back and assesses me.

'New roommate?' he asks, with only a slight accent and no emotion.

'Yes, I got moved here an hour ago.'

He picks up his lighter and tobacco. He's similar in size to me, perhaps slightly heavier, with a thick head of black hair.

'OK, no problem. Do not attempt to fuck me while I am asleep and we will probably get on OK.'

I almost hug him when he says that. 'My name's Ben.'

'Leonid. Like Leonidas, from the film.'

The film *300*, one of my favourites. 'Where are you from?'

'Peterborough.' He smiles. 'Ukraine originally, but I came here to work for my uncle. I take it you are a filthy English peeg.'

I smile.

'Peterborough?' he adds.

'Correct, on both counts.'

My new cellmate is an irregularity in jail. He is normal. Fairly normal, and that's close enough.

'Where are your things?' he asks.

'Still in my cell. They said they'll bring them later.'

He smiles at that too.

'Here, I have spare. You smoke?'

'Sure,' I say. I rarely do now, but it's about building bridges.

We chat all afternoon as we're banged up anyway. I never get my things back, but it's not much of a loss. Leonid is a funny guy. Dry jokes that appeal to my intelligence. He came here a year ago when he was eighteen to work in his uncle's garage. The way he says 'uncle' makes me think he's more family friend than relative. There's something else there, lost in translation. It's his third time inside, which I thought would be bad news for an immigrant like him. Strike three can mean deportation. Strike four would practically guarantee it. I didn't think the Ukraine was in the EU either, but when I say that he laughs and tells me only the British have one passport.

30

They come and collect me at nine-thirty in the morning and take me to the Separation and Care Unit. I'm not nervous, especially seeing as they haven't charged me with anything. The more I think about it, the more I realise Jake will be right. From an external point of view, it's perfectly believable that we were having a cup of tea and were attacked. When you enter another man's cell you are entering his home and similar rules apply. The legal angle around self-defence and use of force is such that Jake will need to argue it was reasonable in the circumstances. That it was necessary and proportionate. If someone comes in your house with a knife you pretty much have carte blanche to do what you like as long as you follow those guidelines. Jake feared for his life, the man was armed, and there were multiple assailants. What will help Jake escape any punishment is that his act of violence was a knee-jerk reaction to the circumstances and was also a single event.

That's what usually gets idiots sent to places like this. Despite what politicians would have you believe, this country is a dangerous place. It is easy to find yourself in a fight and it is acceptable to hit someone in self-defence. Once their foe is vanquished on the floor though, violent people can't resist playing head football. That is not acceptable. None of that applies to Jake in this case. Even if it was a premeditated manoeuvre, which they don't know, what other options did Jake have?

The Sep & Care Unit is where they take those who have been punished with solitary confinement. The mad and the bad. I don't think either get a TV here. No canteen, thirty minutes' exercise, and one phone call a day. Slow time. This is also where they do all the adjudications. It's not unusual for prisoners to get angry when they are told they've lost money or association time. This way it's a short walk for them to be thrown in the cooler to calm down. There is a terrible odour in the unit when we arrive. I'm distracted by it and ask the escorting officer as he puts me in the holding cell, 'What's that smell?'

'Dirty protest,' he says. 'The governor will see you shortly.' He quickly leaves. I don't blame him.

As I turn round, I see there is one other bloke in there. A black bloke. A really big, familiar black bloke. Unbelievably, it's thumb guy. I raise my arm to bang on the plastic window to attract help and prepare to scream the place down. I feel like a chimpanzee put in with a gorilla. He is wary and sees me tense.

'Chill, man. I don't want no more trouble.'

'OK.' I still stay as far away from him as possible. We sit in silence, both holding our noses. Eventually we laugh at the same time.

'Jesus,' I say. 'I don't get it.'

'Throwing your own shit at the officers? No, it's not the way I'd go. I couldn't take the stench.'

'You would have to be pretty fucking fuming.' Or desperate, I think.

A dirty protest is the end of the line. I should think many an officer has been spat on. Quite a few will have opened a cell door and had a cup of piss thrown over them, or even spunk flicked in their face, I should think, on the odd occasion. You use what you've got to hand to make a statement. I've been playing pool and had a TV land on the table from a floor above while I was pondering my shot. A few inches to the side and it would have killed me, but you can't think like that. Once you come to the block you don't have a TV, cutlery, lighter, toilet seat or anything else to lash out with. After you've pulled the sink off the wall and they've moved you into an anti-vandal cell, the only thing you have left to throw at the staff is human waste. If you have ever wondered why our toilets have water in them, do your business on a newspaper and you'll understand. The stink is horrendous.

The other guy clears his throat. 'What you did, man. That was brave.'

'I didn't really think.'

'We all froze.' He flinches as he remembers. 'I hope you saved his face.'

'Strange, isn't it? After the heat of the battle, us two chatting. Typical of this place to put us in here together. You couldn't make it up, could you? Odd though, how, if Jake hadn't done that, we would've got cut up and broken.'

'If you steal from old people's houses there's a heavy price to pay.'

'I had nothing to do with that. I even tried to talk him out of it.'

'Guilty by association.' We grin and nod.

'I don't know why they bring us here. No one's gonna say shit. It's the law of the jungle, and sometimes Tarzan gets got. Hell, man, we were just out to say "Hi", who knows what happened?'

I appreciate the gesture. He's let me know that the powers that be will never know what happened. The door opens and the officer beckons for the man to come out. He stops in front of me.

'Look. Thank you. I want to say it. You won't get no medal, but that was a courageous thing to do. I just want to go home, man. I've got a baby due in two weeks and I don't even have a trial date.' A cloud passes over his face. 'I want to go home.'

The officer locks me back in the holding cell, and I sit and wait.

I've no idea how long I've been waiting. It has been quite a while and I'm bored. I bang on the glass and shout for some water. An officer walks past, cups his ear and squints. Then gives me the finger and walks off chuckling to himself. Bastard. There are some leaflets in the room so I pick up the nearest one, which is all about drugs. I look at the cost of 'brown'. Jake and Lily's little peccadillo.

> The most common effects of heroin abuse are addiction, collapsed veins, pericarditis, infection of the heart valves, liver disease, lung disease, pneumonia, cellulitis, abscesses at injection sites, seizures, heart attacks, accidental overdose, suicide, and death.

Wow! That is some invite list to any party.

> The presence of certain mental illnesses such as ADHD, depression and bipolar disorder dramatically increases the chance of someone becoming an addict.
> Protective factors include self-control, academic achievement and strong parental support.

I think of Jake joking, 'Abscess, make the fart last longer.' The poor boy, he never stood a chance. He has all the nasty, and none of the necessary. I feel so angry and helpless. Who the hell is running this country? I've never seen any of this material or anything like it.

When we're old enough to understand, we should have this shit stuffed down our damn throats every day at school until we bloody choke on it. Whenever any child thinks of doing any kind of recreational drug, a picture of a festering sore-covered skeleton, weeping in agony, should spring to their minds. Not some stunning laughing model rubbing her stinging nose before sashaying onto a brightly lit yacht, brimming with beautiful people, for the night of her life.

The officer comes back and opens the door, I'm hoping with my water.

'In you go now.' He points to the governor's office. 'Be polite at all times. Do not get out of your seat or you will be smashed back into it. Only talk when spoken to.' The officer is so close to me as he tells me this I can smell chocolate on his breath. He even has a small bit of what looks like Smarties shell between his two front teeth. I walk in and sit down.

A big, fat, tired-looking man sits opposite me. There's a long table between us and we are surrounded by officers. Someone is taking notes. Court martial springs to mind for some reason, even though I haven't been to one of those either. He tells me I'm not being charged with anything and that I'm only there so they can ascertain what happened. This is a prison. He doesn't look stupid. He knows exactly what happened, and he also understands it's unlikely anyone will tell him anything. My part in it will confuse them as it clouds the water. Why would I help the people who came to assault us?

'Can you tell us what happened, Mr Jones?'

'Could I have a drink, please, first? My throat's so dry I can hardly talk.'

To my great joy, he instructs the reluctant officer from earlier to get me some water.

He returns and grimly stares at me as I raise it to my lips in victory. I realise, just in time, he'll have spat in it. Our eyes lock as the cup is poised at my mouth, like two chess players in an evenly matched game. I put the cup down untouched and contemplate asking the governor if he would like to have some. Instead, I begin.

'It's all a blur. More or less, Jake and me were making a cup of tea. Some friends of ours came in and the water got knocked over. Some went on someone's face so I dragged him to the shower.'

The man's eyes bore into my soul. I see his jaw tighten.

'That's it?'

'Yup.'

I watch him force himself to swallow and look down. He scribbles on his pad. 'Get him out of here.'

'I have a question. Can I have my things back?'

'What things?'

'My stuff in the cell.'

'That cell is a crime scene. You'll get it back after the investigation.'

'A crime scene you left us sitting in for two hours after the event.'

He continues writing for a full minute and then looks up. He gives me a wry smile. 'Quite.'

* * *

By the time I get back to the wing, lunch is over, and the officers are chasing the last few reprobates around the wing for lock up.

'Behind your door, Jones,' is my greeting at the wing gates.

'Where's my lunch?'

'You missed it.'

'Bullshit. I was at the block. I'm not missing dinner.'

'It was only sarnies.'

'Get me some.'

'I'll bring you one after we've done roll count.'

'I'm not falling for that shit. I'm not banging up without my food.'

We are at my door by that point and I can see the man wondering which would be quicker: to throw me in my cell forcibly, or get me something. He swears under his breath, walks to the servery area and gives me a squashed-looking sandwich in cellophane and a bag of Worcester sauce crisps.

'You haven't got any cheese and onion, have you?'

I think he's going to headbutt me for a second. Then he sees I'm just messing with him. He shakes his head as he locks me in.

'How did it go?' Leo asks.

'No idea, but it looks like I'm off the hook.'

My bunk has a yoghurt, cheese roll, and bag of cheese and onion crisps on it. Leo sees me looking at it.

'I got your dinner for you when you hadn't come back. There's a letter there for you too.'

* * *

Five minutes later, after eating both meals, I'm experiencing a full sensation for the first time in my prison career. I give the yoghurt to Leo.

'The officer came and told me we are being transferred tomorrow to somewhere called Littlehey. Where is that?' he asks.

'It's about twenty miles away, near Huntingdon, I think.'

'I've only been to Parva. Is Littlehey nice?'

'I'm confident nice wouldn't be used to describe anywhere where you get locked up against your own free will. It's a vast improvement on Parva though.'

'OK, we go together. It is better that way.'

I agree. I hardly know him and yet I feel we could be friends, a different type of friendship than the kind Jake can provide.

Leo didn't shout out in his sleep like a crazy person last night either.

'Why are you in, Leo? You don't seem a bad person.'

'First time for assault, second for twoc, this time for shoplifting. The first and third time I was drunk.'

'What's twoc?'

'T-W-O-C. Taking without owner's consent. I had just delivered something for my uncle in a car he lent me. The police pull me over. Turns out the owner hadn't lent it to my uncle. I couldn't say where I got it so they sent me to jail.'

'A bit unlucky, that.'

'Kind of. Uncle Radic was very sorry afterwards. He more than made it up to me.'

'What do you do for him?'

'Some deliveries at night, but mostly I work in his garage. I love cars. He has one guy who knows what he is doing, the rest are useless, and I help him. He teaches me. I hope to one day have my own garage. Uncle Radic says he will send me to school to take qualifications if I can stop taking holiday here.'

'Cool. I'd love to do something like that. My dad and I used to work on cars all the time.'

'You seem like a nice guy, Ben. You should come and see me when you get out. He is always looking for delivery drivers who don't ask what is being delivered. He also needs another mechanic.'

There is the first glint of sunlight in the never-ending night that my life has become. A job, qualifications, or even a future. Surely it can't be that easy? Is this how it works for normal people?

'Are you sure he won't mind?'

'No. It's called Polish Porsche, out at Fengate. Come by. Careful of the secretary.'

'Why is that?'

'You'll see.'

'Is the money good?'

'It depends on how much risk you want to take.'

I was so electrified by the possibility of an actual existence worth living that the last unusual answer doesn't even register.

I lie back on my bed and open the letter. It's from my mum. Her handwriting is usually more pissed than this, but I still recognise it.

Dear Benny,

I'm so sorry to hear you've been sent back to that terrible place. After the shock wore off, I came to the conclusion it's as much my fault as it is yours. I haven't been there for you. So I've come off the drink. I've got a sweat on worse than Jabba the Hutt's masseuse, but I'll be ready for you when you get out. And so will your home.

Love from your crazy old ma.

I am simply overwhelmed. Apart from the weird metaphor, of course, how long have I been waiting to hear those very words? Is my luck about to change?

PART VI

A REAL JOB

31

6TH MARCH 2012

HMP Littlehey seemed more on the ball and genuinely interested in what I'd do when I got out. They put me on introductory English and Maths courses, both of which I passed, and I even had time to do an IT course. I really could have done with being there longer. How messed up is that? Steal things until you get caught and then go to jail and get an education, healthcare, exercise, and fifty quid in your back pocket when you leave. No wonder for some it's not a punishment, but their equivalent of a free health spa and boot camp.

I arrive back home and find two threatening men in ill-fitting suits pressing the buzzer for our block of flats. There's an expensive 4x4 parked on the double yellows. When I let myself in, they try to follow me into the building and I block their path with my body. I'm bigger now too, after ten weeks of weights and exercise. Leo got a job in the kitchen and we must have eaten about a thousand eggs each in that time.

'I don't think so, gentlemen.'

There are two of them, but they back off. There are sharp sides to me that will be clear to anyone who comes into my vicinity. In jail you are ready and wary all the time, poised to fight, as you are living in an atmosphere of repressed anger that can flare at the slightest misperception. You obviously don't leave that in your cell. It will take a few weeks until real life softens those borders and you become a normal person again. That is why some find themselves going back to jail so soon after getting out; the world is not ready for you and vice versa.

'Who are you after?'

'Angela Jones.'

'She's in prison, mate. Out in June.'

I chuckle to myself as I watch them leave.

There's more sniggering behind our door when I get there. It opens to the giggling Portuguese lady who moved into Jonty's flat. She reaches up to my face and squeezes my cheek. 'Jeitoso.' Still laughing, she totters down the steps. My mother is behind her, wiping tears down her face.

'Fallen off the wagon?'

'Not at all. Ana doesn't drink, which is why she's fantastic company for me. Jeitoso means handsome. She also got me a job at her cleaning firm, all cash in hand, like.'

She walks over, looks all over my face and then gives me a hug. My breath is taken away by the strength of it.

'Welcome home, Benny.'

'It's nice to be home. Whose is that?'

There's a very new-looking bike parked in our hallway.

'It's yours, son.'

'What?'

The bike is wonderful. So shiny and pristine. I can't help running my hand along the knobbly unused black tyres.

'Mum, I know you haven't got much money, so you can take it back if you want.'

'Do you know how much I save by not drinking all the time? A lot. Each week while you were away I put some of the money I saved into a pot until I could buy that. It turned up yesterday and I even had enough for a new lock. You should know better than most about all the stealing feckers around here. It's for your nineteenth birthday, a few days late. I didn't think they would let you have it inside. Admittedly, I now eat a lot more and have had to buy a new set of clothes due to my burgeoning waistline so we're still skint.'

I look at her properly and see she's put on a fair bit of weight but it's all over. She looks so much better for it. She has a simple dress on, which is clearly new. It makes my brain search for the last time I saw her in something like that and it comes up wanting. She even has lipstick on, and I also see my mother is still an attractive woman.

'Good for you, Mum. Good for us, in fact.'

'Yes, I've been neglecting you for too long.'

'So you haven't had any booze since I went away? Cold turkey?'

'Yep. My God, it was hard. I had the shakes, sweats, and shits for days on end at the start. I need a new mattress as mine is rotting... I'll spare you the gory details.

'The one good thing is I've finally cleared all of Patrick's debts. He was buying stuff on the never-never, the big shit. The most expensive thing was a sapphire heart necklace I certainly never got.'

I weigh up whether I should mention the fact my dad has gone to 'Patrick' or 'big shit' in just five years, and if I should comment on the fact I've just lied to the debt collectors for her. It also dawns on me who used to wear a sapphire necklace. Sapphires are blue. So was Jonty's mother's necklace. She wore it all the time as well, even after my dad died. I try to smile but my mum gives me a knowing look. I don't know why, but I avert my gaze. It's too late. My mum links arms with me and pulls me into the lounge.

'Sit down and relax. I knew about your father and his roving eye, everyone did. Either Sally was the unluckiest person on the planet for having such a crumbling flat, or your father was going round to screw something other than the loose light-fittings. I don't really know why I put up with it. Some calamity occurred at her house every week and he'd be round that day to fix it. I once needed a hook putting on the bedroom door and it took him six months to do it.'

She crouches between my legs and holds my hands.

'I know he was your hero, but he couldn't control himself when it came to women. He loved you very much though and me too, I think, in his own way. He seemed to think providing for us and having sex with me once in a while made it acceptable to mess about with other women.'

She gives my hands a hard squeeze, one that reassures me and gives me the strength to hope it will turn out well.

'That's all in the past now. I was in a bad place. Something terrible happened, a long time ago, and I've been hiding in the bottle from it ever since. I've a few more home truths to tell you about Patrick, although we can talk about it another time. In a way he saved me as well, but I'll find a time for that story. Now, I've bought my body weight in bacon and white bread and I've got some of that Tropicana fruit juice you loved so much when you had it once. Go watch TV and I'll be back before you know it.'

I turn on the TV but can't hear anything. I remember my mum trying to tell me about my dad in the past and me being too blinded by my worship of him to see it. There can't be any mistaking the necklace. I think of all the upset women at the funeral. I even think of Michelle, drunk and wild, looking for fun, and know my father would have provided some. An enormous cascade of information falls through my brain as I consider my mum over all those years, sitting at home, waiting for him to return. We all have faults though. I'm testament to that. When you go to a place like prison you see a whole stadium of people who have made mistakes and at least he never got sent to jail. He was a good dad to me. I shall leave it at that, as today is a day to look forward. A day of optimism.

When she comes back, it is I who stand up and give her a bone-crushing cuddle. We are both slightly embarrassed. We haven't been this demonstrative with each other for years. It's leaving me with a warm glow inside. In prison, you turn yourself down and lose all emotion. That's the best way to come out with most of what you went in with. These few minutes are swiftly defrosting the frozen mass that my heart has become.

'Your friend called round, the naughty one. He left his number over there. Mind you, I doubt he'll remember being here as he looked like a zombie.'

I know she's changing the subject to hide the warmth she is feeling too.

'I won't be needing that. I might be able to get a job, working with cars. I won't want any distractions.'

'You've grown into such a handsome boy, just like your father.'

We smile at each other, a fresh start.

32

I'm so full I can barely lift my leg high enough to get it over the crossbar. It's uncomfortable to cycle. Eventually, I just push the bike in the hope that my distended stomach will deflate with the exercise. Fengate and Leo's workplace are over the other side of town so it will take ages to walk there, but I don't mind. The best thing about prison is the few days after you leave. The freedom you wanted back is suddenly yours. It is a remarkable feeling. To think I can go where I like, buy what I want, or just sit on a bench and do nothing, makes me grin like a fool.

I walk down Lincoln Road and I'm still smiling, even though it's clogged with cars, rubbish and people.

The smile falls from my face like someone dropping a skip from a great height. Across the road from me, in her hooking gear, is Lily. At least, I'm almost sure it's her. Even from fifty metres away I can see how thin she is, but it's her face that doesn't look right. I'm sure I wasn't inside for ten years. I stand there in shock in the middle of the path, getting a tut from a passing mother followed by something in what sounds like Leo's language and no doubt will not be complimentary. I contemplate going over as it would be good to see

Lily, but she's a part of my life I want to look back on, not re-immerse myself in.

It's too late though as she sees me and wobbles over on impossibly high heels. For the second time that day someone hugs me like I'm about to blow away. I know it's a well-used saying to describe someone thin being a bag of bones, but that is exactly what she feels like. As I squeeze her back I'm sure I can feel her skeleton moving around. I wonder how someone can get so emaciated and still be alive. I can't help holding her in the same way you would an ancient Egyptian relic, gently lifting it out of a dusty tomb. As though too much pressure will cause her to disintegrate in my hands and turn to ash.

She pulls back from me and smiles.

'Ben, you're a sight for sore eyes.' Then I see why she looks so different. The top set of teeth are simply missing. This has caused her face to collapse in on itself and because of that she looks a different person. All I can think is what a horrific waste. If she has seen me look at her mouth in shock it doesn't bother her. As I drag my eyes up to meet hers, I can also make out the yellow of recent bruises underneath the heavy make-up.

'It's good to see you, Lily. You look fine.'

'You too, Ben. I heard you were inside again. Jake told me.'

As she leaves that fact hanging in the air, a loud whistle comes from across the road. I can see that two swarthy gentlemen, arms crossed, have come out of an empty shop doorway. Lily looks back and shrugs.

'I've got to go.' She grins again, that dreadful smile. 'My number is the same. Ring me, we can have some fun.' She teeters away, leaving me incredulous. I remember the warmth of my first time with Lily, and am sure I would rather dip my John Thomas in some hot tar than venture there again. I suspect the result would be much the same.

Full belly or not, I jump on my bike and cycle off as if I'm in the Tour de France.

* * *

I find Polish Porsche at the back of Fengate Trading Estate. I lock my bike a little down the road so I don't feel and look like a schoolboy arriving, then walk into the reception area with a confidence I don't feel. It seems to be empty in there so I walk up to the counter. I'm about to cough loudly when someone's head pops up in front of me. I don't know if there is a saying 'stunned mute by beauty', but if there isn't, there should be. Maybe it's the fact that I've just got out of prison, or that I have just been cuddled by a wraith, but the only part of me that isn't frozen in time are my eyes. They impossibly seem to get wider and wider.

'Good day. What your problem?'

She is about my age, tall, with a red shirt that shows no skin but is so tight it could be a second one. I'm not sure if I'm waiting for a tearing sound and heaven to open up in front of me or I'm actually going to implode with lust. It feels as though my IQ has slipped to somewhere between Rocky Balboa and Forrest Gump.

'You OK?' She gives me a cautious look. She releases me from her stare, opens the door behind her, and shouts something out the back. When she turns around, I notice she has faint acne scars on both cheeks. Focusing on these is the only way I can talk, but I finally manage to say something.

'You should really ask how may I help you, instead of presuming I have a problem.'

She gives me a hard look. She has little make-up on except for an abundance of eye shadow. This makes her green eyes look sultry and compels me to move my head towards her.

'Oh, really? Are you teacher?'

'Umm, no. It's just you're assuming I have a problem, which is a negative way to look at things, when I may just have a query.'

'OK, genius. What is query?' She struggles with the 'r' in query and it slides into a 'w'. I didn't think about what I was going to say when I arrived here, which now seems ridiculous. I didn't expect to be saying any of this though.

'A friend told me you might have a job?'

'I see. You are wrong, then, and I am right.'

'In what way?'

'You do have problem. You don't have job.'

With that, she flicks her brown ponytail and walks past me.

'Wait here, problem boy. I ask.'

I follow her bum as she walks past the coffee machine and out of a side door and conclude she must have been born in those jeans as it would have been impossible to get in them otherwise. Her accent is strong and her voice deep. However, she could have sounded like something in *Poltergeist*, where a possessed girl talks and a five-thousand-year-old demon's voice comes out, and I would still sell my mother for parts for five minutes in a hot tub with this girl.

She comes back and says, 'He will be few minutes. I have question for you.'

'OK, fire away.'

'Did you check me out when I left the room?'

She gives me a huge innocent grin as I fluster around in my vacant brain.

'I was actually wondering if I wanted a coffee.' The relief that I've found an excuse is palpable. I can see where this is going. 'What makes you ask?'

'There is mirror in that corner. I can see your face as I walk out. You must really like coffee.' Sure enough, there is a mirror pointing to the doorway.

I can't help laughing. An open laugh, the kind you stifle in jail. Here, though, I don't care. She laughs with me, something shifts between us and all of a sudden we are having fun.

'You want me to go away, leave you and machine alone. I put the music up loud, just in case is bad machine and you want teach a lesson.'

'Very funny. You seem to know a lot about having sex with machines.'

This time it is her who laughs loud, low and dirty. I'm grinning as if I've dropped a penny and bent over to pick it up and found a pound. A cleared throat next to me drags our gazes away from each other and I look into the visage of an unamused gentleman. He has a green and yellow tracksuit on, which is worthy of piss-taking, but his aura means I definitely won't be doing any.

'Having a nice time?'

I'm not sure what to say to that so I stay silent.

'I am Radic.' He says it with a strong rolling 'R' and a kicking 'itch' at the end.

'Hello, Mr Radic.' I copy the technique.

'Ugh. That rolls off your tongue like two trains colliding. I see you have met my daughter, Karolina.'

I feel heat and worry flood my body as though I have stepped into the boiling sunshine with a fur coat on.

'Dad. Give it a break. Someone has to have sex with me.'

'Arggghhh!' Radic shouts. 'My ears. Take your filthy mouth with its terrible lies and go to chapel. You, come with me.'

It's safe to say I like Radic from the start.

* * *

We walk through to his office via a quiet garage and he gestures for me to take a seat. The man then sits and stares at me with piercing eyes. I return his gaze, even though it's uncomfortable.

'So you met Leo?'

'Yes, we stayed in the same guest house together.'

He smiles and lights a cigar. 'You know anything about cars?'

'I know a lot. My dad taught me, he said I understand them.'

'I don't know what you mean.'

'If a car has a problem, you just need to fix whatever's causing it. You start where it's most likely to be the problem and then work backwards at other angles until you find what's wrong. Usually, it's what you think straight away. Squeaky brakes, new brake pads. Noisy car, blown exhaust. Won't start, dead battery.'

'New cars are a lot more complicated than that.'

'I agree, but you don't seem to have too many of them.'

This time he's the one who chuckles. Of course, it sounds the same as Karolina's. 'You want a drink?'

'What have you got?'

'Water, vodka, beer?'

'Water is fine, unless I have something to celebrate.'

He gets out of his seat and comes to stand behind me. He puts both hands on my shoulders and squeezes. 'I like your confidence. You remind me very much of me. I am number one here. We can be good friends.'

I flinch as I recall my first ever day in prison. He releases me, sits down, and laughs like a clown I remember once seeing at the seaside. Part of me feels like leaving, but I want this job.

It takes a long time for him to calm down. Once he does, he looks at me with watery eyes.

'Leo told me the story, about the guy coming to your cell, wanting to make you his bitch. Very, very funny. Also amusing you went to his cell with your weapon and ended up slinking back with your tail between your legs. I enjoyed the story, very much. Although, better that, than his tail between your legs.'

I have to watch more giggling.

'Here, have a beer. I will give you a chance. You earn my trust, maybe you help out in our other businesses for better money. Immediately, I need another mechanic. Leo likes your women and your strange lager too much; however, you can learn much from Igor.'

Radic opens two bottles of foreign beer. He clinks mine with his.

'When did you get out?'

'Today.'

'Excellent. Came straight here. Keen is good. You beat Leo in today so that tells you something. Family, eh? A blessing and a curse. You have family?'

'Just a mother.'

'Ah, I see. More than some though, eh?'

I finish the beer quickly. It tastes good but my stomach gurgles.

'Another one?'

'No, I'm not much of a drinker.'

'That is good. Me neither. For business, some men need to watch you drink. I'm not sure why that is. Today, have one drink, possibly two and remember. Especially important for you. Feel your freedom, enjoy it. Soon enough you will forget and moan like the rest of us, not even aware you are alive.'

'I'll enjoy it now I have a job.'

'You have a problem, you talk to me, or Karolina, immediately. This is serious business. Many people get hurt or worse. Lot of money at stake. You can get out at any point, remember that. To start, you are just mechanic. I have good feeling about you, you remind me of my son.'

I wonder where his son is, but feel now is not the time to ask. It seems people keep losing them.

'No chemicals around here at all. Beware chemicals. If God wanted you to do that sort of thing, syringes would grow in the garden.'

'What about weed? Does that not grow in the garden?'

'Ah, silly enough to go to prison twice but not so stupid after all.'

There are explicit warnings there. No drugs on the premises and the fact he has done his research on me. There is also information too, which I appreciate. The rules you don't know about are the easiest ones to break. He is up to no good, but it is down to me if I want to get involved.

'Marijuana is too strong now. All this hydro is driving people crazy. Why live your life in a cloud? Experience every moment because like this—' he clicks his fingers '—it is over.'

It's nice to talk to someone with some sense for a change.

'Come tomorrow, 8 a.m. I'll make sure Leo is here. He can introduce you to everyone. Date my daughter if you like but be aware she is special to me. She will give you forms for payroll and things. This is legitimate business. See you tomorrow.'

He crunches my hand with a hairy-paw handshake and I wander out to Karolina. I have a job.

'Here is the form. Fill here, here.'

Her hand touches mine. Unnecessarily, I think.

As I walk out into the sunshine, I smile. Why couldn't she have been a twenty-stone shot-putter?

33

7TH MARCH 2012

Leo is waiting for me outside and smoking a cigarette when I arrive. He admires my bike.

'When I was inside I used to dream of riding a bike. Weird, uh? We should go for a cycle, some woods or mountain somewhere.'

'Cool, that would be brilliant.' I realise I've never done that sort of thing and haven't even had someone suggest it. He'll struggle to find any mountains round here, seeing as we live on the edge of the fens, but just somewhere quiet would be perfect. We could pack some food too. Then the thought that Karolina could come along as well slides into my brain. As I unsuccessfully try to stop my mind playing through the picnic and us kissing on the blanket, Karolina and me, that is, she turns up in a little sports car. She's wearing a short denim jacket, a flowery mini-dress and cowboy boots. Her long hair is loose, and she swishes it over her shoulder as she unlocks the door to the reception. I force myself to breathe. Then I unclench my teeth.

We go in, she slips off her jacket, goes behind the counter and turns round. Arching her back, she reaches up to the high key box on the wall and takes one off its hook. How my penis hasn't burst through my jeans, splintered through the desk and impaled her against the back wall, I have no idea.

She raises an eyebrow at me and then winks. The best I can manage is a Wallace and Gromit type grin and I shuffle off after Leo on what feels like someone else's legs.

We're the first to arrive and Leo makes us a coffee from a dirty-looking kettle in the corner. He regards me with a half-smile.

'The boss's daughter. You are a brave boy.'

'I know. Talk about dangerous.'

'It would be like putting your dick in a pretty mousetrap.'

'Quite. So I won't be going there, don't you worry about that.'

'It's weird though. I've been in this place a while and there are many men who work here and come through. I've never seen her like that before. In fact, I've never even known her have a boyfriend.' He gives me an odd look.

'Here's Igor now. He should douse your fiery passions.' Leo smiles and I see why.

The shutter for the workshop hits the top of its frame with a clatter. A man with a massive head walks in with a strange flat-footed gait. I can only assume Igor is some kind of joke name as he looks like something out of a Dracula film. He comes over and stands in front of me and holds out his hand.

'Igor, this is Ben. Ben, Igor.'

'Tak,' is all he says, and he walks off in the direction of the kettle.

'Tak?'

'Yes. It means yes in Ukrainian. He doesn't say much else until he gets close to you.'

I'm not so sure I want to get very near to him, as he has left a strong smell of body odour in the air.

* * *

Leo was right, Igor doesn't say anything else to me. I'm not sure if he is simple or something but, boy, does he know how a car works.

We only stop at midday for some sandwiches that Karolina brings out. Igor eats nothing, just chain-smokes cigarettes and perspires. He watches the interaction between me and Karolina, and after she has gone he laughs like a drain.

It seems the way things works is either Leo or Karolina speak to the customer and then relay the information to Igor. Then Igor sets about fixing what is wrong. Most of the cars we work on are old BMWs and the like, with European plates. He is organised and professional though. He has a big folder and each car has its own page where notes go.

I have learnt so much today it's unbelievable. My mind is like an insatiable sponge, sucking in everything around it. Sometimes I impress him with the stuff I know and he says, 'Tak,' in an affectionate way. Already I can feel us working as a team. Before I know it he stands up, looks at his watch, and says, 'Tak.' He walks to the corner and washes his hands.

I look at the watch my mother gave me and curse. I will leave that at home tomorrow. I can see through the grease that it's 5 p.m.

Joining Igor at the sink, I wash my hands as well. Igor dries his off and waits for me to look at him.

'You were excellent today. You have shown a lot of potential. We work well together. See you tomorrow.'

He walks out, leaving me spluttering in surprise.

* * *

Leo is in the reception area. He seems to have done very little today.

'What are you laughing at?'

'Igor's English.'

'I bet you thought he was a mute. He must like you if he talks to you. We're off to the pub for a few drinks if you want to come?'

I look from Leo to Karolina. She seems much keener for me to join them. I begin to suspect he has feelings for her. Another reason for me not to go there.

'I promised my mum I would take fish and chips home with me. You know, to celebrate my first day with a job.'

I will remember Karolina's disappointed face.

'Thank you, Karolina. You've made me really welcome today. You too, Leo. See you all tomorrow!'

I unlock my bike in the cool fading sunshine, and whistle as I cycle home.

34

6TH APRIL 2012

A month later and Radic has asked me to do something for him.

'So what do you want me to do? Just give him the package?'

'Yes.'

'Why me?'

'You have been here a month now. Everyone likes you, including me, which is very important. I need people I can trust to help deliver my goods.'

'Like Leo?'

'Yes, like Leo.'

'OK, but why must I see this man?'

'I want you to understand the type of people we are working with. I have been in Russian Military and all kinds of crazy madness in the Balkans, and I have never met anyone as dangerous as this man, Darren Connor, who comes for his money tonight. People like him surround themselves with death so you must consider if you want to be near a man like him.'

'OK, I understand what you're saying.'

'You won't, until you meet him. There is also a present for you to show our appreciation. We have never had so many happy customers and we are getting very busy. It is possible I can become honest businessman after all.'

I follow him out of the front of the building and he shows me to a smallish Yamaha motorbike on the back of a trailer. I know what it is straight away. An RD350. They're old yet brilliantly made, and even though they are two-stroke, they are insanely fast. I love it and I haven't even sat on it yet.

'For deliveries?'

'For you. Whatever you decide. I'll get it serviced, and there's a few parts I need to have custom made, but it'll be yours soon enough.'

As per usual, I appreciate what Radic is doing. He's giving me all the information and letting me make up my own mind. The money is good for the garage work and is more than I've ever had before. I also don't feel as if I'm working. Turns out Igor has a degree in mechanical engineering from the University of Kiev, but just loves cars. He was school friends with Radic way back and came over after his marriage failed. He lives in a village nearby called Market Deeping, and seemingly has a simple life with twin girls. That's all I got out of him about that – what do I know about kids? We just talked shop and were happy.

He has some involvement in the 'family' business, though, as he and Leo are often involved in private discussions. Leo has also told me what he makes dropping packages off around town and it is double what I earn, for considerably easier work. Leo has a green Renault Clio, which he uses to do his delivering. There are two other couriers too, who drive sleek motorbikes, but I never see them take their helmets off.

It is tempting to get involved as the money would be brilliant, but I have no desire to go back to jail. I am also learning so much and don't want to stop. At some point I know I want to be my own boss so I save everything I can.

* * *

I know which man it is as soon as he arrives. He's with another bloke, but my eye is drawn to the person who is clearly in charge. The way he walks is strong and controlled but lithe, like the raw power of an animal. They go in with Radic for a minute, then just Darren comes out.

'Who has the money?' he asks.

Even though there are two of Radic's heavies and Igor here with me, I feel very much alone and exposed. I raise my hand. He strides over and I pass the money to him. He looks at me, almost in a cruel way, from eye to eye and back again. There's something weirdly familiar about him, like looking at an old friend or an evil shadow of a former self. I can feel all the negative emotions in me responding as though I'm looking in a black mirror. There is something else there. Something powerful and ruthless that I don't possess. And then he's gone. As he steps out of view, it is almost as if the temperature rises again and the birds return.

Radic's men look shifty too and Igor does the sign of the cross and goes to wash his hands. I wander through to Karolina, who is laughing at something Leo is saying.

'OK, guys, I'm off. See you at the barbecue tomorrow.'

'Charming bloke, eh?' says Leo.

'Why the hell does Radic do business with someone like him?'

'He is the connect. Radic also said he would rather work with him than against. Apparently, he has seen first-hand what happens to those who cross Darren Connor.'

I'm not sure what a connect is, but he is clearly an integral part of whatever operation is running behind the scenes here.

I shiver again as I step outside, despite the direct sunlight.

'I hope that helped make up your mind, Benjamin!' Karolina shouts.

Weird how only her and my mother ever called me anything other than Ben, but the answer is yes. The further away from malevolence like his, the better my life will be.

35

'Hop in, mate.'

'OK, cheers.'

I jump into Leo's car, trying not to disturb too many of the McDonald's wrappers and boxes all over the floor. 'For someone who makes a lot of money, you would think you would have a nicer car and take more care of it.'

'Ah, young fool. I don't want a car that stands out in my line of business. I want to blend into my surroundings. Besides, if I get rumbled, I can just get out of this car and run away. It's got no engine number and no registration documents. It doesn't exist and is virtually worthless.'

As if to confirm that, the engine races violently for a minute even though we are stationary and in neutral gear.

'So are you going to give the delivering a go?' he asks.

'No. I don't think so, mate. I just want to focus on the cars. Igor has given me loads of manuals to read, and, to be honest, that killer scared the shit out of me.'

'Man, ignore him. That's just Radic trying to worry you. We

have nothing to do with him, he's just part of the supply chain. It's easy. You and me can be a team. One of us drops the product off at various places in the city and then the other one picks up the money later.'

'Don't you worry about them not paying?'

'No one crosses Uncle Radic. When he first started it was a war zone, but his family is originally from Russia. They don't think twice about killing anyone over there. Here he hides the body, or that Darren does. He didn't used to bother before.'

While he pulls away, I try to match this hard person with the man, Radic, who gave me a break. He's full of humour and joy and loves his daughter very much. Although if I look hard enough, I can see that there's some of him not completely in the present, something lurking in the dark. I think that bit of him is the part that's dangerous. I hope I never get to see it out in the light.

Radic lives in Westwood Park Road, one of the best areas in the city. We have to wait for some electric gates to open. They aren't huge like I guess a footballer's would be, but impressive nonetheless. Leo has been here before and lets us in the side gate.

As we walk around to the back, I can hear a hubbub of chatter and muted laughter. It's only midday, yet the people present all seem to be drinking. Understandably I'm nervous, as I've no idea what happens at a barbecue. I haven't been to one prior to this.

I realise, way too late, as Radic approaches, I should've brought something with me. Luckily, he doesn't seem to care. He shows me to the bar, says, 'I will talk to you later,' and then he is gone. I wander outside and see people picking at a buffet under a canopy. Breakfast this morning was toast, and I'm starving, so I get stuck in, trying not to look like a caveman at his first roast buffalo party.

I find a seat in a deckchair next to Igor, who's eating as though he has an appointment with the electric chair in five minutes, and relax. I spy Karolina, who is with a girl who could be her blonde-haired older sister. They both have the same penchant for tight clothes, but even from the other side of the garden I can see there is an arrogance to the other girl that Karolina doesn't display. It's both sexy and off-putting. Radic is like a showman and the garden his big top, doing the rounds and entertaining.

I find myself talking to all manner of people there. Oddly, some police are pointed out, but no one else seems bothered , them included. I also see two guys who I recognise from prison. We circle each other, consciously staying apart, as if the moment we got together everyone would see us for what we really are.

Karolina comes over halfway through the afternoon while I'm beginning to wonder how long these things go on for.

She puts her arm through mine and gives me a soft little kiss on the cheek that makes the hairs down my back stand up. I see Radic looking at us, but before I can extricate myself someone has grabbed my hand in a cool grip.

'Are you not going to introduce us?'

'Ben, this is Nadia.' Her eyes are glacier blue, accentuated by eye shadow. The lipstick is bright red.

'Hi, Ben. I've heard all about you. I know Karolina and Radic from back home.'

Bizarrely, Nadia is still holding my hand and my other arm is still tightly wrapped around Karolina's. The two girls look at each other, like a pair of angry cats. It is Nadia who strikes first.

'Your boyfriend is drunk and messing about with the snooker table.'

Karolina gives Nadia a look that should have popped those blue eyes, and stamps off to the house.

'I didn't know she had a boyfriend.'

'Who knows what her and Leo call themselves nowadays? I'm single though.'

I don't know why I'm so disappointed, but I am. Karolina and I have been flirting safely from a distance all month. There is a part of me that would not risk going out with Radic's prized possession. However, there is another portion that thought the connection we have would mean eventually we would have to be together, whatever the consequences. Until today, I thought the latter would win out. I also feel Leo has let me down. So much for his jokes about the boss's daughter. Still, neither of them owe me anything and I don't remember being lied to either.

'I'm single too,' I calmly say, although I don't feel anything like it. She shows me her big flashy-white teeth in reply.

We chat for a while. She's been over here since she broke up with a partner, came for a better life. It's weird to think that people would come to Peterborough for such a thing. Although, look at me. I have a job – a career, in fact – and I'm at a swish barbecue talking to a girl who I can best describe as coldly striking.

Radic comes over and shoos her away. 'Go powder your ass.'

She sticks her tongue out at him, comfortable with his comedy. He has a small bloke with him who shakes my hand with a thrust that tells of manual labour. As he sips his drink, I see filth under his nails. I see the same under mine.

'This is John. My first partner. He now runs a garage over at Boongate. A professional one where they have the computers to repair all cars. That's where the money is and it's easy too. You plug the car in, it tells you what part isn't working and you replace it. Free money.'

The pair of them laugh together at some joke denied to me.

'Did you think on your career path, Ben?'

'Yes, I would like to stick with Igor, learn my trade.'

He looks at me in a way he hasn't in the past and I know he is thinking of his son. Andriy has been dead many years now. Found shot in the street aged sixteen. Executed, they think, for some unknown slight committed by his father. Radic's rage was biblical. He killed too many of the wrong people and had to flee to England to start again. Leo told me all this and, apparently, I look like him and even have some of his mannerisms.

'I'm pleased, Ben. John here has said he will take you on two days a week and show you how a real garage works. How does that sound?'

'Brilliant.'

Nadia returns and gives me another beer, winks, and walks off. No doubt fully aware that I would struggle to pull my eyes from the most delicious-looking pair of long tanned legs. I have seen less shiny banisters.

'Be careful of that one,' John says.

'Yes, she is an animal.' Radic pronounces it a-nee-marl and they laugh.

'More like a... now what's the word? Grrr.' John pushes his arms out like he is going to attack Radic.

'A dog.' They look as though they are wetting themselves they are giggling so much. Radic is leaning back with his eyes closed and John is bent double. They are like schoolchildren.

'No, like a monster,' John says. Cue more guffawing.

'An angry kangaroo.' Radic whinnies like a horse.

'Is that a monster? Think now, the alien, with Schwarzenegger.'

I wander off and leave them to it. I'm glad they're having a good time. It must be good to laugh like that in your forties.

I hear John shout out.. 'Ah, yes! That is it. A predator.'

* * *

I stroll towards some French doors and peek in, wondering if I'm supposed to be taking off my shoes. No one else has, so I don't bother. Dodging the hordes of children that cannon around, I go for a wander. There's a wooden door under the stairs. That's so commonplace in rich people's mansions that I've seen on TV that I know where the games room is. Sure enough, I step down and enter a gloomy room with a full-size snooker table in the middle of it. Leo is rolling on the snooker table. Karolina is trying to get him off it while using language that I suspect would curl an aged Ukrainian grandma's hair.

'Help me, Benny. Please. He is like made of stone.'

He seems to pass out when I lift him off. I manage to carry him in my arms, like a fireman carrying a child from a burning house. With getting fit in prison, cycling six miles and back to work every day, and the general heavy labour involved in being a car mechanic, or vehicle technician, as Leo says when he's trying to chat up girls, I am in good shape. I manage the weight with no problems. Karolina opens the front door and leads us to her car.

I leave him slumped in the passenger seat, drooling like a geriatric.

'I bet you've never found him so attractive.'

'Always like this. He wants to be pissed.'

'That's pretty normal for boys his age.'

'When does he become a man? I want more than this. I tell him long time ago but he doesn't change.'

'Look, I'll go back in and tidy the mess up downstairs. Radic will never know.'

'Thank you, Benny. That snooker table is the only thing Dad loves more than me. He would get gun, I think, if he saw some asshole had put a beer bottle on the green bit.' She rests her hand on my arm, her eyes search mine, and she is going to say something. Leo chokes in his seat and distracts her.

He isn't sick, but she gives him a filthy look then turns back to me. 'I speak to you on Monday. I better get him home and in bed. If he pukes in my car, I will kill him myself.'

* * *

I return to the house and go downstairs. There's a hint of a ring on the baize, so I rub it and hope Radic won't notice. However, there is also beer on the floor and Leo has knocked over some kind of red broth on the top of a chair. That has dripped down onto the wooden flooring too and I wonder what the hell will clean it up. As I sit back on my heels, I hear the door open and close behind me. I don't want to turn round but there's no hiding the mess as it looks as if someone has gutted a pig. It's an attractive lady with twinkling eyes, perhaps mid-forties, the one I saw holding Radic's hand earlier.

'It's Ben, isn't it?'

'Yes, erm, Mrs Radic.'

She laughs in the same free and easy way as her husband.

'Sofiya. It means wisdom.'

'What's his first name?'

'Only he can tell you that. It's possible he left it behind. He told me about you, Ben. Said you were a good boy, so be careful, please. They are not child's games they play.'

What do you say to that?

'Go and have fun. This borsch will never come off this chair. I'll hide it and blame it on one of his Lithuanian friends. They are always drunk.'

I laugh too and leave.

* * *

'I was looking for you.' Nadia is standing at the top of the stairs. 'I got you another drink.'

'No, I'm fine, thanks.'

'My car's outside. How about we go for a ride?'

The way she says it leaves little to the imagination. As we sneak out of the front door like thieves in the night, I think that on my death bed, many years from now, there is no way I'll regret taking up this opportunity.

My mother and I jostle for position in front of the mirror. It's Saturday night and we are both going out. A new Portuguese restaurant has opened in Millfield and all the cleaners from her work are going there. She's been taken on officially and gets a pay slip and everything. It's minimum wage but, as she says, she doesn't have expensive tastes. It's like living with a different person. I try not to think of all those wasted years as, other than that, it's perfect.

I'm doing well at work too. John's garage has been a real eye-opener. Modern technology and crime-scene gloves, so my hands don't look like I've been digging in a field, make me feel like the technician Leo pretends to be. I've been seeing bits and bobs of Nadia, but she's relaxed about meeting me, which is nice. We don't go round her house because she says it's too soon to meet her family. We don't go round mine much either as when she met my mum it was like putting two explosive chemicals together. Nadia and I screw in her car. It's a different kind of sex.

I'm not sure what the arrangement is between John and Radic but I spend all my time at John's now. I'm like a footballer out on loan. That's fine by me as I learn more and it seems just like a normal job. I thought we were being turned over one day not long after the barbecue when two grizzled-looking men with broken noses and scarred faces walked in. Radic greeted them like long-lost brothers, but I noticed John didn't look happy.

Leo has given up the pretence of doing anything other than the courier work, so I rarely see him, and a barrier seems to have been raised between Karolina and me.

Everyone will be at the Botolph pub this evening though. Radic loves these get-togethers and here is his favourite. There's a park next to the pub suitable for most kids and a big outside seating area nestles in the evening sun. That way, the adults can get drunk and the kids will occupy themselves while their parents have an eye on them. Radic will order platters of food and everyone will have a great time.

Nadia has come to pick me up in her car. She's early, so I tell her to come up to the flat as my mum has left. I open the door and have to look up to stare into Nadia's eyes. She's wearing a ridiculously short skirt and an even more ludicrous pair of high heels. The effect instantly almost makes me snort like a bull. I try to drag her in my bedroom. She's having none of it and says she will wait downstairs if I can't control myself.

'Look at this place. Why don't you work for Radic properly? Then you could live somewhere nice. A new flat in town would be perfect.'

My blood boils for a second time. She is money mad, seemingly able to suck it out of my pocket with much the same skill as another service she provides. I'm not in the mood for an argument so I open the front door and give her a smile. She'd have loved it here before my mum came off the sauce.

When we get outside, Nadia has to take her footwear off and put sandals on to drive. Her skirt rides up though, exposing her thong, and I spend the whole journey biting my tongue. She has a weird effect on me that almost makes me feel out of control, like one of the addictions that Jake has. She knows it too, which makes me feel a little uncomfortable. Either she's a natural at sex or she's had a lot of practice. I know deep down I'm fooling myself as I cling to the former, in the hope it's just great because we feel so crazy about each other.

* * *

When we arrive, we park out the back and walk in together. Her outfit has the desired effect with many a bloke getting a dig in the elbow from his partner. I leave her talking to Karolina and wander into the bar. It's clear there, as everyone is outside and I get served fast. I get a Diet Coke for Nadia and a full-fat one for me.

I stand next to some of the mechanics and join in the chatter. Radic is rolling around on the grass, pretending to eat a little boy's arm. This boy is laughing as though it's the joke of the century. What is it they say? Kids want to be scared by someone who doesn't scare them. Radic is a confusing mix of everything. I know he's taken me under his wing and that has caused some resentment, especially from Leo. However, it was Leo who succinctly taught me with his behaviour over Karolina, that you look after yourself first.

Radic extricates himself from the melee of children and comes over.

'Nice to see you, Ben.'

'You too. Nice to be invited.'

'It's great here, yes?'

'Yes, although I think I prefer it at your house.'

'Really? Why is that?'

'Better toilets.'

He laughs grandly.

'You wouldn't say that if you have to clean them afterwards.'

I can't see Radic on his hands and knees with some Marigolds on, but I smile regardless.

'Some fucker put his glass on my snooker table too. You wouldn't know anything about that, would you?'

'I heard those Lithuanians were drunk.'

He grins at me, like a proud father to his son.

'Look, my wife is over there. Why don't you come and meet her properly?'

I should know that he misses nothing. We wander over and Sofiya gives me a big hug. She's fussing over some children, and initially we're surplus to requirements. She then turns to Radic and commands him in Ukrainian to do something. He protests and she raises her eyebrows.

A minute later, we are walking towards the two swings. Each one of us holding the sticky mitts of a small boy. We lift them on and give them a push. It's a strange experience, doing something so innocent next to Peterborough's (and who knows where else's?) biggest drug dealer. In his own way, Radic is broken too. I can never quite get to grips with his motivation.

'Can I ask you a question?'

'The answer is yes. My wife is the person in charge.'

'I knew that, so, no, something else.' I pause, wondering whether to continue. I think he'll understand my interest. 'Why do it? Surely you have enough. A lovely family, a business, respect.'

'Ah, you mean the drugs. There comes a point when you have gone down a certain path for so long it's impossible to go a different way. There was a junction, a long time ago, when my son died and I still chose to continue. Now this is my life and will be to the end.'

'You could still stop now.'

'It is not an easy business to extricate yourself from. You know too much, too many people. They would feel uncomfortable. I like it too, and we provide a service. It's just a drug, like alcohol. If they made it legal I would pay tax, or more likely do something else illegal. We are men too, we like danger. Certain women like danger. Talking of which, I see you brought your giraffe along.'

Nadia is gliding towards the entrance, leaving a selection of chins on the floor. These chins are like bell-ringers in a line, up and down.

'Yes, you could get a nasty kick from one of those legs.'

'You will learn a lot from seeing her. Let us hope you survive the experience.'

We chuckle together. The kids squeal in delight as we push them higher.

'Pretty boring, this swing-pushing lark,' I say.

'Not for me. I love it. Look around you, at these men. We are all living in this moment because what else is there? In our line of work there are no pensions and gold watches. Yesterday has already gone and tomorrow may never come, particularly for the likes of us. So live life today. Enjoy it all. Or what is the point?'

'Higher, higher.'

'Take your opportunities too, Ben, before they are snatched away.'

I think on his words as we're dragged over to the slide and climbing frame. Taking a deep breath, I gaze around. I'm always looking to the future, not focusing on where I am and what I'm doing. As I watch Radic going down the slide I realise, for the first time since my father died, I feel part of something. I have a sense of belonging and I beam. Although, what does he mean by opportunities? Nadia, Karolina, or making money in his dark pursuits?

* * *

A long half-hour later, I find Nadia, who has a little girl sitting on her lap.

'Who's this pretty little one?' I ask it in good humour even though the kid has a snotty nose that makes me think of the fallout from the overfilled bins at the back of a Chinese takeaway.

'Of course she is pretty. She is beautiful like her mother.'

The penny is a big one. It takes a long time to drop. We both have hard eyes as I say, 'Really? You should've said.'

'I don't just introduce her to anyone. Only when I think it is going somewhere.'

Alarms go off in my head like in a nuclear submarine that has just hit the seabed. She says it all with such chilling finality.

I remind myself I am only nineteen. I don't need this kind of complication. A woman comes across and takes away the little girl. She's about fifty and is the spitting image of Nadia, down to the piercing blue eyes, except she has an ugly expression on her once-beautiful face that tells of a lifetime of disappointments.

Nadia stands up and takes my hand. In silence, we walk to the back of the car park where there is a gap in the fence. She slides through and we are in the back of a garden under a huge weeping willow tree, secluded from sight. She places her hands on the trunk and leans against it in a provocative way. As she does, her skirt rides up at the back and I see her underwear has already been removed.

I promise myself that this will be the last time. I push from my mind, as I push into her, the concern she knows of such a place. I also eject from my brain the fact that I'm being manipulated. She turns round and looks at me. It's so intense, the way she stares, almost willing me to do it harder, to strangle her. I slap her arse, hard, and growl.

37

10TH OCTOBER 2012

I've had my motorbike three months now and it remains one of my simple pleasures in life. I ride it often. Today, I've cruised into town. I walk it the last few metres when I get to the pedestrian zone, as it's not a heavy bike, and park outside Boots, the same place we stole that bike from all those years ago. Where's that child gone?

I allow myself to think of Jake but life has moved on. Control is slipping from me and I'm torn as to how to respond. Leo is back in jail for his involvement in a drunken brawl in town, which left Radic short on couriers.

I did my third delivery night yesterday. They're easing me in gently. It was easy enough. I picked up the package from another rider at a pre-arranged area and went on and delivered it to someone's house. Money didn't change hands. I hardly spoke except to ask for the woman's name as I dropped it off. The other drop-offs were similar. I'm not sure what kind of people snort coke on a Wednesday night but there appears to be considerable demand. I even went back to the same place twice, so it's not like they are getting it in for the weekend. The first night was a favour and then, almost without realising, I offered. I have made more cash from three nights pootling around on my motorbike than I do in a whole week of sweating under a variety of cars.

I'm getting into work later too but no one reprimands me. They know the score. I am on Leo's slippery slope and I wonder if he knew he was on someone else's when he first started out, and, if so, did he worry? Nadia was chuffed when I told her, and it's her I'm in town to meet. God knows why she wanted to meet in Starbucks as she told me recently she's given up caffeine. Always a new diet with her. I'm happy to though, as it is the end of the road for her. I have tried to break up before, but I'm weak. I suspect I will have to be rude, so her pride won't have me back.

She's sitting in the window seat. Without a drink, of course, as she will expect me to buy that. It's only 10 a.m. so the place is quiet.

A few minutes later, I sit opposite and want to complain about paying five quid for two teabags. I know she will bang on about the fact we, and by that I mean I, are paying for somewhere nice to drink it. I'd rather pay a penny and have it at home. The look on her face tells me I have more important things to worry about.

'I'm pregnant.'

The only thing that surprises me about that statement is that I have been so stupid to not see it coming. I want to ask if it's mine but say, 'How pregnant?'

'Three months. If it's a girl, we can call her Willow.'

I stare outside and see normal life going on, knowing that mine will never be quite the same. It doesn't feel real though, almost like I'm in a movie. 'Do you want to keep it?' I ask.

'Do you?'

'If given the choice to bring a baby into this world, which I clearly wasn't, I would have said no, thanks.'

'It's a little late for hindsight.'

'I thought you were on the pill.'

'I was, I am. It's not 100 per cent effective. You know that.'

'So when is the due date?'

'I find out tomorrow, City Hospital, 11 a.m. Twelve-week scan.'

We sit in silence for a minute or two. Time suddenly has little meaning. She gets up and retrieves the buggy with her sleeping daughter, which was next to the radiator. I hadn't even noticed.

'If you are interested, I will see you there.' She looks very different all of a sudden, almost unnatural. Vulnerability doesn't sit well with her.

'Fine. Thanks for telling me.'

She leaves with a flourish, noisily collecting her things together, leaving me alone with my thoughts and her perfume.

As I watch her leave, I ponder a lot of different things. The sneaky cow told me in a public place as she wasn't sure whether I would make a scene or not. She's trapped me, for a meal-ticket. The up-and-coming man in Radic's organisation. What kind of bitch gets pregnant just because she thinks it will help her social standing and provide a roof over her head? Weeks ago, she told me her mum was going back to the Ukraine and she would have no one to look after her child while she worked. I know nothing about children, or babies, for that matter. My mind was on the future, but mine alone.

I watch another parent manoeuvre her buggy to a table nearby. Her partner comes over grinning like the cat that got the cream as he plonks huge cups of coffee down in front of them. They look shattered. With sleepy, dopey expressions, they grin at the baby, who is asleep, and then at each other, like a pair of retards watching tennis. I catch myself. That's one of my father's phrases, one I swore not to repeat. One of the many that upset Sally.

Or, is it me who's twisted? I could have handled that all so differently. Maybe Nadia came here because she wanted to tell me somewhere nice, not just over the phone. I could have been elated, swept her off her feet, demanded we go and celebrate. The pill isn't perfect so it could have been an accident. Who would want two kids by two different fathers when the latest 'dad' was, if not up to his ears in organised crime, then certainly knee-deep and sinking? With no mother in the country, she could be alone if I reject her. With two children to look after and no money. Her looks fading as the second pregnancy and the exhaustion, that no doubt will follow, take their toll.

No, I underestimate her at my peril. She is a beautiful girl who will never be alone if she doesn't wish to be. Therein lies the crux of the matter. Is there something wrong with me? Why wouldn't I want to have a child with an attractive woman? Why can't we make it work? Give the child the best start in life. I know what the alternative is only too well as I have been incarcerated with hundreds of them. No dad and no money means little chance. Look at me, I lost my way. Look at Jake, he never got going. No child of mine will want for the love and guidance of his father. Look at the sacrifices my mother made to keep the family unit together, knowing he was out riding anything that moved.

We will need our own place and that will mean more money than a mechanic earns. There is another choice taken away from me. Still, there are worse holes to be in. I have time too, luckily; these damn things don't just appear. If I do it, I can do it on my terms, and she will toe the line.

I have a lot to think about, many decisions will need to be made. This time I am not alone. I can get advice off John, Radic, and my mum, to name just a few. That's a good feeling. The one decision that has been made is I will be there for the appointment tomorrow.

38

There's a new lad working in Radic's garage. I'm sitting in Reception waiting for them to finish out there. He walks past me with an easy smile and I envy him his innocence. It's two months since the scan. The baby is due on April Fool's Day. That doesn't seem very far away. Everyone has been brilliant at listening to my concerns but not so much on the giving advice. I want to be told what to do. It took me a while to realise, until about ten people had informed me the same thing, that every child is different. It is something we will have to work through. So, we are together and will raise the child that way.

I haven't told Nadia that, in the future, I will take on her other child as well. Until the last possible moment, I just want to be young and carefree. I'll be twenty in March. It seems a lot of responsibility for someone so young. I think my clock began ticking twice as fast as everyone else's when my dad died. Then there is prison. That place will weary you, and then some.

I thought having a child would make me soft, but it hasn't. It has made me hard. Nadia looked overjoyed when she found me waiting outside the hospital. I must admit I was excited and scared at the same time.

To see his heart beating was surreal. However, every step helps in my acceptance. Yes, a boy. That was confirmed a few weeks back. We have a one-in-ten-thousand chance of having a Jonty, which made me think of him after all this time. I hope he's happy. He is better off out of all this madness.

My new take-no-shit attitude is driving Nadia up the wall. She keeps demanding this and that, but I keep putting her in her place. If she keeps on, I get up and leave. I've told her the house will be ready for when the baby arrives and she isn't my responsibility until that day. Inside I know that isn't true. In the meantime, my work for Radic increases at a pace. The packages are heavier and the distances further. As the risk increases so do the rewards. I will be ready for the baby and we will be comfortable. That's assuming Nadia hasn't knifed me in frustration by then. Her sour-faced mother is still about. I have made it clear that the harpy isn't moving in. I wonder whether I am being too harsh but I am so busy, as I'm still trying to keep up my normal work, that I have little time to dwell on things.

'Are you happy to being a dad?'

Karolina's comment brings me back to the present. I smile at her deep voice. She has been in the UK a long time and her English is still the worst of the lot.

'What are you grinning at?' she adds.

'You. It's nice to talk again. We don't see much of each other nowadays.'

'Too busy with my friends, aren't we?'

It's meant as a joke, but she says it too quickly. I catch a frown on her face before she turns away.

'You hear from Leo?'

'Yes, they finally deport him. So he is back in the Ukraine. He says it is dangerous over there. Lot of Russians about.'

'Is he coming back?'

'He has tried once and his new passport failed, so who knows?'

'How about you? Are you happy?'

I shouldn't ask. I know I'm doing it for the wrong reasons.

'My mother and me, we may go back. She wants to run a café in Poland, just through the border. We have family there. We can both see reckless choices being made here.'

I hate the thought of her leaving but what can I say? It is too late and then some.

Igor pokes his head round the door. 'Come on, I want to get home.'

I follow him into Radic's office. He gives me the mobile phone for tonight and tells me the collection locations. He has been feeling the pressure of late and has reverted back to the mute I first met unless speech is absolutely necessary. The other operator tonight is Klaus. He's Latvian, I think, and a total penis. I caught him doing wheelies in a street, while working, as he was waiting for me to turn up. One mistake and the police have you bang to rights. This kind of thing is risky enough without having to rely on idiots like him.

I follow Igor out to my bike, which is being wiped clean of prints by one of the new lads. Turns out old Igor is more immersed in it than I thought. From what I can tell it's Radic and John who are the big cheeses, but Igor is like a lieutenant. A Babybel, if you like. He tells me the first drop-off is on Thorpe Road. It's surprising some of the posh houses we get called to. I guess cocaine is the Rolls-Royce of the drug world, so it's only to be expected that the rich would want it.

Klaus is waiting in the car park of the Hungry Horse. He hands over the package but says nothing. He doesn't even raise the tinted visor on his helmet. Radic tore him a new arse over that stunt and he must be aware it could only have been me who told him. I know Peterborough well now, so drive straight there, no satnav needed. I haven't been to the address previously so I'm naturally cautious. The drive is lit up like a Christmas tree and all the lights are on in the house. Who does that when they're getting drugs delivered? So I drive past and do a U-turn at the *Evening Telegraph* roundabout at the top of the road and have a think. When I get back, some of the lights have gone out. Too many have gone out. So I stop, but don't get off, and leave the engine running.

Something feels wrong. Am I being paranoid?

I lean over to get off and then see the slightest bit of movement on the edge of my vision. There's a car parked in a drive opposite with no lights on. I can see two people in the front seat. I casually lean back on the bike, but I'm rumbled. The lights come on as the car jumps forward.

Swearing under my breath, I stay cool to see what the driver will do. As I suspect, he blocks my path by stopping in front of me. My bike is light and manoeuvrable and he won't be expecting me to reverse. A door opens, I backpedal quickly and let out the clutch and slip past an outstretched arm and roar off down the road. It was a trap. I am in trouble.

My bike will accelerate much faster than any car but it won't corner as fast, not in my hands anyway, and certainly not at this time of year. Even though it has stopped raining now, the air is moist and the road slippery. While the size and lightness of my vehicle has got me away from the initial contact, it also means I have no top end. So I can't outrun them with speed either.

I go all the way round Thorpe Hall roundabout and turn back up Thorpe Road, passing them in surprise. I turn left into West-wood Park Road, accelerating past Radic's house. I should parp my horn and wave, he'd like that. Then I have a flash of genius. The

Grange is a park area with football playing fields with barriers to cars at both ends. If I can get through there in time, they will have to go round a huge circle to catch up and I will be gone. I have to slow to turn in the entrance. The car is only a few metres behind me; a black Audi sign is much too close in my wing mirror. He's going to ram me. He slows at the last minute. I have to stop to slip past the metal posts, only doing so by putting the handlebars through at an angle. One of the men is out of the car, running after me, but I twist the throttle and scare some scruffy lads who are sitting around smoking. I burn straight through the park, out the other end, down Atherstone Avenue and into Buckland Close. There is another pedestrian entrance here, so I go through, past some concrete posts, and into the nurses' quarters of the hospital. It's quiet.

I kill the engine and turn off the lights. The place is deserted. I dismount and ease off my helmet under the darkness of a tree and leave the bike resting on the stand. My ears strain for either a car or, worse, a helicopter. I walk towards the hospital and look fondly back at the bike. That will be the last time I see it. I drop my mobile into a drain, the snapped SIM into the next one. I look up again, watching for the helicopter. I launch my helmet into some nearby waste ground. The kids will have had that by mid-morning. I open a wheelie bin, remove the top bag of rubbish and drop in my leather jacket, covering it with the waste afterwards.

I open the envelope that was under my shirt next to my body, and curse. There is only supposed to be an eight-ball in this delivery; three and a half grams with a street value of around one hundred and fifty pounds. That way if you get caught you can argue, futilely probably, that it's for personal use. There is considerably more than that in here. I empty it onto a puddle. It's spitting with rain now so any traces will soon be long gone.

* * *

When I get to the hospital entrance, my luck changes and a bus pulls up. I jump on, thankful I have the correct change, and we're off. I slump in my seat but don't relax until we are back in town. I get a taxi home and text Radic the code.

Snooker table.

Radic said it would cheer me up if it happened. It doesn't.

My mum is out so I sit on the sofa in darkness with just the twinkling lights of our lame tree, and let my thoughts roam. I could have been arrested by now. I've no idea what the sentences are for this but, needless to say, I would miss my son's birth and a good chunk of the start of his life. Yet again, events have got away from me and things are out of my control. I want out, but I've got a kid on the way and a high-maintenance girlfriend. She's the Ducati of the female world. A breath-taking ride, but is likely to let you down when you least expect it.

My heart is still beating faster than normal but weirdly, I'm also buzzing. That was close, but exciting. I can't remember who said the closer you are to danger, the more you feel alive. He's right. However, there is also a rat. One who has it in for me in particular, as it was yours truly who was hung out to dry this evening. The foundations of the life I've created wobble underneath me as I comb through the past year's memories and wonder who I can trust.

39

'OK, I won't be long.'

'At Radic's house? You sure?'

'OK, I should be back this week some time.'

'Funny ha ha. I want to get my hair done this week, even wash it.'

'Ah, but you're so beautiful.'

I reach down and kiss her on the lips. The dirty little mare has recovered her mojo and slips in her tongue.

'Not in front of the baby, you filth-ball.'

She tries to grab my crotch as I go over to the Moses basket, but I slip past her hands with a swish of my hips, like a grinning salsa dancer.

I kiss Alex on the head. We had a lot of arguments over the name. Nadia liked both Sergei and Oleg. I explained I didn't want my boy named after the toys from the Compare The Market site. She then said she wanted Vlad. Unfortunately, she mentioned that when Radic was here. I explained that Vlad the 'Impaler' was not suitable either. I had both of them on at me over that as he absolutely loved it. After many a bloody skirmish, we settled for Alexander, who is also a meerkat, but spelt in the English way. Turns out it's Radic's first name, so it may have got us the car as he was moist-eyed when he left.

She said she was going on a sex-strike after losing the Vlad argument; however, I'm knackered with all the broken sleep. It took three days for her to realise I was happy with the new arrangement. Then she made me do it loads as she thought I didn't find her attractive any more. There is nothing like being made to do something to suck the joy right out of it.

Strangely, my urges have slackened considerably since Alex's arrival. It's not just Nadia either. I don't feel the urge to have sex with anything, even myself. I'm secretly pleased about that as what kind of man wants to change a nappy one minute and then rut over the kitchen sink a few minutes later? However, I am aware I'm storing up trouble. It's as if my testosterone levels have emptied and I have become some kind of docile womble, happily pottering around the house, making cups of tea. The truth of the matter is that since my near-arrest experience, I've never been more content.

Say what you like about Radic, but he knows his business, and he isn't greedy. As soon as he got the text, he came straight round, still in a dinner jacket, and asked me what had happened. After that, everything stopped. We literally became just two garages. Radic had a lot of meetings and seemed busier than ever, but things settled down. I carried on learning from John and Igor, and, after no one was arrested, even they began to relax. I still don't understand Radic's motivations. He seems happier now that a baby has come into his circle than at any other time since I met him. Seeing as he's a glass-overflowing type character, that is saying something.

He gave me a Toyota Land Cruiser to use to run the family about. It's a few years old but has still got to be worth over thirty grand. Nadia loves it. Obviously. He told me, as he gave it to me, it was to make sure my family is safe. That's pretty fucked-up thinking. Surely the safest place for them would be away from all this.

My close shave with the law, though, has left me seeing life from a different perspective. When I'm getting frustrated with a job, the kid crying, or Nadia bellyaching, I think that I could be staring through some bars right now and it makes me untouchable. On top of that, I paid for a part-time IMI Level 1 Diploma in Vehicle Maintenance and Repair, which was the best part of a grand, and Radic and John paid me back for it. So I've been playing happy families, not been delivering drugs, and am breezing the course. The guy running it tells me I have a natural ear for spotting problems.

Nadia and I are getting along fine. Sometimes I think about asking her to marry me and make it all official, but I regularly get a glimpse of the old Nadia when she doesn't get her way; a cold look, which makes me worry that this is all manufactured. I let her mum move in a few days after the child was born. Pathetic, aren't I? No doubt she was never going back to Ukraine. This keeps Nadia happy and off my back as her mum has all the time in the world for Alex. He will drop off on her weighty bosom as though he's been placed on a heavenly cloud. The unexpected benefit of having her with us is I also get a regular vision of what Nadia will gradually morph into over the next twenty-five years. This tempers any mad thoughts of romantic rashness.

My mum comes round too. I get a sick pleasure from watching the two grannies trying to be polite and show no disrespect, but both having a very different way of doing things. It's lucky Alex hasn't got teeth yet or Baba, as even I call Nadia's mother now, would have knocked them out when she was winding him.

Dasha and I have become good friends. She's three now and a little feisty. I take her swimming and to the park, which her mum never does, so she is more than happy to be with me. I make the time, but even those small breaks are becoming harder to find.

So life is good. Radic has invited me round tonight to wet the baby's head. This is the fourth time we've wet it, but what the hell? The two grizzled men now work in the business. They used to be Special Forces. He said he would use this evening to officially welcome them as they had recently arrived. These two shuttle the cars between the two garages. Ironically, with no effort whatsoever, we have acquired a reputation for reliable, efficient, and reasonably priced work. I don't have all the latest diagnostic tools at Radic's so I work at John's all the time now. The guys bring the cars to us and drop them back at the customer's address afterwards.

You would have to be very cross to tell one of them you weren't happy with the work, though, as they both look sinister. I suspect they are here for when things pick up with the other business. However, they're actually amusing. Karolina has taken to calling them Tom and Jerry and they have taken it in their stride. A more muscular cat and mouse you would struggle to meet, but they have that 'live for today' attitude that makes Radic so engaging.

'OK, I'm off.'

'Have a think about it.'

'I will, it'll still be no.'

Nadia's latest angle is trying to get me to get a tattoo. I know where it will end, with me looking like some kind of circus act. She has a serpent up the side of her leg that, with just a glimpse of the tail, used to get me going like a steam train. Pre-Alex of course. Now I imagine her mother has one just above her cloven hoof. Jake, and his prison art, has put me off tattooing myself for life.

Letting myself out of the house, I still can't believe I live in a three-bed semi on the British Sugar Estate. I am a respectable middle-class person I don't recognise. I even have a mower. I have tried to introduce Nadia to it, but she doesn't want to be friends. The rent is expensive but I can manage it on my wages and savings.

At some point, I will need either a rise or to find a way to supplement my earnings. No prizes for guessing how. The best feeling though, the one that gets me to sleep at night, is one of stability. I know in a while, perhaps a few years, there will be little I can't do with a vehicle. We will take the next step. As a family.

Then, I can do a business studies course. Finally, I will be in control. I'm not sure what my current father figures will think of it all, but I can cross that bridge when I come to it. I hope the barriers will be open.

40

There are only three cars on the drive at Radic's. One is John's, one is Igor's, and I'm not sure who the owner is of the third. I thought there would be more people here. I knock on the front door and I'm also surprised by the lack of music coming from the house. It's a beautiful spring evening, warm and peaceful, but a shiver travels up my spine. I'm startled when Jerry opens the door. He gives me a grin and smacks my back. There is no conviction in either gesture. Mrs Radic takes pride in getting the door. I think she hopes by her greeting the guests they will know this is her domain, and not an extension of Radic's black empire.

'Basement, please,' Jerry says.

I follow him down. Tom, Radic and John are all there. I feel uneasy despite Radic giving me a man-hug that crushes the wind out of me. I can't help thinking it is the type of hug you give someone before they go on a long journey. One from which they may not return. As I enter further into the gloomy room my nostrils are assaulted by an overpowering smell of bleach. John shakes my hand; he was never much of a cuddler. Tom gives me a nod from the doorway where he and Jerry are now standing. I try not to think that they are blocking the escape route, but they are.

'Come here, to the table, Ben.' Radic's face is expressionless.

I walk over, my eyes not leaving his.

'Do you remember that lazy drunken fucker, Leo, ruining my table cover.'

I nod. I do. Eons ago.

'So you know how I feel about the baize and the slate.'

Karolina had said he loves it more than her. I nod again.

'There are few things I value more.' He stops to remember. 'I miss him. He would shag anything that moved, or looked like it may have had a pulse once, but he was loyal. Without question. That is all we have in this business.'

'We know who told the police,' John murmurs behind me. I hadn't even realised he had moved. 'Look down, Ben.'

I look down at the table. As I do, I see Radic's arm come up on my right. I close my eyes and hear a click.

* * *

A second later, I am staggered that I'm still alive. My eyes open and I stare at the table in front of me. The light he has turned on has shown the covering is not bright green any more. It is a dark red or purple. I can sense a coppery tang in the air. This stain covers all of one side of the slab and there's also a piece of matted black hair congealing against a cushion. On closer inspection there are fine cuts in the cloth and I can see the blood has soaked through into the slate. I don't look up.

'Who was it?'

'Igor.'

'What? No way.'

I turn to look in their eyes. They nod solemnly.

'Why?' is all I can manage as I feel stickiness from where I'm leaning on the cushion with my fingertips on the baize.

'He wouldn't admit to it until near the end, but he had problems with heroin back in Ukraine. I've always suspected he got my son involved in it, but obviously he would never confess that to me. I shut down the operation, as you know. Your police are surprisingly honest considering their poor wages and I could find nothing out for a long time. You remember that man who you gave the package to, Darren Connor?' Radic says all this as he makes himself a drink at the bar.

'Yes.' The killer.

'He had a huge shipment go missing that he was moving for us. He said it could only have been inside information that gave it away. He has a few police in his pocket, but they said they knew nothing. It was only after he lost another package that he, uh, applied some pressure on someone's family and they gave him the information it was a Polish Porsche informant.'

'They didn't name Igor?'

'No. I went on holiday last week. Working holiday to Marbella. To keep lines of communication open. They are crying out for quality product over there but is too risky until we find mole. When I come back to Gatwick I bump into Igor's wife. I say "Hey, is Igor here?" She is furious and says, "No. I left him six months ago." He beat her when he was off his face on drugs and she rang the police. They turn up and take a statement and arrest him, and then nothing. She and the twins leave to stay with her sister in London but she hears nothing. It's not even going to court. She was told that the CPS do not think they have a case, which she says is bullshit. She has new boyfriend in Brighton and never wants to hear about him again.'

'Oh, shit. So the police arrive for a domestic. He's off his face on drugs. They threaten him with prison and he offers them some information to get off the hook.'

'Domestic violence is very different in our country. Some say it is your right to beat your wife. Don't mention that to Sofiya, or she will beat me. Igor gave his wife a black eye, basically. So here that is more serious, but still less than one year in prison if anything, so no, he would not have talked for that.'

'After we asked him many times...' John leaves a pause that leaves me in no doubt how the information was extracted. I feel forced to look at the bloody table once more. 'He admitted he got careless and they found about fifty grams at the house. Not much, but too much for him to say it was for personal use. Although Igor said his addiction was terrible and that would only have lasted him a week.'

'So he gave them our names? That's crazy. He must've known what would happen. He grew up with you all. Everyone would've got massive sentences. Why didn't he take it on the chin? You would look after him when he got out.'

'They kept him in the police station for three days. You remember he rang and had three days off for that winter sickness bug, the nogovirus.'

'Norovirus.'

Radic gives me a funny look and I wonder why I thought it was important to correct him. He continues. 'Anyway. That was where he was. We were his phone call. He was climbing the wall, desperate for drugs. He doesn't know what he is doing, so he begins to talk.'

I see how it could be true. I hardly ever saw Igor eat anything. He was always in the toilet. He was sweaty, smelly and furtive. Sometimes though, he could be funny and brimming with energy and other times he was surly and full of hate.

'He gives them a name, so he can leave,' Radic says.

'Your name, Ben,' John adds.

'Bastard,' I involuntarily say. I feel massively let down. I thought we were close, yet it was me Igor sacrificed first. He meant to have me caught in the act.

Something else strange occurs to me. 'He must have known that, even not naming you, he was drawing attention to you.' I gesture to the table but keep my eyes from it, knowing I would be drawn to the clump of Igor's hair. 'Talking was insane.'

'Yes,' Radic says. 'What I do to people who betray me is much worse than what your legal system is capable of. Better to say nothing and take your chances. There is always release day to look forward to.'

There has been so much information entering my brain in the last few minutes, I can feel pressure in my forehead as though it's about to blow. I have learnt many things tonight. If I get caught, my lips are sealed. I don't even want to think about Igor's last few moments on earth.

It doesn't take long for my shock to turn to anger. Sympathy for a drug addict is always in short supply. Ask Jake. More so for one who's also a grass. The violence, though, seems out of kilter with Radic, and John for that matter. It's disheartening to think they would do the same to me if I crossed a line. A line where I don't know the parameters. I wonder if any suspicion hangs over me.

'Still. It is a sad business, but we all know the rules of the game. The stakes are high, but so are the rewards. Here, Ben, drink this,' Radic says. 'Come upstairs.'

John and I follow him. I pass Tom and Jerry, who have visibly relaxed. I wish I could. Radic opens some double doors with great enthusiasm. I dread what I'm about to see. He takes us into an exercise room a hotel would be proud of.

'This gym is for us all to use. The inner circle. I love that phrase. We are a unit now. I let Igor slip away, and we all paid the price.'

I doubt I would have the strength to lift a supermodel's skirt if given permission right now, never mind some weights. I suspect Igor would have something to say, if he could, about who paid the price. Radic gets on a cross trainer in front of us and begins to pump the machine with vigour.

'There are tough times ahead where people have moved in on our business while we have been out of action,' he puffs. 'Polish Porsche will continue but only as a garage. I have bought a new premises in Huntingdon. It's fully equipped and set to go, ready for the new manager.'

He gets off, comes over to me, and offers his hand.

'It is your garage, Ben. You are the manager.'

41

I step outside and take a long breath. Exhale. Then another.

I went through the motions of admiring the gleaming equipment and made my excuses, saying I wanted to tell my mother the news. They gave me some good-hearted abuse for that, but Radic, in particular, looked pleased. There seemed to be no question I would turn them down. Huntingdon is only twenty miles away, so it's no hardship. I'm not sure if I'm being sucked in against my will, or this is what I want. I didn't have any set plans or targets when I started out. Therefore it's a struggle to measure my success.

I decide to see my mother anyway. I've not seen her much except for the occasional coffee or flying visit. We ring sporadically and miss each other. It sometimes feels like we are building a relationship in the same way as two pen pals might: slowly, but with thought. I'm not sure whether I want to tell Nadia the news or not. She'll see it for the promotion it is, but not give a thought to the increase in danger, just the increase in rewards and status.

It helps me towards my goals though. My business course demands experience and I will now acquire it. Radic and John said they will spend time with me so I understand the management side. Igor trained me on ordering and record keeping so I'll soon see the bigger picture. The worry is that I will also see more of the illegal business. I'm getting what I want but potentially the cost is enormous.

As I drive up my old street, I begin to accept my new position as a good thing. Who else would give me this opportunity? I'll do my business course by distance learning if necessary. At some point I will have a choice to make. I can see now that it will be a dangerous one. One that may involve me fleeing and starting again, elsewhere. Disturbingly, the biggest obstacle I can see to that is Nadia. As I slide those conundrums to the back of my mind, I notice Michelle driving a car away from our street. I haven't heard or seen from her since she and Kirsty left all those years ago. I wave, but she either doesn't see me or the evil, angry look on her face is directed at me.

* * *

My mum is sitting on the sofa with her Portuguese neighbour when I arrive. I still let myself in even though I don't live here. My mum said I could keep my key until she started having sex again. I would rather she just took the key off me than tell me that, but there you go. They're drinking a glass of wine when I arrive. I catch my mum's eye and raise an eyebrow but don't mention it. I'm not in a position to make judgements any more. My mum follows me into the kitchen where, as usual, I open the fridge door to see if there's something good in there.

'Glass of wine?' she asks. 'Alcohol free. We were partying until we had a little visit. You must have seen her leave.'

'Good for you, Mum,' I say as I kiss her cheek. I hope alcohol-free wine isn't classified as being on the slippery slope. 'Yes, I saw her. What are you celebrating?'

'Ana and I are going into business together.'

'Really? What as?'

'Domestic Goddesses. We're good at it and reliable. There seems to be no end of work out there so why shouldn't we take the better money? We've saved up to get the equipment and can use Ana's friend's car. One of us will still work for the agency while we build up our business and then we'll both do it.'

'That's brilliant. I'm so proud of you.' When I stoop to kiss her on the cheek, I get a waft of wine that takes me back to unhappier times. I notice my mum isn't ecstatic. 'Michelle's visit wasn't good news?'

'No. I don't know how to say this to you, Benny. I'm not sure how much of a blow it will be.'

'If I had to guess, I bet she wanted to complain about something.'

She is now the one who takes a deep breath.

'Michelle came round to tell me she won't be keeping our secret any more. She says she's going to tell her the truth.'

'What truth? Who are we talking about?'

'Your father, Patrick, is also Kirsty's father.'

That can't be right. My eyes close as my brain frantically tries to look for a different result to that statement.

'So, she's my sister?' I eventually ask.

'Yes, half-sister. Your dad had a roving eye from the start.'

My mum looks shifty, is it just guilt, or is it something else?

'All that time, you let us play together, without knowing?' Letting her give me a blow job without knowing is the troubling memory. 'Why? How?'

'You remember what Michelle was like. She didn't know who the father was to start with. It was only when Kirsty got to about five that she started to resemble him. She had some of the same gestures too. Loved to eat while she watched television. She was also left-handed. She loved Brussels sprouts.'

'What? That's hardly a fucking DNA test.'

'Language, you. No, I guess not. It seems crazy now I'm thinking straight. We didn't know for sure and time flew by. Then it didn't seem worth telling anyone. It would have painted all of us in a poor light. Them for doing it and me for putting up with it. It wasn't like we'd be families. Your dad helped out, but did it all with a few quid here and there so it didn't affect Michelle's benefits.'

'I'm not sure I believe I'm hearing this. Don't you think Kirsty had a right to know she had a father? Whatever kind of reptile he is, was, it's got to be better than not having one. I had a sister. Didn't I have a right to know that?'

'I'm so sorry, Benny. It was a long time ago, and we didn't know any better.'

I stare at her. She has moist eyes, but that is all. For her it's the past. I'm not sure alcoholics remember life in the same way. In fact, I bet it feels like a dream to her, the state she was in. Surely that's no excuse, though, for any of them. My brain can't take any more.

'Look, I'm going. I'll talk to you another time about all this. Let it sink in.'

'OK, but make it soon, will you? There's an old envelope at the door. Jake came round and left his number and address again. I said I'd pass it on.'

For a nanosecond, getting off my face with him appeals. I am lucky, in some things. I have what many addicts don't: the ability to remember at the right time that when I wake up tomorrow all my problems will still be there. If I weaken, I will be in a worse condition to resolve them.

I walk out of the flats, still stunned by the lie my parents maintained for all those years. I know where I'm heading. Into the abyss with Radic. I recall the only phrase I remember from the Bible. I stand next to the car, look up to the heavens, and try not to think back over the last decade. I fail. As the years roll by, there is a steady chant in the background. 'Let him that is without sin, cast the first stone.'

Who am I to judge, to condemn? A small powerful voice inside me states that at some point in the future, I will need my mum.

42

24TH DECEMBER 2013

I can hear the sound of a big lorry pulling up outside. I check my watch and it's 4 p.m.

'Saint Nicholas!' Nadia's daughter, Dasha, shouts out. She lifts the curtain where we're sitting in our new lounge. More likely the police, I think. Who or whatever it is clears off quickly, and she sits back down to continue to watch Peppa Pig, unconcerned. Maybe it was Saint Nicholas. She doesn't need anything, as she gets everything her eyes rest on for more than a few seconds, so she would be as excited by seeing him as I am a milk float. Except a pony, I drew the line there. She turns the volume up to an irritating level and I regret, again, showing her how the remote control works. Sometimes I think this is why Nadia and I argue. The jingle of the intro seems to be a permanent soundtrack to my life and I'm constantly on edge. Perhaps I am permanently stressed because I finally understand what I'm involved in.

The quantity of drugs being moved is staggering. I know because I am moving them. We toddled before we walked. Now we run. It is exponential. There's still a lot I don't know and for that I'm grateful. Tom and Jerry are neck deep in it. Someone has bitten off a piece of Jerry's ear and broken his nose, and Tom is down a finger. I work out with them twice a week but our new house has a gym so I guess I won't do that so much now. Three new guys have arrived from back east. They hover around Radic and John like flies. Leo, who has evaded the UK Border Agency, calls them Bert, Ernie and Beaker. This would be funny, but they don't speak English, and are clearly just guns for hire. Leo hasn't said what he was doing while he was away. However, he's different now. Radic hinted that he had been in a Ukrainian prison. They are not holiday camps. He has been sent to help me and is all business. Radic calls him 'Benjy's little helper'. Only he laughs at that. Leo works long hours and is money motivated. As though time is running out. I have a sense of that too. Still, we have fun together and it helps to have a friendly face about.

The money has got us the new house. Even that has caveats. We rent directly off Radic at an extremely reasonable rate. It's huge. I give the money to some slippery fellow who comes round to collect it each month. He calls himself an accountant, but he doesn't look like he could run a bath, never mind someone's tax fiddle.

You would think Nadia would be happy, but she isn't. She's like an enormous baby bird. Every time I arrive at the house she is waiting with her mouth open, with her claws clutching and scratching. This afternoon I came home and all she said was, 'I am taking Alex to see my mother. You babysit Dasha. I need one hundred pounds.' Yes, her mother is still in our old house and I'm still paying for it.

I give her the money. There's money everywhere. We have a bank account with my wages going in, which I never need to touch. Unfortunately, Nadia had a card, so it was pounded. I eventually changed it so no more than two hundred pounds could be spent each day. She blew up like an egg in a microwave when her card was rejected in John Lewis. Verbal abuse sprayed to the four walls.

Despite me telling her she had a problem, and the limit was there, the majority was flung at me.

So, things are out of control. I'm so deep in the 'business' I can't see a way out. I haven't touched my study books for months. I have a half-sister with whom I have a sexual history. My always-unhinged partner is now so irrational she has become certifiable. I never see my child as I'm too busy working. People are dying. Money can't buy you happiness. I thought it was a lie, told by the poor.

Alex is a sweet child with whom I would love to spend more time. Yet, when I'm at home, Nadia keeps him pinned to her. It's as though if she has him attached, I won't see through her crazy machinations.

I hear the back door open and close, and know they are home. I'm not sure if I want sex or not. As she descends into her personal pit of psychosis, the sex is getting more violent and sadistic. I can't say I don't enjoy it as she's still a beautiful woman, but it doesn't seem to sit well with me afterwards. It's not the sort of thing I imagined doing with the mother of my children.

Thomas the Tank Engine comes on. Leo even ruined the only theme song that didn't drive me up the wall. His version is:

> *Radic, he's the number one,*
> *John is shy and not much fun,*
> *Tom delivers the drugs on time,*
> *Jerry shoots straight down a line,*
> *Benjy really knows his stuff,*
> *Nadia hoots and huffs and puffs,*
> *Leo takes all the girls to bed,*
> *Igor, let's just say, he's dead.*

Very witty, considering English isn't his first language, but despite the upbeat rhythm the ending hardly leaves you in a happy place. I even caught Dasha singing 'Radic and his friends,' once. It was spine-chilling.

'Do you know you have a Christmas present outside?' Nadia asks.

No 'hello, darling' for me.

'No, what is it?'

'Come outside, I will show you.'

She puts Alex down and I follow her out. I should be in bed. I'm tired and I have a lot to do tonight. Christmas Eve and white powder go hand in hand for many.

I don't see the bike at first as it is parked near the house and is all in black. Nadia sits on it and gives me her best porn smile.

'You can take some pictures of me on it, if you like?'

'Cool, I'd like that. I'll get a helmet.'

It's a cheap shot and I know the effect it will have. I watched an old film called *The Vikings* a while back. Near the end, Kirk Douglas says to the woman, as his foe rushes up the concrete steps to fight him for her hand, 'Look at him, how he hastens to his death.' Sometimes I feel like that.

'You motherfucker. You don't fancy me. Your child sucked the life from my body, gave me stretch marks, and now you say cruel things.'

'I was joking.'

'You should marry me, if you love me.'

This is another recurring theme.

'Go in, please, Nadia.'

She spits on the floor next to me as she walks past. An unusual gesture from a striking woman that strangely turns me on. Am I as messed up as her? What do I say? I don't want to marry you because you are mad, mean, and money-grabbing?

It's a beautiful motorbike. A Triumph Daytona. 900 cc. Swift does not do it justice. I've admired it in his garage for a long time. A double-edged present as usual. Here is a lovely machine. It will help you commit crimes for me in a faster, more efficient way. Perfect. I sink another notch in debt to Radic.

I grab my helmet, gloves and jacket from the garage and remove the key out of the envelope taped to the tank. The handling is heavy at low speeds, so I take it out on the parkway and open the throttle.

For the first time, in a long time, a smile of pure joy animates my face. It soon fades as I think of the reality of my situation. I know I am damned. We all are. We can't continue like this; something has to give. There is nothing I can do and there is no escape. Lives will be ruined. Mine will be one.

PART VII

AN ADULT

43

1ST MARCH 2014 (TWENTY-FIRST BIRTHDAY)

Nine a.m.

I blink the sleep out of my eyes and stare at the slit between the curtains where I can see raindrops patter against the window. I snuggle into my warm duvet, stretch my feet out to the bottom corners of the bed and groan in pleasure. A creeping sickness pervades into my temporary state of happiness as I note that, even though it's gloomy outside, it's not as dark as it should be to enable me to get to work on time. I'm also on my own. I crane my head to look at the watch my mother bought and which I use as an alarm clock. It's more or less in the place it is supposed to be, except it's encased in glass. A tumbler full of water to be precise. She understands the history of that watch. Knows what it means to me. So instead of being angry, I am afraid.

She has always been wild and prone to irate outbursts with no thought for their consequences. This dunking indicates she is mentally unstable and capable of anything, as she should be aware how angry it would make me. That's concerning.

Last night's argument was about money. No surprise there. I was looking for the power company's paperwork. Foolishly, I had thought that, seeing as Nadia had nothing to do all day except look after the kids, she would make sure all the bills were paid. She had said she would run the house, bills and all. I came home unexpectedly as I had left a car part in the garage and caught the postman on the drive. Judging by the red reminders, British Gas wasn't the only utility company being given the cold shoulder. Nothing had been paid. Threats of disconnection and other legal shaftings abounded. That wouldn't have bothered me too much as you can just settle them and problem solved. However, she had been asking for, and receiving, the money to pay for them.

When I was looking for the paperwork, I came across a bank statement for Santander. We use HSBC. Turns out Nadia also banks with Santander. Her account has over eight grand in it. She has more or less been hoarding money like a psychotic squirrel for months. Needless to say, in true Nadia style, when I discussed it with her, it was all my fault. If I won't marry her then she has no security, so she is only looking after her and the children's future as currently she could be slung out at any point. I was coolness personified and bellowed back to her, 'That day is coming.'

When queried about the fact we would freeze to death and have to wash with cold water when they cut us off, she said 'Why don't you pull your finger out and share the load?' I'm not sure where she got that little English titbit from. Although she does love her daytime TV. When she should be hoovering.

I calmly replied, 'I'm fucking paying for it. I'm not bloody cleaning it too.' More terrible things were said. More spitting. Then the usual madness of hard-core porn sex after the dust had settled. I fell asleep, thinking the matter finished with.

I remember it's my birthday, twenty-one. I feel much older as I get out of bed and turn on my phone. What are others my age doing? Many will have never even have had a job, either through education or a lack of one. If experiences and stress age you, then I'm already a withered man. Sometimes I find it strange that I'm managing people much older than me, yet it comes naturally. 9 a.m. – the time I'm supposed to be at the University of Radic. He can be a funny bugger about timekeeping too. Other people's obviously, not his own. I text him to avoid an instant confrontation and go into the bathroom.

* * *

Ten a.m.

I'm not doing any hands-on garage work today so I put on my best jeans and a new shirt. That is another source of annoyance. Nadia knows my size but never buys me any clothes, stating she doesn't have time. Yet her wardrobe is so full of new things you would need to be a magician to get any more in. As if I haven't got enough to do I have to go into Next and deal with their maddeningly enormous range of denim wear. I've been dropping a few hints about getting her mum to have the kids for a weekend, so we can go away and celebrate my birthday and the fact I passed my motorbike test last week. Funny how I am happy to break the law in other ways, yet want to be a legal driver now.

It was strange but, like when I passed my driving test, I got a huge buzz afterwards. It was as though I had been given a giant boost to my self-esteem. I want to enjoy success that has no negativity attached to it. When we do a good job at work or we have a great deal go down, we also celebrate, but it's tinged with regret and fear, as what we are doing is drenched in illegality. I can hear the kids coming up the stairs, no doubt with my favourite wicked witch. The door opens and I brace myself for the inevitable onslaught.

She gives me a stone-chilling smile, the kind Medusa would pay good money to master. She's dressed in a black and white business suit and looks imposing.

'I am off to pay the bills. Do some shopping for food. Get you some clothes. Get my hair and nails done. All the things I have been putting off as I'm so busy.'

'OK,' I quietly reply. What am I missing? Apart from some presents, obviously.

'I'll see you later, honey.' She kisses me on the cheek.

It takes five seconds.

'No fucking way. I've got a business meeting.'

I chase downstairs after her but remember the stair gate hasn't been put up. My job, apparently. I glance back and see Alex's head coming over the top stair, with the look of an overly enthusiastic lemming. I stop him from his suicidal descent as he slides past the fourth step. I pick him up, put him under one arm, grab Dasha and put her under the other. I hammer down to the hall, cursing as I have to put them down as the bitch has locked the front door behind her. Alex crawls away as I open it. When he is caught, I race outside. She has the car off the drive, engine running, with the window down. As I rush towards her, she shouts out of the window, 'Try to keep them alive!' and then she is gone.

* * *

Eleven a.m.

My God. What an hour. Turns out there was no stair gate for the lounge either, so there was nowhere I could trap them both. I gave them a bag of Maltesers to distract them while I got the box for the stair gate that I remembered seeing in the dining room. How long has it been there? I seem to recall seeing it in that cardboard at the old place. She really is a lazy mare. It's taken me half an hour to put it up and some rude words have been said, but they are now corralled in and I'm feeling much more positive about the experience. I mean, how hard can it be? Admittedly, I had to rest my foot on Alex's back at one point to stop him moving, which would not have been a good photo for child services to receive.

They are staring over the gate at me now, wide-eyed, as if they are expecting me to perform some kind of trick. A disappearing act springs to mind. I remember snippets of Nadia moaning when I get home from work and she has been on her own all day. 'Feed, change, sleep, feed, change, sleep.'

'Are you hungry, Dasha?'

'Yes. Crispies, please .'

Do a four-year-old and an almost one-year-old eat crisps? They do today. I need them quiet to ring Radic. I pass two bags of Walkers over, ready salted for Alex and prawn cocktail for her. She looks at me as though I'm trying to poison her and then they toddle off to the TV. I note that the little shit can walk when he has food he's interested in.

'Hi, Radic. I've had a mare.'

Silence. 'Go on.'

'Nadia has cleared off to get her hair done. However, she didn't take the children with her.'

I can hear a big booming laugh and him telling whoever he's with. I can hear him laughing too. Gits.

'When is she coming back?'

'She didn't say when she would be back.'

More explosive laughter.

'OK, we see you tomorrow. If you're still alive.'

* * *

Twelve p.m.

I decide to sit in the lounge with them. I can't get anything done due to the constant bickering. There's a terrible smell in the room too. Dasha comes over and hands me the ready salted crisp packet. 'More.'

'Where are the prawn ones?'

'What's a prawn?'

'The pink packet.'

'They were too spicy. Alex ate them.'

I steal a look at a pasty-looking Alex.

'I'll get you something in a minute. I don't suppose you've farted?'

'What's a fart?'

'Erm. It's a bit like a cough.'

'Mummy said Alex was poorly and should only have toast.'

'Really? Why didn't you tell me that earlier?'

'You didn't ask, so I'm telling you now.' She is definitely Nadia's daughter.

I stand next to Alex. He hums like a two-foot-tall bumble bee. I pull back the elastic waist on his jeans and then hook my finger in the back of the nappy. I gasp in shock. It smells like a toxic leak at a biochemical factory but it's the incredible amount of produce that's astounding. If I created that much shite I would take myself to A &

E. Letting the nappy close, I wipe my brown fingertip on the inside of his jeans. It's already too late for them to be saved. I'm out of my depth. I pull the jeans back and see both legs are covered in manure.

I pick him up, run with him to the bathroom and put him in the bath. I don't know what to do. His shock at being manhandled by me has subsided and he starts to cry.

'Mummy takes our clothes off before we get in the bath.' Dasha has followed me up.

'Really?'

I figure he's crying now anyway so I just pull all his clothes off. I feel like crying too. There is shit everywhere. I can taste it almost. He starts to sob. I can feel it in my spine. I shower him off. It's not like he can cry any harder.

After a few seconds, I realise I'm wrong. Dasha is looking at me as if I'm preparing her brother for the pot. I'm in hell.

* * *

One p.m.

'Are you sure you have sandwiches every day?'

'Yes.'

'Cheese sandwiches.'

'Yes.'

'And more crisps?'

'Yes.'

I'm weakening. I should ring Nadia, but know I'll never live it down. Alex only stopped crying when I gave him more Maltesers. I've only got one more bag. I sweat at the thought of not having any left and wonder about the irony compared to Jake's addiction with bags of heroin and his fear of running out.

I do four rounds of cheese sandwiches and take them into the lounge. Dasha follows behind me, like a judgemental shadow. They are now watching a cartoon called *Pocoyo*. It is monumentally irritating. They love it though, so it's on repeat. I put the food on the floor next to them and sit down on the sofa, exhausted. Alex is wearing one of Nadia's T-shirts as I couldn't find any of his clothes. I didn't look too hard. It's a new one as well by the looks of it, or was before he began to soil it. I have to take my rewards where I can today.

'We can't eat that.'

'Why not?'

'It's got the edges on.'

'Leave the edges.'

'No, you take them off.'

I get a glimpse of why people hit their children.

I get up, walk to the kitchen, cut off the crusts and return.

'We can't eat them either.'

'No? Why not?'

'That's orange cheese. We only like yellow cheese.'

'You watched me making it. Why didn't you say something?'

'I thought they might be yours.'

44

TWO P.M.

There is food all over the place. Sticky chocolate stains all over the TV and some on the carpet. The carpet chocolate stain seems to be a different colour though. How do you tell? I will have reached rock bottom if I have to get down and smell it. Alex has been crying. I tried milk, changing him again and putting more clothes on, then taking some off. All that resulted in was different types of crying.

It turns out giving a four-year-old blackcurrant in a cup without a lid and then not supervising is not a good idea either. She has dropped everything I have given her today. That included.

'Alex wants to go for a sleep.'

'Does he usually have a sleep?'

'Yes, after we have sandwiches.'

'Why didn't you say that before?'

The look she gives me indicates I'm not worthy of a reply. Someone is cruising for a bruising, but if it shuts him up I will bow down to a superior intelligence. I put him upstairs in his cot. Put a crochet blanket over him and close the door.

I sit downstairs next to Dasha on the sofa and we listen to him squeal. She passes me his bottle. I fill it up with milk, take it upstairs, give it to him, walk downstairs, sit next to Dasha and we listen to him scream. Dasha turns up the TV. I allow myself the dream of having a gun. I'm not sure, if I did have one, whether I would use it on them or myself.

* * *

Three p.m.

It must be the fifth time I have been upstairs to see him. He is snivelling now. Heartbroken. I pick him up and slowly sit down on the weird rocker-chair next to his cot. He stops crying. I put the bottle in his mouth and he sucks on it like mad, while his small hand holds my little finger. I gently rock back and forth, watching his eyes slowly close. He fights with all his remaining strength and then they shut. He carries on sucking for a good minute and then he releases his grip on my hand and the one on the bottle. All the tension drops out of his body, then out of mine. I can feel my heart breaking too.

* * *

Four p.m.

Alex wakes up as the pizza delivery guy arrives. I'm not sure if children like pizza so have got a variety of chicken products and some chips as well. Thirty quid to feed little kids seems excessive, but if it works I would have paid three hundred. I wasted the hour that Alex napped trying to clean the carpet. Like his jeans, it is beyond economical repair. There's a weariness creeping into my bones that is making me want to lie face down on the filthy floor.

We sit on the sofa in a row with Alex wedged in the corner so he can't fall over. I pull the coffee table over, cut some bits up and put them in front of him. I go in the kitchen to look for some sauce and find a load of puréed veg pots. That seems to make more sense than pizza. I begin to realise how little I've helped out over the past year. I changed a few nappies at the weekend but only so I could say I'd done it. Bath time lies in wait, like a mugger down a dark alley.

* * *

Five p.m.

They are in the bath but that's where the control ends. How can two children make so much noise? They are constantly irritating me and each other in equal measure. They have every single doll and figurine possible in the bath with them so it looks as if they are in a toy soup. At least undressing him was easy. I just peeled off the filthy T-shirt, which looks like I've cleaned some car tyres with it, and dropped him in with a plop. She has just got out of the bath.

'What are you doing?'

'I need a poo.'

'OK.'

She sits on the toilet while I wash the crevices of the foul thing in the tub. He wouldn't eat the super-smooth carrot, apple and parsnip medley when there had been goujons on the menu. He did spit it out though. Then smeared it over anything he could get his sticky paws on.

'I'm finished.'

'Good for you. Get back in the bath.'

'My bum hasn't been wiped.'

'Wipe it, then.'

'You do it.'

'Erm, how about you do it?'

'I don't like to.'

'I don't like to either.'

Needless to say, she is wet from the bath so my fingers go straight through the toilet paper. She climbs back in.

'Right, you stay here. I'll go look for pyjamas.'

There is stuff everywhere. The filing system from hell. I have found a sleepsuit, but it looks tiny. Is that what they sleep in?

'Arggghhhh!' Dasha screams from the bathroom.

I rush back in a panic. Judging by the horrendous, high-pitched screech only something like an enormous snake must have got in the bath.

It is a snake. A big brown one. And lots of little ones.

'Alex has pooed in the bath.'

It's the happiest I've seen him. This boy could poo for England. There are small brown turds everywhere, all intermingled with the toys. It's as if I've had a thousand nervous rabbits in for a wash. I make a noise between a laugh and a cry. Where's the manual?

I hear the front door open and close, and peer down from the top of the stairs. Nadia has come in with a load of Tesco bags. She looks up at me and smiles. She glances in the lounge and while the smile fades, she doesn't seem surprised. I have never been so happy to see someone. Not even Jake, when he was waiting for me at the prison gates.

'Miss me?'

My tongue is frozen with gratitude. She walks upstairs and looks in the bath.

'Momma,' they sing, the bottom broth temporarily forgotten.

'Dadda said fart.' Dasha smiles.

'Alex, have you pooed in the bath again? Stand up, kids. You know the drill.'

They stand up as though they have a rifle pointed at them. Neither of them utters a peep as she lets the plug out and showers them off.

'Tough shift?'

'Challenging, I would say.'

'Do you understand?'

'Yes, Nadia. Yes, I do.'

'Go on, go, before you fall over. I'll give you your presents later.'

I stagger out of the house and into the back garden like a survivor from a high-speed train crash. There is a swing in the corner I didn't even know we had. It's cold and I haven't got a coat on, but quiet so I don't care. It feels like a doctor has removed two parasites from me, which were leeching the energy and sanity out at a prodigious rate. I want no stimulus whatsoever, just to enjoy the unappreciated ecstasy of silence.

There is happy squawking from the house as they go back to the lounge looking all clean and fresh in their pyjamas. I smile; they are safe and still alive. I should get a medal.

45

We arrive at The Anne Boleyn public house just after 6 p.m. This evening's activities are a continuing theme for us to have some time together without the kids. It's working, to be honest. I'm glad at least one part of my life is going well, because the noose is tightening on the rest of it.

Nadia can still be huffy, but she loves being taken out to a nice restaurant. I tend to get a few days of peace afterwards. To be fair I enjoy them too. Unfortunately, tonight, because Radic asked me to, we have to make a stop off at a pub run by Darren Connor. His and Radic's relationship has broken down. We are struggling to get product and I've even had people come to the garage asking for it. You know the police aren't going to be far behind when people are asking for a gram with their MOT.

Radic wants a final meet with Darren to agree a resolution. I've been sent to make sure the message gets to him personally. I've sent one of my own couriers in to the establishment about half an hour ago, so I know he's there. He's only a young lad, but he's playing the fruit machine at the moment. Not much back up, I know. I could fill a book with the warnings I have had about this man. Surely they can't all be true. I've taken Nadia as I suspect there will be less chance of any drama with a woman present. However, from what I've heard of this cold-hearted murderer, I shouldn't discount anything. I know it's weak to take a female. This is Nadia though. A force no one would be expecting.

'What are we doing at this shit-hole?'

'It's not. It's a decent bar, with some good wines. I thought we'd have a quick drink before we went to Topo's.'

She smiles at me. She loves it at Topo's. Great food, good value, friendly Italian waiters fussing over her, me paying. Perfect night out for her. My favourite part is wandering through the square and past the cathedral with a full belly on the way back to the car.

'Your dress is lovely. Red suits you.'

'It's cerise.'

* * *

The sign declaring the pub The Anne Boleyn a free house creaks menacingly in the breeze. There is a presence at the entrance. A giant. He looks half asleep, but I know from prison that if you are so mismatched you have little chance. I might as well have a garden gnome planted inside for assistance. When we reach the door he gets off his seat and I realise he's a good six inches taller than me and what I thought was a belly is a coat. He looks unbreakable.

I don't usually frequent places that need a bouncer in the early evening, but he is very polite.

'Evening, sir, madam. I think you would enjoy it more in the lounge.'

He directs us into what is an expensive-looking area. An empty one. Darren is behind an oak bar. Nadia walks up to him and smiles. He grins back.

'Good of you to come in, Ben, and I'm pleased you have your beautiful partner with you too.'

He gestures for her hand and kisses the back of it. She thinks it's normal.

'Champagne?'

'Yes, please.'

'Not for me, I'm driving.'

The silence as he pours Nadia's drink is deafening. I have to say something.

'Darren is a friend of Radic's.'

'I see. It's a lovely place you have here.'

'Thank you.' Darren smiles at Nadia. 'Would you be so kind as to give Ben and me a minute for a quick chat? There are some olives over there. Everything's on the house.'

She picks up the bucket as though he's going to change his mind and moves over to the booth that has been laid out for us.

'We meet again, Ben. Still hanging around with Radish, are you? I've not spoken to him for a while. You should have asked him to come.'

'Perhaps if you answered your phone you could ask him yourself.'

'He seems agitated at the moment. It's nice to have his protégé instead.'

'That's why I'm here. Where's the delivery you promised?'

He takes his time drinking the pint of lager he has just below the bar. Half of it disappears. I notice a trickle of sweat run down his neck. It's cool in here. He's on the edge. I've been around drugs for so long now I can see someone who's losing the battle as clearly as if their T-shirt declared that fact. He is fit and lean, but too many veins show. He has bags under his lifeless eyes, and the almost imperceptible jerks of someone who is wired. It wouldn't take much for him to lose control. This is his domain. I know, for a fact, I would lose if we fought. As if to confirm my fears the giant from the door comes into the room and stands quietly near the window.

'Ignore Aiden. He gets cold on that stool.'

He pauses again before he answers.

'The shipment was lost. Again.'

'We pay you to deliver.'

'The police seem to know every move I make.'

'That's your issue. I thought you had contacts.'

'I did until your fucking junkie mechanic grassed us all up. You and your crew have caused these problems. I'm out.'

The vein on the side of his head pounds rhythmically with his speech. Luckily, I'm not here for solutions, only to provide information.

'We all have our problems. You were given half the money. Radic wants it back.'

'Like the shipment, the money is gone.'

'He says you have a week.'

Darren drains the rest of his drink and smiles.

'I thought I recognised you when I first met you.'

'I did too. Maybe from prison?'

'I haven't been to jail. Not in this country anyway.'

'Not that, then.'

'No. It's the way you talk. Surprisingly well spoken for a mechanic. You remind me of someone else, from a long time ago. Although there's nothing like cocaine for dissolving your memories. As for Radish, leave him. Work for me.'

'I think my loyalty is clear.'

'This is a hard game, Ben. Make sure you're on the right side. Losing is dying.'

'So I understand.'

I turn and walk towards Nadia, who is pouring herself another glass of champagne. His last words are growled at my back.

'I never lose.'

* * *

Nadia insists on finishing her drink, so I have to sit there for another thirty minutes. A few more people come in and the atmosphere actually seems convivial. As we leave, Darren comes over and hands me a mobile.

'I sent your friend home. You can give his phone back when you see him. If anyone else turns up, to play the fruit machine, there won't be any free drinks.'

Polite words, told with a menace I can hardly fathom.

The bouncer is nowhere to be seen as I pull open the door. The jukebox sparks into life and 'Lady In Red' comes out of the speaker above us.

Nadia waves to Darren. Darren blows her a kiss back. As we step into the street, she looks up at me. 'What a nice guy. I really liked him.'

Welcome to my world.

46

Leo is waiting for me in my office when I arrive at work, which is unusual as it's still very much the morning and it's rare for him to show his face before midday. He looks worried and shifty, which is at odds with his usually determined expression of late. He's in my seat, but gets out when I walk in and sits opposite.

'All right, Leo. Did you sleep here?'

'Very funny.'

'No girls under the desk, or suspicious fluids I should look out for?'

'I can't sleep. I'm shitting myself about Saturday.'

Radic is having a housewarming party then. He recently bought a new place near Whittlesey. The house is actually between Eastrea and Coates, which are even smaller villages in the fens about ten miles from Peterborough. Basically, it's a huge farmhouse in the middle of nowhere. His paranoia has ratcheted up these past few months as more and more shipments have gone missing. He's going through cigars like Bugs Bunny does carrots.

'Really? Why?'

'You aren't nervous?'

'I have concerns about the strength of the punch. I only had a cup last time and my eyes wouldn't focus for twenty minutes.'

'Not the party, you idiot, the meet.'

That's unlike Leo. Since what he called my 'promotion', he has been extremely deferential. He must be losing it too.

'The barbecue? No, I don't have any real concerns.'

'You don't know, do you?'

At my confused face, he continues.

'Radic is worried he is losing control. People have been letting him down all over the place. That Darren owes him big but won't pay. He says he's been let down too. Radic thinks it's gone too far and if he doesn't resolve it with him, you know, take action, he'll lose face and it will all fall apart. He has to come down hard or the respect will be gone. You know how Radic likes respect.'

'So what's happening?'

'Radic called me and told me he wanted to meet as there is something important going down. He met me at the Rowing Lake. You know how he loves the fact it can't be bugged. He was out of the car stretching against the back of it when I turned up, puffing away on his cigar at the same time. Very weird, man.'

Leo shakes his head as he remembers.

'You don't know about this?'

This is the unusual part of our relationship. I run the garage but Leo is still closer to the inner circle as he has been involved for so long. He shrugs.

'It was unlike him. He was nervous. I never thought I would say that about him. He's going to tell this Darren to meet him over at Maxey pits on Saturday. He knew this was going to happen. That's why all these heavies are here. Bert, Ernie, Beaker, Tom, and Jerry. They will all be there. I'm going. He told me I should be prepared.'

'Shit. I went to talk to that Darren a few weeks back.' Him with the cold, familiar face. 'I think if Death came calling, you would feel the same when you looked at him.'

'I know. He is a total madman. He scared me when we were on the same team. He's a trained killer as well. S A Bloody S.'

'There'll be loads of you. Radic will know what to do.'

'Not you, though.' A look of dawning realisation comes over Leo's face. 'He doesn't want you to come, does he? You're his favourite. The son he lost. It's too dangerous to get his precious Ben involved.'

'That's enough. You don't know that. I'm meeting Radic later today. He must be going to tell me about it then.'

I'm not seeing him until Saturday. He said exactly that, 'See you Saturday', to me last night on the phone.

'Will you go?' Leo asks. 'I haven't shot a gun since I was a kid with an air rifle.'

'Of course I'll go.' I will have to go or it'll be me losing face. I can't say I fancy it either. The SAS are the best soldiers in the world. A crazed ex-member is not a nice prospect. 'The others, our guys, they're all ex-Special Forces too.'

'I know, Ben, I know.'

He doesn't look convinced, and neither am I.

* * *

I let Leo out of my office, tell him not to worry, and that the bloke probably won't even show. I order Leo to go home and get some rest. Whatever happens, he'll need to be alert.

Before he leaves, he looks me in the eye and then hugs me. 'I have to go. I have to be loyal. If not me, then who does he have? Then, I'm going to ask Karolina to marry me. I'm done with all this shagging around. I want what you have. I'll see you tomorrow.'

I ponder my choices. He can probably have what I've got if he's so keen. I'll drop them off tonight, Actually, that's not true any more. Since 'poo Saturday', or, as Nadia likes to refer to it, 'Shitterday', we've got on much better. I hate to admit it, but it was kind of my fault. I get home earlier now, or go in later, and generally help and *communicate better*. What an awful phrase. No doubt she picked it up from *Loose Women*, which she watches avidly.

The reason for me being at home more is that we have had less product to deliver. Oddly, with me being around, the heat has gone out of our sex life. Although I worry less about her killing me while I sleep. My relationship with the children is developing too. Dasha called me 'Dadda' again a few days ago. I said nothing afterwards, and she seemed not to notice. It gave me a lovely feeling.

Our date nights help too. Nadia seems to have relaxed more. I don't think I understand women. Nadia is like a delicate flower. She needs constant tending. Without nurture she goes bad. In her case, instead of dying, she mutates into some kind of violent triffid. She is very protective of the children, though, so that's something.

I guess it's them who temper my arm from ringing Radic and demanding to be involved in the 'meet'. I had a terrible feeling from the start when I first came across that man and have no urgent need to meet him with a gun in my hand. If I don't go, I will look bad, but will it be worth it? I have children who I'm responsible for now. I remember I have two big packages to drop off. One tomorrow in St Ives and one in Sandy on Saturday morning. It sinks in now. He is, in a way, protecting me. Both these envelopes contain a hundred grams of pure coke. The last of the previous shipment. That's a lot of money. He can't afford to lose any more. This is a double win for him. He gets his most trusted courier to take charge, and he also takes his adopted son out of what could well be the gunfight at the OK corral.

I decide to let things ride. I'll do the drop tomorrow evening and then ring Radic to see if he mentions it. There's something else tugging at my mind like a bird at a juicy worm still clinging to the mud. I focus and realise I am thinking about Karolina. We have been getting on so well lately I'm surprised she didn't tell me she was back with Leo. She's a pretty, normal girl, the type that would make you feel lucky every day you were with her. I allow myself a minute to imagine a different world in which we're together. I walk out to my bike and put on my helmet.

As I pull away and fly up the road, I fight the image that is filling my mind. It's her, in those cowboy boots. I lose.

47

I pick up the package from an innocuous-looking white van parked down a quiet road in Stukeley Meadows Industrial Estate. I don't even get off my motorbike. Just open my shirt, put it next to my skin, redo the buttons, and tuck it back into my jeans. My leather jacket is a tight fit to keep the wind out so it will be secure. As usual, no words are said. The guy who gives it to me has white overalls, a beanie, and sunglasses. It could be Tony Blair for all I know. I put on my thick leather gauntlets and gun the engine. I know the guy who the drop-off is for. He has a motorboat on the river. All I will need to do is pull up alongside for him to get off and collect. Then I will roar away. Easy. I'm early so I stop further up the road and wait round the corner near a church. The path is busy with people going out for the night. I recognise one shambling towards me with a curtain hairstyle, drinking a can of Red Bull.

I can't believe it. It's Jake. I haven't seen him since I left that jail cell over two years ago. Surprisingly, he was moved on after the kettle incident. Unsurprisingly, I heard through the grapevine he'd only been out a few months when he went down for another burglary. Strike two, that would be, so he'd have served at least a year. He walks past me with his head down, and I'm about to let him go on his way when something stops me. He looks so despondent and down on his luck that I want to help. If it were me, I would want Jake to say hello. I guess there's also an element of guilt still present for leaving him high and dry.

Before I have time to decide if I'm better off in the current hole that I am in, or the simpler one I was in with him, I shout out his name.

He turns and stares at me. At least he doesn't look off his face. I raise the visor on my helmet.

'I heard you like a good ride.'

'Ben, is that you?'

He's missing half of one of his front teeth, which is not a flattering look for him.

'Yes, mate. Are you on holiday from the 'boro?'

'Shit. It's good to see you. Where've you been?'

'It's been a roller coaster, man. I've had a kid, run a garage, renting a place. Some work, just busy, you know. How about you?'

'Not much, to be honest. I got nicked again, twice since then. Really unlucky I was, too.' He has the good grace to grin. 'I've only been out a few weeks now. They got me a room here away from all the trouble. At least I didn't leave homeless again. They did help this time. I'm off the drugs finally. Well, still on methadone, but you know, not high. I've got a big old licence too, so I've got to keep my nose clean. One fuck-up and I'll get full recall.'

'How long did you get?'

'Two years. It was long, man.'

Two years mean you serve a year inside and a year on licence. The second year is spent in the community but you have to work on your behaviour with the National Probation Service. If you make any kind of cock-up you can be sent back to prison for the remaining time. It depends a bit on your relationship with your probation worker. All Jake's hate him as he doesn't give a shit about anything. So he is on very thin ice. It's the nightmare all cons fear. To do your time, get out for a few weeks and then get nicked again and have to serve the rest of your sentence.

'I heard you were doing well. Lily said. Others told me too. You have quite a reputation. She's in and out all the time now too. She wrote to me in jail. I have to steer clear of her or she will drag me back down again. Have you got any work for me?'

What a mess we are all in. Can any of us be saved? Jake cutting Lily off after me doing the same to him. A circle of doom. I can imagine how much Radic would love Jake. Typical Jake too. First, he says he needs to keep his nose clean. With the next breath he's asking for work, which he must know will be crooked.

'It's not really my gig, Jake.'

'Come on, Ben, don't make me beg. Look at you now. Look at the size of you.'

I'm not sure what he's driving at. I'm not aware I have any kind of reputation, yet I think of how Leo treats me. How everyone treats me. My new apprentices worship the ground I walk on. I think of how much weight I can move around in the gym now and it's a lot. I can't remember the last time I bought myself a drink. I guess I still see myself as a boy. I thought that some of the heavies were distant. Could they just have been wary, or even nervous? What have I become? Before I can think of an answer I can see a policeman walking towards us.

'No way,' I say under my breath. 'I'm carrying.'

Jake looks round, sees him, then turns back to me. 'Drugs?'

I nod. Then the policeman is next to us.

'I knew it wouldn't be long until you and I became acquainted.' He looks at Jake with a leer.

'I've done nothing wrong. Leave me alone,' Jake says.

'Pay for that drink, did you?'

The world goes silent for a moment as Jake turns to look at me and our eyes meet. All those years of stealing and running from the police, the time spent in places no better than slums, sharing food and money and anything else we could get our hands on, pass between us in an instant. Jake knows the score, so I know what he is going to do at the same time he does. I'm pleased to see there isn't a glimmer of doubt on his face.

'The squad car is round the corner, so don't even think about running.' The policeman points a gloved hand in my face. 'You can stay and we'll see what you have to say for yourself as well.'

I press the start button and rev the engine at the same time as Jake jumps on top of him. It's a pathetic manoeuvre, although it takes the policeman by surprise and they fall to the floor. I wait for the revs to drop, pull in the clutch lever, stamp the bike into first gear and pull away. I can take my time and be careful not to stall it as they are rolling around like children in a playground. A police car comes round the T-junction at the top of the road and I watch it in the mirrors as I drive past. I see the policeman get to his feet and give Jake such a driving punch into the stomach it bends him in half and I utter an involuntary 'oomph' myself. As I begin my turn, I see him point after me and know the chase is on.

There are cars tootling everywhere, but I'm on a fast bike and can easily manoeuvre around them. I need to get back to the motorway without having an accident. How can I have been so stupid? To be cautious all these years and then make a schoolboy error like that. I'm in the shit if they catch me. Years in jail unless I can get away. I see the flashing lights behind me as I'm forced to stop for a red light. If I go through Huntingdon, perhaps I can lose them in the one-way system, so I race off into the next gap.

The traffic in the town is terrible; however, I think I've lost them.

As I go past a junction, a different car puts its lights on and pulls out after me. There is an accident just to my right, which I hope is their destination and the cause of the delays. I am wrong. I'm starting to sweat in my helmet at the seriousness of my situation. There isn't time to take off my gloves and drag out the package while the police car is so close.

I make it to the slip road for the A1 with one car only fifty metres or so behind me. For some reason, I have Jon Bon Jovi's 'Blaze Of Glory' playing in my head. It makes me think of Jake, who always wanted to go out in a flash of fire. I open up the throttle as I get onto the A1 proper. It's often referred to as the 'A1 racetrack' as this stretch opens into four lanes of new tarmac. I press my body down onto the tank and kick through the gears.

About a minute later, I'm doing over one hundred and fifty miles an hour. The flashing police lights disappear from the view of my mirrors. I am going insanely fast. If I come off at this speed and hit something, I will disintegrate. It's madness. Adrenalin is coursing through my body almost as fast as the traffic is zipping past.

The cars in front aren't expecting me, so I have to weave through them, undertaking and overtaking, catching the odd glimpse of startled faces as I zoom by. I see one man mouth 'Fu...' and I am gone. My cheeks ache through grinning. The bike is handling superbly and I appreciate the weight that I cursed when I was driving in town.

After a few minutes, I join the slip road to Peterborough and take stock. I seem to be on my own and alive. A miracle. I power round the parkway and get onto Oundle Road, where I slow down to the speed limits. It's around 10 p.m. so the roads are quiet. I know where I'm going. There is a secluded car park near the town bridge where the fair sets up when it's here. I will leave the bike there and run to the river to get rid of the package.

I can drop my helmet too and slip over the bridge into the centre. I'll get a taxi home or go into one of the pubs and have a drink. My new mobile has nothing incriminating on it, but that can go to a watery grave as well.

As I get closer to my destination, I wonder now whether I should hang onto the drugs. The package is worth five grand at least. Radic, though, always says not to hang around and bin it the moment you get chance. You never want to get caught with anything. Especially if it's pure. I realise, too late, that there's oddly no traffic coming the other way. At that moment, I notice a black 4x4 accelerating hard towards my rear. I wonder how the hell they knew where I was.

I look up, knowing I will see the helicopter. Confirmation still makes my bowels lurch. As I get to the traffic lights next to the park, there is a police car in the distance stopping the traffic. There is also one much closer at the crossing on the other side of the road. My lane is clear but I can imagine a stinger tyre deflator, sharp steel spikes shining sadistically, waiting for me in the dark. Bad news on a motorbike.

I can't outrun the helicopter. My brain buzzes like a wasp in a glass as I try to process all this new information. The only thing I can do is go somewhere busy, lose my bike, drop the identifying clothing, and hope to mingle in a crowd. The only place I know that will be busy at this time of night is The College Arms. If I can lose the patrol cars by driving through the pedestrian zone in town, and park round the corner of the pub, I might be able to pull it off. If I go in with my helmet on through one door, keep my head down, leave it and my gloves and jacket next to a fruit machine and walk out of the other door, cross the road and get straight in a taxi, I may just have a chance. I drive into the park next to the road just as the X5 is almost upon me. Ironically, it is the place where Jake and I used to spend so much time when we were bunking off school.

Suddenly, I remember the alley way out to Queen's Road. Dog shit alley.

I race through past the swings and roundabout. The grass is slippery and I have my legs out to the side even though I know if the bike slides, the weight will drag me off whatever I'm doing. I only have to reach the passageway as it's just wide enough for a big motorbike and they won't be able to follow in a car.

I follow the path towards it. There is a searchlight on me from the enemy overhead. I lift my steamed-up visor so I can see what I'm doing as the streetlights down here have all been broken with stones as usual. I have to be quick so I speed down the straight lane, trying to dodge the litter in front of me. There is slippery rubbish all over the path – ubiquitous dog waste, greasy takeaway wrappers, and beer cans, none of which I want stuck to my front tyre.

When I near the end of the path, I look up and realise there are new posts at the bottom, to no doubt stop idiots like me doing this very thing. You couldn't get a bicycle through them without getting off so there's no way my conveyance will fit. I grab at the brake lever with my hand and press hard on the rear brake pedal with my foot, a notoriously destabilising act. But the bike seems to hold well and I think I'm just going to make it.

As I come to a stop, the bike slips out from underneath me and I hit the path with a bounce on my arse. My head smacks on the brick wall next to me with such force my visor pings off and I get dust in my eyes.

I jump up, clinging to the posts to stabilise myself, and try to run but as soon as I stagger through into the road I'm so woozy from the impact I can't keep straight. I veer to the right, as if I've been playing a drinking game in the sea, and bounce into the parked cars until I fall to the floor.

Scraping my helmet on the pavement, I turn my foggy head to

the side. A police van comes round the corner and stops with a screech of brakes. From my prone position, I can see sprinting black trousers. I am spent. The first heavy arrival jumps on my back, knees first, and it's over.

PART VIII

ADULT CUSTODY - HOSTAGE?

48

27TH AUGUST 2014

The huge officer kicks over the mattresses and stamps into the room. I'm not sure if it's the people behind him, who nudge him in their fervour to get involved in the action, or the baby oil that causes him to slip. The result is the same, and it's an unfortunate start for them. The big man falls forward onto his shield and flops on top of Donny's lower half. Jake launches the TV with a natural force that surprises both me and the officer whose chest it smashes into. The falling shield man and poor field of vision from the helmet must have caused him to be blindsided. He's propelled backwards and goes down as though his spine has been ripped out.

Not to miss an opportunity, I hammer the broken pool cue into the big guy's shoulder and feel something give. He rolls into the corner of the room. Either the weapon broke or his shoulder did. The next man, who is tall and thin, lurches forward, eyes wide in his helmet, shocked at the scene of mad devastation around him. He comes at me with his arms up like the mummy in a cheap horror film. I turn round and take a big step backwards – a move Jake and I used to practise as kids. My leading foot ends up between his legs and at the same time I punch my elbow as hard as I can into his midriff. The move is so successful he folds up like a cheap deckchair and butts me in the back of the head. I stagger forward and tread on Donny's hand.

With the roar of an enormous wounded animal, he jumps to his feet. I see another shield man advancing on Jake. Jake, his chin forward, is shouting abuse. The officer has the shield at an almost horizontal angle and cracks it straight onto the bridge of Jake's nose. I see blood spray in the air as though a water balloon has exploded and then Donny charges past me, bellowing, screaming, and throws men around as if they are rag dolls. He forces his way through them, grabs the one in the doorway, picks him up by his armpits and tries to throw him over the balcony. I see Senior Officer Cave snarling in fury, pounding his clenched fist into the side of Donny's head as others try to pull the falling man back from the chasm.

Jake is out cold, and the team who dealt with him turn to me. They shuffle across in a tight arrowhead formation, the men on the sides tucked behind the front man. I only have the tabletop left and throw it at the lead guy's groin. His shield comes down and blocks it and then it's raised to the nose-bursting angle from a few seconds ago. I've no wish to lose all my cartilage. I have to grab the edge of the shield with my hands and pull it down as he stabs it towards me. As I do, the men on either side of him bring their hands round and grab my forearms. I am yanked back and pinned like a crucifixion against the wall as the flat face of the shield is bashed against my face and chest. I see Cave's distorted furious face advance on me through the dirty plastic and then the shield is pulled out of the way. He has the wild-eyed look of someone out of control.

He pulls his arm back and I realise he is going to punch me in the face. I'm pinned and cannot move. As the fist arrives, I turn my face to the side, knowing my head is against the wall and this will hurt. There is a brief stinging impact and then blackness.

* * *

My head clears, and the noise that sounded as if it was playing on a muffled radio is clear and vivid. I hear the kicking of prisoners' doors and the groans of men. An entire tooth is loose in my mouth, sticky with blood. I briefly hope it was the one that hurt. I am still pinned to the wall but my head is free. I look up, which seems to take the same amount of energy as pulling a lorry with my chest, and see Cave being manhandled out by other staff, some in riot gear, others in white shirts, speckled with blood. He is throwing his head around as if a beetle has crawled into his ear. A helmeted man comes back, and grabs my head and pushes it down. He holds my chin and secures my head against his chest. I feel the men on either side twist my hands behind my back and then into a strange position by my side with my thumbs pointed outwards. Blood pours out of my mouth and the tooth comes free.

'Lock on!'

'Lock on!'

I hear the men shout as I realise I can't move my upper body at all.

'Get him out of here!'

'Prisoner, you will walk forward now at my pace. If you resist you will be taken to the floor.'

I shuffle and slosh towards the door like a geriatric in slippers. Jake is being attended to by a nurse next to the door. There is a lot of blood on him. I'm so weak I can hardly get my legs to move and the men are virtually carrying me. The tooth is still in my mouth and as we reach the top of the stairs I spit it out. I can hear shouting and radio chatter, but it's distant again, as though you are at the cinema and standing just outside the door to the screening as the film reaches its dramatic conclusion.

'ZB. I repeat this is a code blue and two code reds.'

'Give me an ETA on those ambulances.'

'Sierra one receiving, the emergency vehicles still have to be searched.'

'Get someone on those gates so they're let in the minute they arrive. Clear the route.'

'Mike six, where the hell is that second defibrillator? We need it now.'

'Delta four, I need landline figures for the director.'

'What are you doing? Let me look at him.'

I find the grip on me is released. I sink to my knees and am propped upright. My head spins lazily around, as though I'm stretching it before exercise, while I try to focus on what appears to be a nurse in front of me. I catch glimpses of pinched expressions. Men and women with helmets removed, slumped on the floor with sweaty hair. The main show is over and as the adrenalin drains away, so does the colour in people's faces. They realise the dreadfulness of what just happened. Pointless and violent. Prison.

'Put him down! Look at the state of him. What do you think he is going to do, run off?' The nurse screams the words. Even I can hear them clearly.

Without the support, I fall to the side, as if I've been shot through the heart. The last thing I see is a man in the corner surrounded by staff. He is being given CPR chest compressions by a sweating, ashen-faced lad not much older than me. By the look of abject terror on his face, my hopes for Donny are slim.

49

10TH SEPTEMBER 2014

I wake to the sound of a man snoring in the bed in the far corner. He is an old, old man, a man with sixty years of child sex offences. I should stuff my boxer shorts in his mouth, but I promised the officers I would behave. The insane fire, like burning magnesium, that was raging in me two weeks ago has been doused as though dropped into the deepest, iciest ocean. The seriousness of my situation weighs heavy and cold around me, making me lethargic and compliant.

I'm in the prison's healthcare department. The single cells were all full, with nutters, judging by the shouting throughout the night, so I was put in the four-bed ward with this fine specimen of the human race. He's actually extremely pleasant and charming, and remarkably good company. That is why he is so dangerous. It's still closed conditions where we are locked in every night at 6 p.m. but we have relative freedom on the unit during the day. Despite the weirdos, it's a lot less stressful than being on a wing of eighty.

'Here you go, Ben. I'll take you over after work movement.'

The officers here are more relaxed. It is easier for them as well. I

open the letter and see it's the notice of my adjudication this morning. Two weeks have gone by since it all happened. I have been here
recovering. I spent a few days in hospital after the incident and was
then brought here. Thanks to the delightful SO, I had a suspected
broken jaw. It wasn't; however, the entire left-hand side of my face
went a deep purple colour. I still look like an angry clown. It's hard
to get a good view in prison as the cells don't have proper mirrors.
Otherwise, one hard tap and you have an instant lethal weapon.
One of the officers told me about Jake's unsurprising broken nose,
as I haven't seen him since. By the officer's account I probably won't
now as Jake is going to be transferred to HMP Highpoint soon.
Knifepoint is its nickname. That will be nice for him.

There were notices on the kiosk for the week after. I thought it
was a strange thing to announce, but it's a required procedure to
notify all prisoners and staff that there's been a death in custody.
The demise of someone in close proximity affects people in
different ways. Anyone already on suicide watch is particularly
vulnerable, but it's the ones who aren't that need watching. They
are the ones they find in the morning. Donny lived a short,
wretched, violent life. What does that say about our humanity?
How can we say our society is cultured and developed when people
are dying like this? A heart attack, they said. That phrase barely
scratches the surface of any kind of explanation. It must be a
terrible call to receive saying your son or husband has died in
prison.

Prisons are full of gossip, most of which turns out to be false. I
remember one year we were all going to get fans, as it was so stifling
in the cells that 'residents' were saying they were struggling to
breathe. A few were given out but shortly afterwards the amount of
homemade tattoo guns they found in the prison went up. The fan
motors had been dismantled and sold on. The word on the street,

though, is that SO Cave is suspended or has had a mental break-down. I suspect the former as he has not been right in the head ever since I've known him.

They put my tooth back in and filled the cavity in the one next to it. I don't remember much. Neither feels right, to be honest, but a lot of lives were altered that night and I suspect I have come off lightly. So far.

I met my Radic-appointed solicitor. He didn't say as much, but getting caught with that amount of cocaine is not easily explained. I was kept in the police station for an entire day with very little food and drink due to the fact I would say nothing to anyone until my solicitor arrived. When he did, he advised me to maintain my silence. I asked him what was the worst that could happen. Luckily, the amount I was caught with was less than 150 grams. This makes it a category three offence; the maximum they can sentence me to is ten years as opposed to sixteen for a category one. Excellent, huh?

This time he explained how the sentence would depend on my role in the organisation. That was what he would work on as I'd plead guilty regardless. It was, after all, stuck in my shirt. It's a terrible thing to have that hanging over you: the possibility of five years in prison. I hate not being in control of my destiny. There is nothing worse than having that metal door locked on you in a hot cell when you want freedom.

I realise I've been standing in the middle of the room, unfo-cused, like a crazy person. Maybe I will fit in here after all.

I pull on my jeans and trainers. My clothes got sent in, so at least that's one element of normality I can cling to.

I was remanded on the Saturday at Peterborough Magistrates' Court. The crime was too serious for them to deal with. Poor old Jake was kept at Huntingdon Police Station until Monday. Then he was returned to HMP Peterborough. He said he pissed himself in the prison van on the way here because it was taking too long. Typical of this place that we were still allowed a cell together.

Something happened on that Saturday when Radic and his crew went to meet Darren. The solicitor confirmed as much but wouldn't be drawn any further. He said it was not for him to say. The only telephone numbers I know off by heart are the solicitor's, as Radic made me remember it, and Nadia's. I put them both on my prison pin phone. Neither have picked up when I've tried to ring. Nadia knows I'm here as it was her writing on the box that the clothes were sent in. The solicitor said to sit tight – almost laughable.

I'm interrupted from my stupor by the officer returning.

'Come on, Ben, I'll take you over now.'

* * *

When we get over to the Separation and Care Unit, I am placed in the same holding cell as the last time I was here. At least this time the place doesn't smell like excrement has been smeared on the walls. It is eerily quiet. I find this more unsettling than if there were angry voices.

The man who comes and gets me is a big man. I can't tell for sure, but I'm pretty certain he was the first man into the room on that night. He doesn't have an arm in a sling, so at least he didn't get hurt.

'It's quiet,' I say.

'We shipped out all the pricks.'

He puts a big paw on my shoulder before we go into the room. 'Most of them, that is. Any funny business in there and you are jam. You understand?'

I look into unforgiving eyes and nod.

He opens the door and I walk in. I sit in the seat to which I'm directed. My big friend and one of his equally helpful-looking companions sit directly behind me. I feel their boots rest on the back legs of my chair as I sit down and push my seat under the table in front of me. That way, if I lose my temper I can't leap out of it since it won't go backwards. They will just smash my face into the table if I try to stand. I doubt they'll need much of an excuse to do that. His words hit home though. I could be transferred anywhere in the country. I can't get Nadia to answer the phone at the moment, so she's unlikely to bring my kids to Manchester or Newcastle.

It's the elderly deputy governor who's running this investigation. He involuntarily grimaces when he sees my black eye and puce jaw. I've heard he's a pragmatic man, and that's the best I could hope for.

'Ben Jones, confirm your prison number for me.'

'A4711AK.'

They read me the charge. It sounds reasonable.

'We are here today to ascertain what happened that night. You have been charged with "barricading" at this point. However, we acknowledge that there were mistakes made on both sides.'

'I would like to take legal advice.'

The deputy governor looks at me in annoyance. I have the right to ask for that. It will slow the whole thing down for weeks. He knows I understand the system now and could spin this out for a long time. They'll be under pressure from way on high to clean this up, or make it go away.

'Will Senior Officer Cave be here for this investigation?' I add.

The man puts down his pen. 'Mr Jones, you are on remand here. Is that correct?'

'Yes, sir.' He likes that.

'What is it you want, that will enable you to co-operate?'

'I want these charges dropped and for me to remain here until my trial.'

'And then we will have your full co-operation?'

'Yes, sir.'

He smiles. He knows he has a hook. Prisoners will complain to the heavens about the conditions in their local jail but they will rarely want to leave that place. Better the devils you know than the gangs you don't. Most prisoners' families can barely summon the energy to get on the bus for a visit. The chance of them paying fifty quid for a train ride is virtually non-existent. I've known inmates hide razor blades in their mouths and then cut their own faces to bits in the prison transfer van. They know the transport staff won't take them in that condition, so they get brought back into the prison. I also know he hasn't agreed to anything yet. The wily old fox leans in.

'So tell me what happened that day. In your own words.'

I give him a confident look.

'I was visiting Donny in his cell. He's an old friend of Jake's and mine. He went mad. It was clear he had taken a load of drugs and he set up the barricade. He wouldn't let us leave.'

Confusion flares on the governor's face. I feel myself being pushed into the table by the pressure on the chair legs from behind me.

'I thought he was the hostage?'

'No. We told Mr Cave we wanted to leave. He ignored it and said we were going to die.'

'So why did you fight?'

'Someone comes in your cell to attack you, you fight. This is a prison. It's what you do, you know that.'

He bridges his hands and ponders the information. I press home my advantage.

'Obviously, if you ask Donny he'll tell you himself. He's an honest man like that. I wouldn't ask Mr Cave. I mean, he lied to you, and look what he did to me.'

He is about to explain to me that Donny has died when he

realises I know that already. He looks at me for a few long seconds with an air of exhaustion.

'That will be all, Mr Jones. Escort this gentleman back to Healthcare.'

You're so sly, but so am I.

50

30TH SEPTEMBER 2014

I look at my watch in anger. It's half six in the evening, so there are only ten minutes of association left. I've been queuing to use the phones for over an hour. A note was put under my door with a pin and phone number to ring tonight at six. It has to be Radic. I haven't got hold of him or Nadia yet and it's driving me insane. It's been over four weeks now. I've written letters, but what else can I do? They sent me my date to plead at Crown Court; however, I'm unlikely to be sentenced before Christmas. So I'm stuck in limbo for months. Money is arriving in my account each week so I'm not short of anything, but the only person I can ring is my mother and she seems to work every hour God sends. Typically, tonight there are only two phones working on the wing. There have already been two fights. I can sense another one brewing.

The wing officer stands next to me and shouts, 'Last call phones and last call water!'

I'm next in line and the guy in front miraculously finishes his call.

'Time's up,' the officer says.

I look at his name badge. Paul Ellis, it says. He doesn't look like a prison officer, more some kind of free-spirited hippy with longish wavy black hair.

'Paul,' I say. 'Please, I have to make this call.'

'Two minutes, then.'

I am so surprised and thankful I almost cry. Radic picks up on the first ring.

'Cutting it fine, aren't we?'

'You don't want to know.' I don't have time to waste on small talk. The rules are no names, no detail. He will know what I want.

'I've heard nothing from her. I need to see them and her. What's going on?'

'She is a cold fish. You know this. I will have a word.'

'Get her here, please.'

'I will. How is it apart from that?'

'Fine, peachy.'

'Excellent. It doesn't look too good at this point. There isn't much to say, I'm sorry, Ben.' Radic never avoided bad news.

'What happened at the meet?'

'It's all sorted.'

'Is everyone OK?'

There's a pause. I hear, 'Behind your doors, gentleman. Time's up. Off those phones now.'

'No, there were losses.'

'Who?'

'Now is not the time.'

I strain my mind for what he will know.

'Beaker, Bert, Ernie?'

'All gone.'

'Tom and Jerry?'

'OK, mostly.'

'J?'

'No.'

'My little helper?'

There is another pause.

'No.'

'Have the issues been resolved?'

Another stretch of silence. The longest yet.

'It is sorted, yes.'

Officer Ellis reaches over and takes the receiver out of my hand. I was dropping it anyway. He flinches at the look I give him but says, 'Bang up, mate.'

I stumble back to my cell in a trance.

51

15TH DECEMBER 2014

I wake up knowing I am in prison. I've been here nearly four months now and it's no longer a surprise. At the start they were some of the worst moments, the time between sleeping and waking. Then the sounds and smells of my predicament would creep into my awareness and I would experience the sinking feeling all over again. A terrible start to a new day.

This morning I also woke to the sound of a slight gasp. I look down from my top bunk and watch him do it again. He slides the razor blade across the top of his thigh and I see a red line appear, almost as if he's drawn it with a felt-tip pen. It's the first time he's done it for at least a week. I watch him slide the blade back in an old tobacco box he has just for this very purpose. He reaches over to some tissues and then holds them on the wound like a dressing. The tops of his scrawny legs are a patchwork of fine white scars with the occasional recent red one. I watch him pull on his jeans, holding the 'bandage' in place, and then he turns to look at me, as he always does, to see if I'm awake. Our eyes meet as they often do.

'Bad night?' I ask.

'Yes, terrible. I haven't slept at all.'

'Feel better now?'

'Yes, thank you. I'll get your breakfast for you, so you can see the officers and try to get your children sorted.'

'Cheers, Chris. I don't hold much hope. This place is so disorganised, it's no wonder we kick off.'

I have a visit on Wednesday. Nadia, the bitch, is finally coming in to see me. Reading between the lines, Radic forced her. I am still more than a little stunned that she hasn't written or sent in money, never mind not coming to see me. Maybe there is an explanation, but I can't think of one. She's bringing the kids too, for which I should be grateful. It's not unusual for women to refuse to bring a con's children into the jail, especially if they are young. It isn't a nice experience. They obviously need to be searched, as many scumbags in here have taken the opportunity to smuggle drugs into the visit hall via a pocket on their child's coat, or in the folds of the baby carrier. Even hidden in a dirty nappy is not unusual.

My problem is I didn't know the children need to be registered on the system too, or they won't admit them. There's no way I can use the conventional route and rely on the paperwork to be done. There is zero chance of that happening in time. So, I need to get an officer to say he'll do it. No easy task.

More importantly, I need to find one who will actually follow through with what he's agreed. Some will say they'll do it just to get you off their backs. We are on the remand wing, so it is mad busy with inmates demanding their rights, often with the caveat 'I'm not even supposed to be here'. Everyone feels hard done by as we are still innocent until proven otherwise. To be fair to our legal system, in my experience, we don't lock up many people who aren't guilty, but you use whatever weapons you have.

Chris is on remand too. He's been telling everyone he is in for fraud, but I know otherwise. If you spend enough time in places like this, you kind of know. To use Jake's little game, you have a 'paedodar'. Apparently, he never self-harmed prior to being sent to prison, he is just under phenomenal stress. To maintain a lie in these conditions must be tough. He's been here the same time as me and says it's the only way he can cope. It gives him a release. Funny, what you get used to. Him doing it, me watching, and neither of us thinking it unusual.

They put us in a cell together after we left Healthcare. He collapsed at court as they sent him here. He was saying he had angina or something, but I think he just wanted to stay out of main circulation. They are wise to that old game. He was so scared when he came on the wing that I felt sorry for him. I waited for him to be away at a doctor's appointment one day after we arrived and went through his legal paperwork. As I suspected. Index Offence: Making indecent images of children.

It had been a few days by that point and I had found him an intelligent man who loved to chat about the news and, more importantly, business. He's middle-aged, I think, but it's often hard to tell here. Six months on remand for a serious offence can easily put ten years on you. He's run numerous companies of his own and is a rich vein of information. Crucially, he doesn't snore. So I failed to mention what I'd found out about his offence. That may seem cold or even wrong, but, as I said previously, prison is a strange place. I don't judge people by their offences. We are all broken. How is that offence worse than murder, or rape, or burgling old people while they lie in their beds above, too scared to move? Or selling the drugs that ruin so many lives? They are all terrible. The finality of murder has to be the worst. No amount of therapy will bring Leo back.

Paedophilia seems to be a sickness. I can't imagine anyone would choose to fancy children and they seem to know it's wrong but are unable to control their urges. Sending them to prison won't cure them, it just stops them getting anywhere near any more children. I can't think of anything more dangerous than a man like this after he's been released from a long stretch. All of us in here had choices, we just chose poorly. Anyway, in a sick way he's good for my mental health. When my course books arrived we would spend hours chatting over them and it is perhaps the only thing that has kept me sane. Besides, who knows? He may even be innocent.

For Chris, though, it's only a matter of time. I won't be the only one who's noticed. This is a remand wing, so the population ebbs and flows. It may take a while. They will watch first and see who he's with. The fact he shares a cell with me will stop many, but not all. It will be a bad reflection on me, but I don't care. Very few look me in the eye here. They know who I am.

Our cell door is opened and I sprint to the office. There is already a big queue and I curse under my breath. They only do queries in the morning, or they would be doing them all day. It's the hippy officer, Paul, who let me use the phone that night, who is on duty. That is a good thing as at least he will do what he says. You shouldn't have to rely on the professionalism of someone else to be able to live your life, but that's the way it is here.

Eventually, I'm next in line. I tune into the conversation in front of me.

'Where are my bloody trainers?'

'When did you order them?'

'Two months ago.'

'That's how long it takes here.'

'Un-fucking acceptable. I've had enough. I want them today.'

'This isn't Argos.'

'Fuck you.'

'Nice. After your kind encouraging words, I'll be sure to look into it for you, as soon as possible.'

'You're all the same; no one gives a shit here.'

'Correct, I don't care.'

'You'll fucking care when I smash the wing to pieces.'

I can see people waiting at the gate for exercise. Time is almost up.

'That's enough. He said he'll look into it, now leave.' It comes out louder than I expect, but I do need him to get the message. The 'leave' is drawn out, long and low.

He's a little rat of a bloke with broken blood vessels peppering his nose. He turns round to kick off and finds a man on the edge. His gaze reaches my eyes and is then dropped. He doesn't want any of that, he just wants his trainers.

He turns to the officer, growls, 'Prick,' at him, and sidles past me like the weasel he is.

Paul looks tired. His shift only started twenty minutes ago, and he has already had ten full-on shout-in-your-face arguments. No wonder his hair is curly.

'Paul. I know you're busy, but I'm desperate. Please can you help me?'

He's coming out of the office so I back up. The three people behind me in the queue start cursing. I silence them with a look.

'What is it?'

'My kids are coming in to visit me in two days and I need them adding on the system. You know it won't get done if I follow the official route.'

'Is it all written down?'

I hand him the form with a big beaming smile. 'Thank you, Paul. You are a star.'

He bellows, 'Exercise to the gate!' down the wing, then turns to me.

'You know what? You were the only one who said please.'

52

17TH DECEMBER 2014

I pull the orange netball bib on over my shirt and walk into the visit hall holding room. There are about twenty men in here and they all look as anxious as I am. An officer walks in with a list.

'Macstravick, Barton, Peacock, Buckingham, Lovett, Mansbridge.'

They all file out. The lucky ones. One farts as he walks past me. He must be particularly nervous.

The officer turns to leave. An angry man gets to his feet.

'Gov, is my visit out there? I've been here ages.'

'Did I read your name out?'

'No.'

'No, then.'

'Jesus Christ, where are they? Fuck this, I'm not waiting.'

He throws off his bib and stomps to the exit door. He looks a tool as he obviously can't let himself out. It's hardly the officer's fault his visit hasn't shown, but it's the worst feeling in the world. I'm all keyed up for mine and I too would be devastated if they didn't show. Another officer comes in.

'Jones, Bates, Graham, Nowell.'

I leap out of my seat like a salmon.

As they open the door to the hall, my eyes frantically search them out.

'ID card.'

I hand it over.

'Desk thirty-three. Your hour starts now.'

I follow the numbers and they are there at the back... well, two of them. Nadia doesn't get up. Her make-up is so light-coloured and thick she looks like a geisha. She displays no emotion. Little Alex is squirming on her lap to get off. She eventually lets him go and he toddles over. I pick him up. He smells so wonderful that my vision blurs with happiness.

'Where's Dasha?'

'I was told to bring your children. I have done.'

There, the pleasure died.

I sit down opposite her. She hasn't bought anything for me from the shop. She is all business, like a funeral director. I know I will be buried now too.

'Why haven't you been to see me?'

'I do not want to come into a prison. I certainly do not want to bring my children into one.'

'Nobody does, but that's what being a family is about.'

'You will get a long time, Ben.'

'I know, but when I get out we'll be a family again.'

She doesn't even break stride to plunge the knife in. 'I'm seeing someone.'

'What? Who?'

'Does it matter?'

'Of course it fucking matters.'

'Mind your language, Jones. That's a warning.' A passing officer stares me down.

'A good man,' she snarls.

Alex begins to cry. He goes back to his mother.

'I've only been inside four months.'

'You could get ten years. Shall I wait for you? Would you wait for me?'

'Where's your loyalty?'

'Do not talk to me about loyalty. You left us with nothing. Who is paying the bills while you are in here? Who will look after us? Did you think about that while you were dealing your fucking drugs?'

'You knew exactly what was going on. You enjoyed the life.'

'Yes. Now the money has gone and so have you.'

'There's five grand in the current account, more in your own one.'

'That is all gone.'

'You are a treacherous snake.'

Her eyes harden as she leans in. 'This is how I survive.'

The look of murderous rage that twists my face finally causes hers to display some emotion other than disinterest. It is fear. She involuntarily puts her hand across our son's chest.

'I won't be in jail forever, Nadia.'

Threats never worked with her. I regret it as soon as I say it.

'I will be long gone. Be a man. Face your reality.'

She stands up and shouts, 'Officer, I am ready!'

* * *

The walk back to my cell is an awful one. How I didn't lash out in frustrated fury at one of the staff I will never know. Now the adrenalin has left me, my legs feel dead and heavy. I barely have strength to lift them. I've lost the son I only recently found and there is nothing I can do about it. There is truth, though, in what she said. Delivered with a sledgehammer, of course, but that has always been her way. I shouldn't be surprised. I gave up the right to be a good father when I broke the law. Do I really want him growing up and thinking it's normal to visit your dad in jail every week? Would I have been faithful to Nadia if she had gone to jail? My life is a mess. Only I can be responsible.

I make a pact with myself there and then. No more crime. I am at rock bottom. It cannot get any worse. I will climb out of the depths I've dug for myself. Whatever time I receive will be spent productively. I will breeze that course and learn everything I can from anyone I meet. Then, when I'm free, I will build something that can't be taken from me.

* * *

The officer called Paul lets me back on the wing.

'Good visit?'

'Yes, great. Thank you.' I don't want sympathy.

It's association and I have to walk past the pool tables and laughing idiots to get to my cell. I wish Jake were waiting for me. His life was so chaotic that he made me feel normal. Instead, I feel very alone. No one has written, except my mother. I've made friends in here all the times I have been sent down and even a few on this sentence. They all promise to write but no one ever does. I guess you want to forget this place as soon as you've left it. You would write though, if you could remember the crushing boredom and hopelessness that fills your hours. Maybe if you didn't forget, then the deterrent would be forefront in your mind when you next went out to break the law.

Any kind of letter would be welcome. A letter from an ex-con is such a rarity, but it gives you a glimpse of a different future. Perhaps they don't write as they have nothing good to say. 'Hi, guys. I'm homeless again and having to sleep on my mum's kitchen floor.

We're all back on the drugs again. I feel really down. See you soon, Paddy.'

I approach my cell and note the door is open. That is unusual. Chris is paranoid about getting anything stolen, for obvious reasons, so always keeps the door shut. There's a lad next to the door looking shifty. I realise immediately he's a lookout. He spots me too late to warn whoever is in the cell but is quick to disappear himself when he sees the instant anger on my face.

I stand in the doorway and look down at an unpleasant scene. Chris is lying on the floor, unconscious by the looks of it, but there's so much blood on his face it's hard to tell. The guy astride him is still hitting him though. There is paperwork everywhere. That's how they tell. They come in and demand to see your court documents. If you refuse, you're a wrong 'un anyway. My folder, with all my coursework, is scattered everywhere too. Some of my papers have fallen in the bog.

'I think he's had enough, don't you?'

The man turns round with a start. It's the weasel from the office two days ago. He gestures at the bloody pulp.

'He's a kiddy fiddler,' he pants.

I smile and so does he. I point at the mess he's made.

'That's my homework in the toilet.'

The grin slips from his face like a blind that is gently closed.

Just one more crime.

53

20TH MARCH 2015

It's late by the time I get back to my cell. The wing is locked down and for that I'm grateful. It has been a long couple of days at court. It was a long time waiting for today to arrive too, but I'm now a convicted drug dealer. That is a depressing fact, but it's a relief to know my fate and for it to be over.

Radic's solicitor did a brilliant job. He was up against it. Not only the offence itself, but the aggravating factor of my attempted escape. I didn't even think about that. I was caught with a lot of product and then drove like a dangerous lunatic trying to prevent myself from being arrested. However, he made me sound like a poor wretch from a broken home. He got my old probation worker to talk in my defence and testify to my generally being a good person. I'm glad I didn't tell my mother when the trial was. Her dirty linen was aired too. The only person I knew in the public gallery was Karolina, who came every day. She was the spy who would report back to Radic.

I wondered whether Jake would get pulled into it under some kind of conspiracy link, but my solicitor said they were happy to just leave him in jail. Apparently, an eye witness said the policeman had punched Jake repeatedly, so it was best to let that one drop. Besides, the beauty for the police of someone being on licence is that anything like this triggers an immediate recall to prison and, due to its seriousness, the individual will serve the full sentence. The state doesn't even have to bother with a trial. Poor old Jake, who still had a year to go, will serve, give or take a few weeks, two years of a two-year sentence. Two whole years of what should be the best time of your life.

As for me, I thought for a few blessed seconds I was going to get released. 'While it's evident that you've had a hard start to life, you have not helped yourself. However, it cannot be easy growing up in that environment and you are, by all accounts, a decent human being. While I don't for one minute think you are the ringleader in this and, in all probability, played a minor part, we are still talking about class A drugs. The scourge of society. I see the damage they cause every day. Any credit to be awarded for an early guilty plea is also diminished due to you declining to name any other parties to assist the police in their enquiries. You have, though, saved the state considerable time and money. Therefore, you are hereby sentenced to three years. Take him down.'

There's some post on my cell floor, which I pick up as I enter. I turn round to the officer, wondering why he hasn't locked the door. I've got to know Officer Fletcher quite well over the last six months.

'How long did you get?' he asks.

'Three years.'

'Not too bad.'

'No. Although your life has definitely gone off the rails if you're happy with that.'

'Better than ten, mind.'

'Yes, better than ten.' I finally smile.

'You've done six months on remand, haven't you?'

'Yes, so I only have a year to serve.'

'That'll fly by. So I don't need to tell the night officer to look in on you?'

'No. This is the start of the new me.'

'Excellent. I'll see you tomorrow.'

He shuts the door and I look at the four walls surrounding me. I sear the moment on my brain. The last time.

I lie back on my bed. I have a single cell now. I thumped the weasel straight in the mouth after that visit back then. Bad timing from him as the blow had a lot of history in it. I had to remove a tooth from my knuckle afterwards. That got me a week in the block. It was fine. I got my head together. I got my own cell afterwards as none of us talked about either beating, and they weren't sure what happened. They can't double me up now, in case I kill my pad-mate over an argument about whether we watch *Homes Under the Hammer* or *Jerry Springer*. I sometimes see Chris on the nonce wing, queuing for his dinner. I heard he got fourteen years. Rape of a child under thirteen. So, he was guilty, and some. He hid that paperwork better than I thought. He doesn't wave.

The post is a postcard from Portugal. It's from my mother. They've gone on holiday to the Algarve, her and the neighbour. I'm beginning to think they are more than friends. I'll save it for later, read it slowly, but I look at the bottom of the card and laugh.

Wish you were here.

54

Time is passing. I'm doing more Maths and English exams and at night I read my business studies book to death. My mum sends mechanic manuals in although I have no idea where she gets them from. I keep busy to stop any dark thoughts from gathering. I'm an enhanced prisoner now, on an enhanced wing. It's calmer and I keep my head down. I often think of Alex and tonight have a chance to find out more. A foreign guy has come to our wing gates and given me a mobile number. It can only be Radic. There are two mobile phones on the wing at the moment so I will take the risk to ring him tonight. It's a big danger as I have heard they're now prosecuting anyone caught with a phone and looking to give them an extra six months. I have to know though. I also have to tell him my plans. A conversation I am not looking forward to.

I sit on my bed after bang up and wait.

Ten minutes later, roll count is finished. Now is a good time to ring as it's shift handover and the night staff won't be wandering around with mobile-phone detectors.

'Tak.'

'It's me.'

'Excellent. How are you?'

'Good. Not too long now.'

'I have news for you.'

'Yes.'

'Nadia moved away, not long after her visit. It took me a long time to find her. She is in London, in Richmond. He is rich, and old. They have a nanny. The children look happy.'

'OK.'

'This is not the best news, but it is good news. You were never suited to her. She has ice in her blood. Dasha's father went to jail too. For a long time. Nadia also left him in the same way.'

'OK.'

'Don't worry about it now. When you get out we can, uh, look into things. I have had someone speak to him. It was made clear. He will look after them as if they were his own.'

Let us hope he's not too old, or that conversation will have hastened his end.

'Look, Radic. I've had a lot of time to think. I'm only twenty-two and I've been to prison three times. I don't want to end up a lifer. That's enough. When I'm released, I want out. No involvement at all.'

'I always said you can get out. Run the garage, it will be fine.'

'No, completely out. I'm going to move away. Make a fresh start. I'm sorry, but that's the way it has to be.'

He always liked his pauses on the phone. This is a long one.

'OK, Ben. I understand. I, too, would like sometimes to leave.'

'Take care.'

'I do want you to know that when you went away, I paid for everything for her and the children. Nadia was looked after. They wanted for nothing.'

'Thank you.'

Bitch. She had my money and his. Again, I'm not surprised.

'Say goodbye to Karolina for me too.'

When I look back and remember the conversation we had about missed opportunities, she's the one I will rue.

'Of course. Good luck.'

The phone is dead, but I feel alive. I'm a hot-air balloon, tethered to the ground. Radic was a rope to be snipped, Nadia was another.

My lack of education and freedom is all that is holding me down. I will cut them myself. As for the rest, will I be able to forget?

55

4TH NOVEMBER 2015

I relax on my bed and open my mother's letter. I'm tired, but in a good way. The best paying job in the prison is a red band. These are trusted positions where you empty bins and help out where needed. I've taken one as you earn around thirty pounds a week. I try to save as much as possible although I've been going to the gym, and it's almost impossible to get enough protein to bulk up. I spend half my wages on protein shakes and tuna from the canteen, but it's never enough.

Dinner is a waste of time for that. There must be some poorly chickens round here, judging by how little meat there is on their legs. I don't want to have to rely on anyone when I get out though, so I put away ten pounds a week. It's not much, but it helps. I am twitchy already. It's a common thing if you have done some reasonable stir and you're getting out soon. You count in years first, then months. I am on weeks now, with about sixteen left. It won't be long and I will count the days.

Dear Benny,
    I hope you are well and got the paper I sent in. This is only

going to be a quick letter but I have some dramatic news. I actually have two bits. One is new and one, I guess, is old. The latter concerns your father but it is not something I can tell you in a letter. I am free for a visit a week on Sunday, so book me in and I will definitely explain. It is something I should have told you a long time ago, but I didn't know how to. It's a long story and let's just say you aren't the first Jones to end up in prison.

The second bit is exciting and scary. Perhaps you had better sit down. I hope you don't think I'm abandoning you, but I'm moving to Portugal, to the Algarve. It's where Ana is from. We've saved some money and are going to take our cleaning company over there, to do people's apartments and holiday homes. She says there is 'big business' and we'll be able to converse with them in most languages. . I went to check it out and loved it. Things will be tight, but I think we'll be fine. It's a new start for me. I'm sure you can understand me wanting that. Somewhere with no bad memories and the sun will help.

We will be going in January. She wanted to go now, but I wanted to carry on visiting you until the new year as you'll be out shortly afterwards. Please don't think I am deserting you as I'm not. Come and stay with us when you get out. You can join us in the business. Ana has already said she would be more than happy with a strong man to help with the lifting. Or you can do your own work, they have cars there too, you know.

Anyway, I wanted to tell you before I come so you could prepare any questions for when I'm there.

Lastly, I cleared the few remaining bits out of your room. There was a Fyffes bananas cardboard box full of stuff. Your friend dropped round, so I've given it to him for when you get out. It's mostly just odds and ends. Your birth certificate is in there too, along with some photographs from years ago that I had forgotten about. He gave me some money. I tried to say no, *but he insisted. I'll put some in your prison account. The odd envelope gets put through the door with money in it too. It must have been him.*

    All my love,

    Mum.

It's lucky I'm lying down as it's surprising news. Brilliant news for her, but I can't escape the fog of desertion that has descended. My disorderly life has meant I'm doing poorly for friends: a motley collection of drug dealers and drug addicts, neither of which are any use to a rehabilitated man like myself. My teetotal mother was the star attraction. I planned to go back and live with her until I got on my feet. I can't help feeling proud of her though. She deserves it. I'm a survivor. I will be fine.

It was good of Jake to go round and see my mum. I'm surprised he gave her money. He must be up to no good. Long may it continue, or he will either sell or smoke my belongings. What the hell is this about my dad too? It will be a long few days until I see her. There's no way I'll be able to sleep now. I get off the bed and turn the television on, but I'm not watching it.

56

15TH NOVEMBER 2015

My mum is sitting at the table. She looks both nervous and happy this time. I've had a nagging worry since I read the letter. I have been carrying the news around with me like a cape made of lead, dragging all the enthusiasm and energy from me. One of my fellow red bands described me as being like a 'rat with a sore arse'. No amount of work or exercise has let me forget it. I'm not sure why either. I can hardly be judgemental about my dad having gone to prison, but I can't help thinking there's something else she wants to tell me.

She's been to the counter and got some of the cakes they make in the prison. They're actually made by the female cons on their side of the jail in an NVQ training kitchen. The cakes are wonderful and a glimpse of the outside world. My mum asked whether I thought they would spit in them. That made me laugh out loud, especially considering if they had I would most likely still eat them.

'How are you?' she asks.

'Good. Keeping busy.'

'Not long now.'

'No. A hundred days or so.'

We smile at each other, understanding the need for small talk before we unveil the dad-faced elephant in the room.

'So, your dad. It's probably best if I just keep talking and you stop me if you want to ask anything.'

'OK, good idea.'

We take a deep breath.

'Around 1991 he was involved in a road accident. He was driving and he'd been drinking. I don't know if he was drunk or not but it doesn't matter because he hit a girl pushing her pram. She was more or less fine afterwards. Well, a broken leg, I think. Her son was only one. Tragically, he was instantly killed. Your father came from a small community in Ireland. A place called Kilrane, in County Wexford. It's near Rosslare Harbour. The woman only lived round the corner from him and his family. Everyone knew.

'He went to court and got five years. He came out after two and a half with nowhere to go. He was ostracised by everyone and felt he couldn't even walk the streets where he grew up without people judging him. It wouldn't end, as he was guilty of something no one could forget. So he moved to England and eventually found his way to Peterborough and me in 1994.'

She stops talking and looks at me, waiting. I'm eating the cake but I can't taste it. What's she waiting for? What am I missing? Then it hits me.

'But I was born in 1993.'

'That's right.'

The last piece of cake actually falls out of my mouth.

'What?' is all I can manage.

She has tears in her eyes now, but takes another deep breath.

'I was very young when I had you. Younger than you are now. It was rape, I suppose. I didn't really see it as that at the time. He forced himself on me, but we'd been fooling around. I'd been kissing him and he would say I led him on. I should've been more determined in stopping him. He was a strong man though, your father. Your real father. He had a temper too. Anyway, he disappeared, went into the forces, and I never heard from him again. I didn't know what to do with the baby. You, that is, and even considered, you know. I had no support or family and lost my job in the pub where I was working. Keeping you was the best decision I've ever made though. You have made my life worth living.'

She reaches over and holds my hand.

'When your dad came on the scene I was really struggling. I'd just moved into our flat on benefits and begun to drink heavily. Your dad was down the pub on one of the few nights I went out after a neighbour babysat for me. I fell for him instantly. He was the world's most loveable rogue. I'm not sure what he saw in me. I couldn't believe my luck when he asked to move in and wanted to marry me. It's most single mothers' dream. He was brilliant with you, and Jonty. We all loved him.

'He had his demons though. It was quite a while later that he told me about his past. I hope he loved us as well, but I think he saw it as his penance. We were on our own and needed help, and he provided it. He had a roving eye all right, but he treated us brilliantly and raised you as his own. For a while we just socially drank together at home. I didn't want to go out as I had everything I wanted in the flat. My drinking got worse as the years slid by. He began to stay out, kept saying he was working late, but we never had any money, so how could he have been? I should've done something about it a long time ago, but I was too scared. I didn't want you to lose him either.'

My mouth is still open. I pick up the cake that I dropped somewhere during her delivery. I look at the young inmate at the next table. It's clearly his dad visiting as they look just like each other. No wonder I didn't look like him. Like Patrick. Does that make him

Patrick, or does the fact he was my father for all those years mean he's earned the right to be called my dad?

'Say something, Benny. Are you angry?'

Numb would best describe how I feel. That's a lot to take in, especially in one go. It does beg the million-dollar question. 'So who is, was, my actual father?'

'He was a lad I met in the pub. I didn't know him that well and don't even know if he's alive or where he lives now. I can understand you wanting to know. It brought it to a head when I found your birth certificate. His name is on there.'

'Who is it?'

'It's Darren Connor.'

57

1ST DECEMBER 2015

To say the next few weeks were weird was a massive understatement. It felt as though the world was a large grey balloon and I was on the outside, gently chafing on the surface. Looking in, but not participating. I must have been in shock. I certainly couldn't get my head round it all. Look at the father figures in my life. Patrick, Darren, and Radic. A womanising, baby-killing alcoholic, a psychopathic maniac and a ruthless drug dealer. Incredible. And I thought Jake never stood a chance. What did Radic say after the meet with Darren? 'It's sorted.' If I hadn't been arrested I could have been unknowingly shooting at my biological father. What did Radic say? 'It's sorted.' What does that mean? Is he dead? Do I care?

I have to convince myself it doesn't matter. I must believe I'm in control. Otherwise, I might as well top myself to save the world from the damage I will inevitably cause. That's why I'm in a place called 'the link' today. I've been in the gym playing doubles badminton, of all things. I liked it. The guy I was playing with is in for running a cannabis farm. Manufacture and distribution (us) were victorious over the team from acquisitions (two burglars).

'Yes?'

'I have an appointment.'

'Who with?'

'I don't know. It says resettlement.'

He checks his list. 'You're here to see Richard Graze. He's in the corner.'

I walk into the room and cannot help but think that it's like trying to get into a posh nightclub. However, as soon as I get inside I can feel a different atmosphere. An officer in the corner on the phone, aged about fifty, mouths 'two minutes' to me. I sit down on a comfortable clean seat to wait.

The prisoners in here are laughing and joking with the staff. There's a steady stream of relaxed inmates going in and out of rooms with civilians. It feels like I'm in a library. Not a prison library either, as nobody seems to be dealing drugs.

'Ben, sorry about the wait.'

'No worries. That's all right.'

'Come into my office.'

I sit down next to his computer and think for a minute he's going to offer me a coffee. He doesn't though.

'What happens in here?'

'The link? All the outside agencies come in here to help. Drug workers, foreign national helpers, family welfare, that sort of thing.' He smiles and continues. 'You asked to see me. How can I help?'

'I'm out soon and have nowhere to live.'

'No parents or friends?'

'No.'

'Why not? Where were you living before you came in?'

'I lived with my partner but we broke up. My mum is moving abroad before I get out and everyone else I know is either a criminal or a drug addict. Or both.'

'Right. That's a common problem. If you go back to the same

environment that brought you here, with the same people, you don't need to be a genius to see the outcome.'

'Exactly, I want a fresh start.'

'How old are you?'

'Twenty-two.'

'Right, the good news is that for youngsters like you, there are some charities in the area. There's a shared house in St Ives. There's also a new one in Cambridge.'

I think of Jake. It must be the same one he was in. That one didn't work out so well for him. Cambridge sounds good. I don't know anyone there.

'How much are they?'

'We get you in and then housing benefit is paid directly to them. There's just a weekly charge of about a tenner. You pay that out of your Job Seeker's Allowance.'

'How long can I stay for?'

'Generally, not longer than six months. You should be able to get on your feet in that time. I know it all sounds daunting, but they have a support worker who will help you look for work and take you to appointments if necessary.'

'That sounds great.' Too good to be true. 'Can I say yes now?'

He laughs. 'It's not quite that easy. I'll book you another appointment. There's a form to fill in. There's strictly no drugs or alcohol in these places.'

'That's fine. I was delivering it as opposed to partaking.'

He gives me a funny look.

'I don't think they'd like that either.'

I smile as I shake his hand. It's been like an appointment at the bank. Very professional and, more importantly, I can see the first chink of dawn for my new life.

* * *

When I arrive back at the wing, I still feel optimistic. The officer lets me on with a rueful smile.

'Where is everyone?'

'Banged up. We're spinning the whole wing.'

Cell spins are cell searches. Intel states there is something on the wing and your cell is combed through.

'You're next, I'm afraid. In fact, you're last.'

I look at him, unsure whether he thinks what they're searching for can only be in my cell as they haven't found it yet.

'My cell is clean.'

'Yes. Just routine.'

I stand in my small cell and nod to give them permission to search my legal documents and religious items, despite not having any of the latter. I remove my clothes for the inevitable strip search. The tears are coming. It's not the humiliation of two grown men in uniforms, wearing medical gloves, staring at your privates, as I'm well used to that. One of them takes me inside the cell next door to mine.

'Wait in here. We'll only be ten minutes.'

I choke back the lump in my throat, just nodding again as I'm scared what sound I will make if I try to talk.

A guy called Eric was transferred back to London for local release yesterday. There isn't a single item in the whole room but it still smells strongly of the pipe tobacco he used to smoke as normal cigarettes. It's harsh stuff, but cheaper. Even the mattress is gone. No doubt someone is lying comfortably on two now, in one of the other cells.

I sit on the metal bed. As soon as the officer locks the door, I sob. Like a child denied its favourite toy. All the stored-up misery and misfortune that I've locked away has been released by a kind man, treating me like a human being and offering me hope.

58

My cell looks sparse to say the least. I have given everything away except my clothing. The bits of food I donated to new arrivals. My remote control, stereo, and games console to some close acquaintances. In here, they all have value and were appreciated. Don't think that prisoners are usually full of such altruistic actions. That was the way I had come by them, left by one of the lucky ones. They weren't on my property card anyway so I wouldn't have been able to take them away even if I wanted to. 'On the out,' as they say in jail when referring to being free, they have no value so people leave them behind. I bet some kids nowadays have never even seen a PlayStation 2.

It is a good feeling for most, though, when someone leaves. Time does go by, wherever you are, and this is a reminder we all get released at some point.

I've spent most of the afternoon in my cell, which is unusual for a Sunday. It's early bang-up tonight so thirteen hours until you are unlocked again. Therefore, people are in no rush to spend any more time in their kennels than necessary. If there's anything more depressing than Sunday night television, I've yet to discover it. I've been kind of dozing and reading on my bed as the closer I come to release, the less sleep I manage.

A key clicks in the door. I assume I'm being locked in, even though it's a good ten minutes early, so don't even turn round.

'Ben.'

It's Richard, from Resettlement. He looks serious.

'Hi, I thought you were seeing me tomorrow to give me all the paperwork.' There is no stopping the dread that's rising up my body from the soles of my feet. Strangely, it's not dissimilar to when I first took crack. He already gave me the address of the place in Cambridge. I will get a travel warrant in the morning, so there's no need for him to see me today.

'I'm afraid I have bad news.'

'Go on.'

'I'm doing overtime today so had a chance to check my emails. The support worker for the house emailed me yesterday. Apparently, one of the other tenants set fire to his curtains. There's smoke damage throughout. It was lucky no one was hurt.'

'So what does that mean?'

'There won't be a room for you.'

'Anywhere?'

'No.'

'I leave tomorrow. So are you saying I'm homeless?'

'No, we have options.'

'Let me guess, I visit the council in the morning.'

'Yes, I'll ring them first thing for you.'

'I see. That's fantastic news.'

'I'm so sorry, Ben. I don't know what to say.'

'Me either.'

'I don't suppose you have any money?'

'Just over three hundred quid.'

'That'll help. You can pay a small deposit and it will give them more options. Go into town and have breakfast in the morning. That will give me time to ring them and they'll be ready for you. It's their job. They can help.'

I let out a deep breath and lie back down. 'I know it's not your fault. Thanks for telling me too. You didn't have to come over and do that, knowing it was not going to be a champagne moment for me. It's better I know now, so I can prepare myself for what lies ahead.'

There is a pause. Then the sound of someone leaving the cell and locking the door. Oddly enough, here I am warm and safe. The likelihood of me being so tomorrow night has just rapidly diminished.

PART IX

FINALLY FREE?

59

22ND FEBRUARY 2016

There are only two of us leaving today so the reception staff are in a good mood. I look over at the other man in the holding cell. He appears as enthusiastic as I feel. He's propped a window open for ventilation so he can smoke out of it. An illegal move but he doesn't look the law-abiding type. He only has a few drags and gives in because the already-cool temperature in the room plunges as the icy wind swirls in. All he has on is a thin sweater. He catches me looking over.

'Not a great day for it, is it?'

'No. Looks like it could snow.'

'Aye. It was summer when I first came away. Over five years ago. You would have thought I'd have had plenty of time to get a coat sorted.'

My leather bike jacket turned up here a while after the trial. There was no sign of the gloves and helmet, or the bike for that matter. I'm guessing the fact it wasn't insured or taxed would mean it was long crushed by now.

'Haven't they got any second-hand coats here they can let you have?'

'They said they'd look.'

As if on cue, an officer comes back, unlocks the door to the room where we wait, and passes a light-blue sports jacket to the man next to me. 'Here you go, Ian.'

As he tries it on, the officer leaves. I assume that means there isn't a selection of garments to choose from. It fits fine, perhaps a little short in the sleeve. It would be ideal for a summer evening as you strolled home from the pub. Not much use on a Baltic morning in mid-February.

As the officer goes out of sight, Ian hammers on the glass. 'I've got thicker fucking underwear than this.'

* * *

We step out of the prison together. There's a female officer based outside to help with travel warrants and phone calls. She's trying to explain something to a young girl who, judging by the possessions she is carrying in a plastic bag, has just been released from the female side of the jail.

'Where did he go?'

'I don't know. He just said he was going.'

'You said he could wait here.'

'Your father was drunk. I didn't have any choice.'

The girl breaks down and is helped to a seat. The officer looks over at us.

'Where are you two going?'

'Council,' I say.

'The off-licence,' Ian says.

Neither response is a surprise to her. 'Do you want a taxi? We pay for it.'

I just want to get going, so I decline. Ian explains the offie is only round the corner, so he doesn't need one either. I think we regret it when we stand outside. It's freezing and damp. A chilling blast whips any vestige of heat from us in seconds. We put down our heads and walk.

'Fancy a bevvie?'

'Bit early for me. You got anywhere to go?'

'Nope. I'm gonna get so drunk that I'm not going to know where am.'

We pass a man lying in the bushes. He doesn't seem to know where he is either. I briefly consider going back in to tell them but don't. It's just gone 9 a.m. and it's grey and gloomy. The prison hangs over us in the background like an evil watching presence. If I had somewhere to go to, I would run.

There's only one vehicle parked in the visitors' car park, a dark-blue Ford S-Max people carrier. Its lights are on, but the windows are tinted and in the poor light I can't even see if anyone is inside. The horn sounds. We look round but don't break pace. It can't be for either of us. It sounds again. I turn to see the window coming down and see Radic leaning out with a smile. I stop and stare. Temptation looks back at me like a roaring open fire on a cold day. I'm stronger than this. I am about to turn round and continue walking when the rear passenger door opens.

Karolina is sitting on the first row of seats. Next to her is the Jyffes cardboard box. The one my mother mentioned she had put my things in. Did I really think that it was Jake who'd been looking out for my mother and going round to make sure everything was all right? I turn to look for Ian. A hand is raised, he turns, and continues on. He knows the score. As he reaches the other side of the car park, he's almost running. He has somewhere to go, I suppose. I wonder if the box or Radic are part of why I look back at Karolina and stride towards the vehicle. They're like a bonus.

I clamber in and sit next to her. She is the reason I would've come regardless.

Radic looks in the back and puts a cigar in his mouth.

'Do not even think about igniting that in here, you oaf,' Karolina snaps.

He looks at me, then smiles. A warm and genuine interaction I've been deprived of these last eighteen months. 'Can you believe pay for the English lessons that teach her such things?'

She gives me a serious stare. She looks the same; beautiful Turning to face the front, she adds, 'Let's just get out of here.'

As Radic puts the car in gear and we pull out of the car park Karolina reaches over and finds my hand. She squeezes it hard.

60

The drive back to Radic's is a slow one. It's almost as if he knew it would be alien to me. The normality though is lovely. I don't stop holding Karolina's hand until we pull up outside the gates to his house. It looks bigger than before, but that's probably because I'm used to a cell. Radic speaks into the intercom and we're permitted access.

'There are people waiting for you here.' Radic honks his horn as he talks.

The door opens and Sofiya, his wife, ushers out two children. I leave the car and walk slowly towards them. They've grown so much. Dasha runs towards me and throws herself at my legs.

'I missed you,' she says with a beaming smile. As though I've been away for the weekend.

Alex is more bashful.

'Go on, that's your dadda,' Sofiya says.

Emboldened by his sister's display of affection, he toddles over.

'Dadda?'

I almost drop Dasha as sobs wrack my body.

I kiss Sofiya on both cheeks, the way she likes.

'Welcome home.' She looks concerned.

Dasha shouts at us both. 'We're watching Thomas the Tank Engine. Come and watch too.'

My mind instantly thinks of Leo. I remember the promises I made to myself about living a different life. I think of his poem. Radic interrupts my train of thought.

'Come, Ben, into my study. We have much to discuss. Children, we'll be there soon, watch TV and then we'll have the late breakfast we promised. Coffee, please, Sofiya.'

I follow Radic further into the house and through some double doors while childish shouts of 'Yeah, sausages' echo around us. Tom and Jerry are waiting to greet me in what must be his study. Things have been tough. They've aged more than I have. There's something wrong with Tom's right eye, but the men seem upbeat. Maybe they are just pleased to be alive.

Radic has tried to make the room look like something he's seen on TV with books along one wall. I can see straight away they're new and unread, so it has more an air of Waterstones than somewhere cosy.

'Strange to be free?' Radic asks with a grin as we sit on the two sofas facing each other.

'Very.' I decide not to think about the future for one more day. 'I never thought my children would be here for my release.'

Radic doesn't flinch, but I see Jerry tense out of the corner of my eye.

'How did you manage that, then?' I ask.

'She moved back here. There was a car accident.'

'Really? The kids were safe?'

'Yes, they weren't there. With Nadia's mother at the time.'

'And Nadia?'

'Just her in the car when it happened.'

I can't help thinking revenge has been taken for the disloyalty she displayed. However, the fact she will always be the mother of my children quells any satisfaction I may have started to feel.

'So, she didn't make it?'

'No, somehow she got out. She survived. Very lucky apparently.'

This time Radic does look away. Not guilty, but responsible. He looks at the others, then back to me. 'Changed. She is changed.'

The other question that's screeching around my head, desperate for release, is what happened when Leo was killed? How did John and the others die? Did Radic murder my father or did he have no choice? 'Tell me about Leo and John.'

'We went to the brick pits to meet Darren to discuss lost shipments. I wasn't sure what would happen. He owed us so much money, but he was losing too. The thing with Igor was our fault. I thought we were clear to continue but everything was rotten. The police knew too much.'

'So there was a fight?'

Jerry laughs at that, and says one word. It sounds like 'diablo'. A bitter cry, while Tom shakes his head. Radic continues with a rueful look.

'A devil, is what he just said. We went prepared. This Darren was very dangerous. We knew that. It wasn't enough. He came with two friends but they were outnumbered. I don't think they knew what he'd involved them in. The gunfire started. He shot the three soldiers I had brought over, in less than a second. Bang, bang, bang. He hit John through the window of the pick-up, and Leo too, who was in the back. One shot for each, straight in their heads. He only had a pistol and was thirty metres away. Incredible really. I thought he would kill us all.'

'But you killed him.'

'No, actually. His friend shot him in the stomach. It was a nasty wound.'

'So he's dead?'

'I don't think so.'

'You don't think so? Surely you must know.'

'I deliberated long and hard as we drove away. As his life faded, he promised me he would get me my money. I know an old army surgeon who retired here after his family settled in the area. We took Darren there. I'd told him we might need his help. He was in a bad way with an infection afterwards but gradually looked like he would probably make it. He disappeared one night soon after, told the guard he would be back to sort things out. I worry a little. Is that a good or a bad thing? Maybe I should have killed him. There was so much money tied up with his operation though, and I thought I would have time to make a final decision.'

'Is big mistake.' Tom shakes his head.

'Why didn't your man stop him?'

'He was careless and his gun got in the wrong hands. He is lucky to live.'

I lean back in my seat. I'm not sure what to think about this news. There's a small but significant part that's pleased. These are also thoughts for another day.

'How long are the kids here for?'

'I don't know. Ask Nadia.'

'She's here?'

'Yes, in the garden.'

I stand up immediately. 'I should talk to her.'

The three of them say nothing. They look worried.

* * *

I find the way out to the back garden through some French windows. What the hell is she doing out here in the drizzle? I can see her on a bench next to a long hedge, staring into the distance. I'm nervous as I approach. She looks striking still. She's wearing her usual tight jeans and heels with a thin coat that can't be keeping her warm. I'm almost with her when she notices me and turns her head. Then, I see how she is changed.

Her nose has clearly been broken, but it is the right side of her face that shocks. There is a long livid scar that seems fresh. Sore-looking tissue glints in the rain. The hair is sparse there and her face droops at the mouth. I can't stop my eyes widening at the horror of it. A monster.

'Pretty, aren't I?'

What do you say to someone who trades on their looks and has lost their business? I sit next to her on the left so I don't have to look at her damaged features.

'Come inside. It's freezing out here.'

'The cold helps cool my pain.' She takes a deep breath. 'And my anger.'

'I'm sorry, Nadia. Thank you for bringing the children. It means a lot.'

'Do you think I could have said no?'

We sit in silence for a few minutes as I consider those words. All this time I believed I was in control, that Radic had given me choices, but I never knew the whole picture. So I was guided through those decisions, by him, like a parent with a child, a hand on each shoulder.

'Can anyone escape this life, once they become immersed in it?' I eventually say.

'This is your life, not mine. Just because you were inside, don't think you are innocent of what happened to me. My new partner left. Of course he did. Scared to death, so now I'm here on my own. With nothing.'

She is so furious she is shaking.

'The brakes failed on a new car I'd been bought. Less than six months old. The police said they are investigating as it must have been tampered with. What a joke. People will be paid off, no one will get justice.'

As she spits out each word, she stands, puts her ruined features next to my eye and whispers in my ear. 'He will suffer for what he has done to me.'

She stomps away, her heels plunging into the grass like the dagger I imagine she would love to wield. Stopping halfway to the house, she turns and smiles. It is an evil grin. In the mist, she's become the two people she always was, both inside and out. 'And so will you, Ben. So will you.'

AUTHOR'S NOTE

The inspiration for this book came from the many teenagers and youngsters in their early twenties I met when I worked in the prison system. The young are often some of the more depressed and angry members of prison society. It's easy to judge them as law-breakers and accept that they are in the right place. However, many of them are simply doomed to fail. A toxic environment and poor or non-existent parenting often means jail is inevitable.

Once someone has been in the police and prison system, it's hard to keep out of it. Impressionable teenagers aren't going to learn valuable life lessons from career criminals in adult jails, but that's where they often go when they are first sentenced. If they are remanded, it's often where they will remain until their trial. This could be as long as a year. A further descent into criminality can be almost unavoidable. Easily impressed, they can be exploited and a pattern is set for the rest of their lives.

When they are released they often do not have the skills, knowledge, support or finances to climb out of the hole they've found themselves in. We expect the most from the people who have the least. Who would you rely on if you went to jail? Who would help when you got out?

They become careless, chaotic and have no expectation of any kind of settled future. They are a burden on society and there seems to be little appetite to deal with these issues. There are many who work tirelessly with young people and try to get them back on track, often without being paid, but it's hard work and often unsuccessful.

Ironically, to paraphrase *The Shawshank Redemption*, a life without hope is a terrible thing. Many of these issues are brought up in *Lifer*, but it's also a book about persistence, determination and luck. In some ways, it is also a modern love story. Some do escape the clutches of the prison system. Will Ben be one of them? For others the unpleasant thought is whether it's too late to save them. Would our money be better spent focusing on the very young? Those who still have a chance.

As for the answers, personally I don't think anyone is beyond saving, but the financial cost in fulfilling that statement would be vast. I hope to have changed some of your perceptions of the young adults who end up in prison, but after reading this novel there is one thing I can be sure of. You will never want to go there yourself.

ACKNOWLEDGMENTS

I would like to thank, in no particular order, Yvette Smart, Nicola Holmes, Kev Duke, Alex Knell, Rachel Brightey, Mark Blackburn, Kate Symonds, Louise Holmes, Emma De Oliveira, Jo Curtis, Jamie Jones, Steve Mansbridge, Barry Butler, Jono Hill, Sharyn Rutterford, Richard Burke and, of course, Amanda Rayner. You all played a part! Alex Williams, yours was a big one. Paul Lautman has also been a great help.

There also needs to be a special mention of the Bloodhound Books gang. To be in such a team is one of the best parts of this experience.

Someone once told me writing a book is like raising a child. Creation is the easy part. It's the years of tweaking and correcting that matter. That's where the hard work begins. Eventually, though, you have to release them into what can be a harsh world. The years of sacrifice and usually the contribution of many people over time is what makes it a success. Thank you for reading.

MORE FROM ROSS GREENWOOD

We hope you enjoyed reading *Lifer*. If you did, please leave a review.

If you'd like to gift a copy, this book is also available as an ebook, digital audio download and audiobook CD.

Sign up to Ross Greenwood's mailing list for news, competitions and updates on future books.

http://bit.ly/RossGreenwoodNewsletter

Why not explore the DI Barton series.

  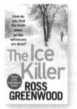 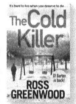

ABOUT THE AUTHOR

Ross Greenwood is the bestselling author of over ten crime thrillers. Before becoming a full-time writer he was most recently a prison officer and so worked everyday with murderers, rapists and thieves for four years. He lives in Peterborough.

Follow Ross on social media:

 twitter.com/greenwoodross
facebook.com/RossGreenwoodAuthor
bookbub.com/authors/ross-greenwood
instagram.com/rossg555

ABOUT BOLDWOOD BOOKS

Boldwood Books is a fiction publishing company seeking out the best stories from around the world.

Find out more at www.boldwoodbooks.com

Sign up to the Book and Tonic newsletter for news, offers and competitions from Boldwood Books!

http://www.bit.ly/bookandtonic

We'd love to hear from you, follow us on social media:

facebook.com/BookandTonic

twitter.com/BoldwoodBooks

instagram.com/BookandTonic

9 781802 803907